A Dangerous Favor

A Dangerous Favor

A Jenna Stack Mystery

Hanna Wren

ISBN: 979-8-9878098-2-2

Cover Design: Jessie Horsting

Contents

Chapter 1
A Pressing Proposal

Internship Proposal
University of Manhattan
Name: Jenna Stack
GPA: 4.0
Degree Concentration: Criminology / Minor in
Sociology

Proposed Placement:
Bell River Police Department, Eastmoor County,
New York

Project Description:
I want to intern with local law enforcement in
a small-town setting where I can learn through
hands-on experience while applying practical
knowledge to various tasks and situations. I
have selected my hometown of Bell River, New
York. In addition to meeting the small-town

criteria, the crime rate in the county is
higher than those of similar size and
demographics in the region. I plan to study
county archives and community dynamics to
ascertain the causes of this anomaly.
Additionally, there are practical
considerations, such as familiarity with the
area and affordable living arrangements.

Project Duration: Winter Quarter
Project Completion: Spring Quarter

I pull the cover sheet for my internship proposal out of the printer and clip it into a folder. At eleven a.m., I have my quarterly evaluation with Professor Wolfson, head of the criminology department at the University of Manhattan. I plan to submit my proposal to him then, *in person*.

I've filled out all the paperwork, taken the required courses, and submitted a Student Enrichment application to the Bell River Police Department. If BRPD accepts me and Wolfson approves, I'll start my internship in twelve weeks. The truth is, I can't afford to be turned down—my brother's life depends on it.

For inspiration, I've propped my crime board up on the chair in my bedroom. Red, yellow, and blue threads crisscross the surface. Like a colorful spider's web, they connect the evidence that convicted my brother of first-degree murder. But Tyler is innocent, and I plan to prove it.

For one thing, I have a new piece of evidence, a lab report that was never presented at Tyler's trial. But to figure out exactly how this new information factors into the case, I'll need to search the police files where the murder occurred. My only chance to do that is from the inside. And I'll only get inside Bell River PD via one of Professor Wolfson's famous internships. He's already assured me I'm a shoo-in for the program. It's my choice of location that will pose a problem. I need to convince him that Bell River is the ideal location for this budding criminologist to hone her skills.

"Jenna?" A loud rap on the door startles me, and I almost spill my coffee. It's Dave, my best friend, roommate, and proud owner of *Tails of the City Pet Sitting Agency*, making him my part-time boss.

Instead of waiting for an answer, Dave barges right into my room. He looks polished and put together, as always, even when invading my personal space. Today he's wearing a light orange polo shirt that accentuates his tan and slim khaki pants that flatter his physique. His styled blond hair appears effortlessly disheveled, and he's cultivated a light stubble on his cheeks and chiseled jawline, giving his face a less pretty, more rugged look. His high-voltage smile fades when he sees what I've been up to this morning.

Dave does not approve of my crime board. He thinks I spend too much time staring at the same notes, colored strings, and photos with nothing to show for my efforts. I try to shove the offending materials under my bed, but it's too late.

"Oh, Jenna, what am I going to do with you?" He scowls at the enormous piece of foam board. "That thing is a crime against your mental health. And your room looks like an actual crime scene. I can't even stand being in here. Come on." He motions for me to follow him.

I have to admit, my room is a mess. Clothes are scattered all over the floor, and the desk is piled high with papers and empty coffee mugs. Between school, two jobs, and working on Tyler's case, I don't have much time for housekeeping.

"I can't talk right now." I nudge some dirty clothes under the bed with my foot. "I'm getting ready for my evaluation with Professor Wolfson."

"Well, I'm on a tight schedule, and there's work stuff to go over. So do you think you could make some time?"

"I *really* need to figure out how to talk Wolfson into letting me intern in Bell River *before* I meet with him. I know you don't approve…"

Dave's expression softens.

"Honey, I know you're trying to help Tyler. But do you really think spending three months working at that backwoods police department in that awful town is such a great idea?"

"It's the only lead I've got, Dave. I *really* need you to be supportive."

"Okay. Okay." He throws up his hands in surrender. "But right now, I *really* need you to focus on the business. It'll just take a minute."

Our eyes meet, and suddenly, I feel terrible. When my relationship blew up six months ago, Dave took me in, no questions asked. He gave me a place to live and nursed me through the heartache. All he asked for in return, all he continues to ask, is for some help running his business.

Feeling contrite, I follow Dave into the living room, which, since I moved into his spare room and former office, has become the nerve center of Tails of the City. Out of the corner of my eye, I spot three enormous pieces of brand new, matching luggage inside the front door.

Oh no! Today is the day Dave leaves on a long overdue, much needed, Parisian vacation with his recently acquired, glamorous boyfriend, Matty Cooper.

"Oh Dave, I forgot you leave today. I'm so sorry!"

"Yeah, I figured." He brushes it off with a shrug. "Give me five minutes to get you up to speed, and then you can get back to *Operation Small Town Invasion*. Okay? Matty is literally on his way."

"Absolutely! I'm all yours."

Dave points to a massive bulletin board with a map of Manhattan covered in colored push pins. "These are the pet sitters assigned to various clients. Gary is out of town until tomorrow. Then he'll take care of Mrs. Brochelle and Erik Tran. His pins are green. If anything new comes in, ask him first. He's always looking to pick up extra work. Gina's watching Matty's place and has a few simple dog walking routes. Her pins are yellow. Sandy is covering all of her usual clients. She's red. All you have to do is make sure everything runs smoothly."

"Got it," I reassure him. "Everything will be fine."

"I left a list of contacts in case of special requests. The regulars have your info, but don't forget to check this too." He hands me the official Tails of the City cell phone.

"You're not bringing this with you?"

"No, Jenna. I'm going on vacation, and you are in charge. You can handle this, right?"

Dave built Tails of the City into a thriving business in just two and a half years. Dog walking, pet meal prep and meds, exotic animal care, full-service apartment sitting, even pet travel arrangements and the occasional errand; whatever the client needs, Tails of the City handles it well and discreetly. But he's had zero downtime since the whole thing started.

So, when Matty went from client to boyfriend and invited Dave on vacation, he jumped. Still, leaving his business for even a short time must be nerve-wracking.

I nod firmly. "I will not let you down."

His broad shoulders relax, but only for a few seconds.

"Oh! One more thing." He plucks a large manila envelope off of his crowded desk. There's a name written on the front in Dave's precise handwriting: *Natalie Swanson.* No address or sign of a postage stamp. Uh oh.

"What's that?"

"Some paperwork for a client. A legal document." Dave quickly scrawls an address in the east 40s under Natalie Swanson's name and hands the envelope to me. "I was supposed to deliver this myself, but I ran out of time. Matty upgraded our tickets, and we're on an earlier flight." His eyes light up at the mention of his considerate boyfriend.

"Okay." I set the envelope down. "I'll do it tomorrow."

"No!" Dave snatches it up again. "Natalie needs this letter ASAP, and I promised. She's a total sweetheart, and she's in a terrible situation."

I raise an eyebrow skeptically. Dave can be a bit dramatic at times.

"Seriously, she's in the middle of an ugly divorce. Her husband is a lawyer and a total prick. He kicked her out and moved the girl-friend in practically the next day. He even had Natalie followed by a private eye and is threatening to make her look bad in court. Worst of all, he took her babies."

"Her children?" I stare at the envelope in Dave's hand, horrified.

"No, her *dogs*. It's a pet custody case. I'm trying to help her."

"Pet custody?" I've never heard of a pet custody case, but it does explain how Dave got involved.

"Her ex is going out of town, so she gets Olive and Pepper for a few days. But she needs this document to make it official, and she's very anxious." Dave thrusts the envelope at me. "So you need to bring it to her *today*, Jenna! Before you do anything else!"

I'm a little suspicious of Dave's explanation. It seems weird that someone would need a legal document to watch their own dogs. And I have my own problems.

"I just can't. Not today. I need to prepare—"

There's a sudden loud buzzing noise. Dave rushes over to the front door.

"Who is it?" he calls nervously into the intercom.

"Who do you think, silly?" Matty replies.

Dave triggers the door release and waves for me to join him. We stand side-by-side while Matty makes his way up in the elevator. I feel ridiculous, like I'm in a receiving line to greet royalty. But it is sweet that Dave is always so excited to see his boyfriend.

Moments later, Matty Cooper walks through the door wearing casual slacks, a black T-shirt, and a fashionable, but well-worn, khaki jacket with dozens of pockets. His short, dark hair is freshly cut, and his beard is neatly trimmed. He is dragging a single, rolling, carry-on suitcase. The overall look is travel chic and ready to go.

"Hey, Jenna." Matty gives me a warm hug. "Thanks for watching the shop." Then he turns to Dave. "Ready?"

"Yes." Dave points to his pristine and excessive luggage.

Matty cringes.

"You know we're not *moving* to Paris?"

Dave ignores Matty's teasing. "We just have to make a quick stop in the forties."

"No way." Matty shakes his head. "We don't have time."

"I'm sorry." Dave throws up his hands. "But I promised, and Jenna's just *too busy*."

They both look at me. Damn you, Dave!

"Please, Jenna." Matty tilts his head hopefully.

"Pretty please," Dave coos, suppressing a smirk.

"Fine! I'll do it."

Dave grabs me and kisses me on both cheeks, French style.

"You're the best! Tails of the City is in your hands, mon cherie! Whatever you do, please don't drop it!"

"I won't let you down. I promise. Now go have fun!"

Dave blows me an exaggerated kiss and shouts, "Au revoir!"

Matty maneuvers the luggage down the hallway as Dave runs to catch up. I shut the door behind them and smile to myself. I should be mad at Dave for putting me on the spot. But I'm not. Knowing he's happy and off on a romantic adventure feels good. And sure, dropping off Natalie Swanson's paperwork is inconvenient. But the apartment is on the way. I can make a quick stop.

My stomach rumbles, reminding me I haven't eaten yet. But with an extra task on my plate, there's no time to waste. I race around the apartment, gathering my things—backpack, internship proposal, laptop, my phone, the Tails of the City phone, the envelope for Natalie Swanson, a protein bar, and an apple.

Then I make sure everything's turned off, lock the door behind me, and head out. I'll have to eat, and rehearse my conversation with Professor Wolfson, on the subway. I've got to find a way to convince him to send me to Bell River.

Chapter 2
Natalie's Story

If you asked most New Yorkers their favorite time of year, I think they'd say springtime when the winter freeze breaks and everything is blooming. For me, the best time of year is fall—once summer's oppressive heat and humidity are finally over. The air is cool and crisp. Everything feels clean and comfortable.

I step out of Dave's apartment building on this fine October morning. It's fifty-nine degrees with a soft breeze, my idea of heaven. Cool enough for jeans, a lightweight sweater, and a cozy scarf. But warm enough for my favorite lightweight Converse sneakers. I'd love to walk the thirty blocks to Natalie's, but I don't have the luxury of time. I need to deliver her papers and get to school.

When I reach the subway, rush hour is over, but the platform is still crowded with people. A warm gust of wind announces the arrival of the Express 4 train. After jostling into a seat, with barely enough time to read the graffiti, the train arrives at Grand Central Station. Thanks to the New York City subway system, I'm running early.

A promising sign for the day. I hope my luck holds.

The doors open with a whoosh. The station is busy with tourists and commuters rushing between trains. Outside, the street is just as chaotic. The corner of Lexington and 43rd is congested with taxis honking in frustration, bicyclists whizzing by, and people rushing to appointments.

Natalie Swanson's apartment is in an odd part of town. The United Nations building is basically *on* the East River at 42nd Street. So Midtown East, also called Turtle Bay, is a cluster of Consulate Generals and Permanent Missions, punctuated with quick lunch spots, corner bodegas, and old steakhouses. Traffic grinds to a halt when dignitaries visit, but the city keeps the neighborhood reasonably clean and cheerful, so those same dignitaries have a nice view through their limousine windows. With all of the official buildings and diplomatic activity, I imagine this area might be a strange place to live. Still, I wonder what rent prices are like in the area. I can't stay at Dave's forever.

Natalie's four-story building comes into view, and my heart sinks. No doorman. Probably no elevator. Hopefully, she's on a low floor. I find *Swanson* on the intercom and press the buzzer.

"Who is it?" a soft, timid voice floats from the speaker.

"Jenna Stack from Tails of the City. Dave sent me—"

"Oh. Okay. I'm 4B."

The door buzzes open with a jolt. Inside, the black and white tiled lobby is tidy but dingy. And as predicted, there's no elevator, and the stairs are steep. I look up with dread and begin my ascent to the fourth floor. When I arrive, winded, Natalie Swanson is waiting at the door.

Petite and pretty, with curly dark hair, she's bundled up in a baggy pink sweatsuit. Her big brown eyes are swollen and red, her delicate face streaked with tears. She looks positively miserable.

"Where's Dave?" Natalie nervously gestures for me to enter.

The apartment is tiny and full of boxes, the furniture sparse and mismatched.

"He's on vacation. Didn't he tell you?" I hand Natalie the envelope.

"No. He didn't." She opens it, glances at the papers, and bites her lip anxiously. "But... Dave promised he'd deliver this for me."

Natalie is clearly upset, and I don't want to make it worse. But Dave has a habit of bending the truth.

"What, exactly, are those?" I gesture to the papers.

"Did Dave tell you I'm getting a divorce?" Natalie sniffles back a tear. "And my ex already moved in... with the other woman?

"He told me a little bit."

"It's been so awful. Her name is Elena Solaris. And, of course, she's everything I'm not. Sophisticated. Well-traveled. Flashy. You know..." Her voice trails off sadly.

"That's rough," I say, remembering how I felt when my ex-boyfriend Liam cheated.

"Well, this"—she waves the envelope—"is a Temporary Custody Order for our dogs, Olive and Pepper. My ex is keeping them to spite me."

Before I can ask why her jerky ex is so spitcful, Natalie's frustration erupts. She's not done talking yet.

"He doesn't even like dogs! And that Elena woman, I doubt she pays my babies any attention." The pitch of Natalie's voice escalates before she catches herself. "It's just, I miss them and... I'm terribly worried about them."

My pulse quickens at the thought of someone hurting an animal.

"He wouldn't—"

"No. Nothing like that." She shakes her head. "But Olive and Pepper are high strung. They get nervous when they're left alone.

Dave's lawyer friend arranged a hearing as a favor. When Rick didn't show up—"

"That's your ex?"

"Yes, Rick Muraro. I was awarded the temporary order when he didn't show up for court. So, I can *keep* them, at least for now."

"Well, that's good."

"Yes, but when Rick realizes what's happening, he'll get angry. He hates to lose."

I wait a moment while Natalie catches her breath. I get the feeling she doesn't have many people to confide in. When I'm sure she's finished talking, I ask what feels like an obvious question.

"Can't you just hire a process server?"

"I would, but money is tight, and Dave, well, he *offered*."

Natalie takes a deep, mournful breath, and stares off for a moment. Then her focus returns abruptly, "Oh, where are my manners? Please, sit down. Can I offer you some coffee?"

Natalie gestures to a heavy maroon wing chair covered with the Sunday *New York Times* crossword puzzle. I glance at my phone. There's plenty of time to have a quick coffee and still get uptown. I move the puzzle, which I notice is mostly filled out, slip off my backpack, and sit down. She walks into the kitchen, pops a coffee pod into a small machine, and hits start.

"Cream and sugar?"

"Just a splash of milk, thanks."

Watching Natalie prepare the drinks, I'm struck by her manner. There's something dignified and measured in the way she moves, pouring milk, stirring carefully. She's delicate, almost bird-like, but focused and intent. Finally, she places a cup of coffee in front of me and sits down, cradling her mug.

"Are you the girl studying to be a private investigator?"

I'm taken aback by the shift in topic, but I like her directness.

"I guess you could say that. I'm studying criminology."

"That sounds dangerous."

"Not really. Unless you know something I don't?" I sip the coffee. It's hot and strong with just the right amount of milk.

"Well, my husband...I mean, soon-to-be *ex-husband* has a private eye working for him. He's nothing like *you*."

"What's he like?"

"I don't know. He's..." She pauses, struggling to assemble her description. "Abrupt. Suspicious. And I guess the word would be jaded? Like his whole purpose in life is following people, expecting to catch them doing bad things."

"Well, as far as I'm concerned, most people are basically good."

"Really?" Her eyes widen with surprise. "You think so?"

"Definitely." I smile. "They just get into awful situations."

Natalie laughs, but the sound is hollow, as if she's out of practice. Her eyes drift to the envelope. I can tell she's upset by the way she bites her lip.

"Did Dave tell you my ex is a lawyer?"

"He mentioned it. What firm?"

"Muraro and Hill. He inherited the practice from his father, then brought in a partner."

"What kind of law?"

"It's a neighborhood practice, so a bit of everything. Criminal cases, personal injury, wills and trusts, divorce. Try divorcing a *divorce* lawyer. It's a nightmare. He's an expert at hiding things. And he's just become so... mean."

There's a flash of fear in her eyes.

"Are you scared of him?"

"A little. But when I left I took some papers that will protect me, help me negotiate with him. I hope."

"That was smart."

"Thanks." Her face brightens before fading back to sadness. "I want Olive and Pepper back so badly. I need to find someone to deliver the custody order, someone he won't expect...."

Dave was vague about Natalie's situation, and now I understand why. She's a nice person in a tough position. He knew I wouldn't leave her hanging. Now that he's out of town, I'm pretty much stuck.

"I'll do it." The words tumble out of my mouth before I consider what I'm agreeing to do.

Natalie's face lights up.

"Thank you!" She seems lost in thought for a moment, then adds, "You should serve him at his office. There will be people around."

I nod. Her logic is solid.

"Tomorrow morning?" she asks.

"I'll make it happen. Just give me the address."

"It'll be easier if you pretend you're a potential client." Natalie picks ups her phone and makes a call. "Paul?" Something in her demeanor changes. She blushes a little and twirls her hair. "Listen, Paul. I have a friend who's come into some money. Um hmm. She needs a trust. And you know how good Rick is with that kind of thing. Could you make an appointment for her? Tomorrow morning?"

She holds up her index finger to signal that she's waiting.

"Great, nine a.m.?" She looks at me, and I nod my approval. "And maybe don't mention I sent her? Great. Thanks, Paul. You're the best." She hangs up.

"Who's Paul?"

"Paul Hill. Rick's partner. He's so sweet. I feel bad tricking him, but I knew he'd put you on the calendar without asking questions. Just tell the receptionist you're looking for someone to protect your interests, and Rick came highly recommended. He won't be able to resist."

"Sounds like a plan."

"Oh... And Jenna?" Natalie looks at me with eager eyes.

Uh oh. What now?

"After you serve Rick the papers, maybe ask him when he can drop Olive and Pepper off?" She wrings her delicate hands.

"I will. And Natalie?"

"Yes?"

"You said he's going to be mad. How mad?"

"He has a terrible temper, but I doubt he'll pull anything at the office. Maybe yell a little? But Paul will be there."

"Okay. As soon as it's over, I'll text you."

A smile spreads across Natalie's face. "You're a lifesaver." She exhales and leans back in her chair. It's the first time I've seen her relax.

With Natalie comforted and a plan in place, I check the time. Yikes! If I don't leave right away, I risk being late for my appointment with Wolfson. I shove the envelope in my backpack and rush to the door.

"Don't worry. We'll get Olive and Pepper back."

Chapter 3
Operation Internship

The clock is ticking when I reach the University of Manhattan. My rubber-soled shoes squeak on the marble floor of the criminology building as I race down the empty hallway. Finally, Professor Wolfson's office door comes into view. I skid to a stop, lungs burning, and check the time.

Five minutes late. Ugh! I knock softly.

"Enter," comes a stern male voice.

Unlike the modern, aggressively lit university building, Wolfson's office is old-fashioned, dark, and musty. Bookshelves sag under the weight of volumes on subjects ranging from fingerprint analysis to occult rituals. The ratty tweed couch is scattered with folders and an array of gruesome crime scene photos. Seated in the middle of the chaos, behind a large, worn desk, is a small, wiry, balding man in his fifties.

Professor Karl Wolfson runs the criminology department at U of M. He's also a consultant for the FBI, CIA, and who knows where else. He's written several tomes on criminology and law enforcement methods and appears regularly on CNN as a crime expert. But you would never guess any of those facts from his appearance or the state of his office.

"Late again, Miss Stack." Wolfson glares disapprovingly with intense black eyes. "And on such an important day."

My stomach clenches. This is not how I'd hoped to kick off my evaluation. "Sorry, Professor." I sit in the only chair not stacked with files and books directly across from my displeased advisor.

Wolfson turns back to a leather journal on his desk and continues writing for what feels like an eternity. Is my evaluation canceled because I'm late? Am I supposed to say something?

Finally, he looks up. "No excuse?"

I've learned the hard way that Wolfson does not like excuses unless they involve danger, criminology, or some combination of the two. I don't think a pet custody case qualifies.

"No," I try to glance away, but he holds my eyes with a stern gaze. He's expecting more. "There's no excuse, sir."

"Precisely." Satisfied, Wolfson opens a blue folder with my name on the tab and glances inside. Then he looks up to begin his critique. Okay. Here we go. The knot in my gut explodes into a flutter of nerves.

"Your habitual tardiness shows an egregious disrespect for others' time. You often show up to class tired and distracted, as do many of your classmates. And while I know your financial situation requires you to work, that's not an excuse."

Uh oh. My quarterly grade, and possibly my brother's future, depend on this meeting going well. If only I hadn't stayed at Natalie's so long. Damn Dave for making me his messenger girl.

"I realize I've been—"

"What does weigh in"—he flashes an icy stare, warning me not to interrupt—"is my knowledge of your family situation, which is a legitimate concern. And unlike your classmates, you, Miss Stack, are already living the life of an investigator."

I'm slightly relieved, but I know he's not finished yet.

"Your classwork, participation, and marks are excellent. My evaluation is that you show great promise. I suggest you buy an old-fashioned wristwatch and set it ten minutes ahead while learning to compartmentalize the various aspects of your life. Understood?"

I exhale gratefully. "Yes, sir. And thank you."

He snaps the folder shut.

"Fine. Let's move on. Have you completed your internship proposal?"

My heart skips a beat. This is the moment I've waited for. I sit up in my chair, ready to make my case for Bell River. He even opened the door by mentioning my "family situation," aka the fact that my twenty-one-year-old brother is in prison for a crime he didn't commit.

"Yes, sir…"

Professor Wolfson leans forward as if to hear my plans more clearly. I lean in, matching his body language. But before I have a chance to continue, he speaks.

"As you know, Miss Stack, the internship is a privilege reserved for my most gifted students. It relies on my relationships with law enforcement and the forensic communities. If accepted, you will, in effect, be representing me. Do you understand?"

I look down at my lap. I know what he wants me to say next and find myself unable to make eye contact. I take a deep breath.

"I do. I will not disappoint or embarrass you in any way." And I mean it. Or at least I'll try my hardest not to do anything to damage his credibility.

"I should hope not. You are intelligent, curious, and committed to justice. In fact, I would say you have superior instincts and enormous potential."

"You really think so?" My cheeks flush at his encouraging words.

"But you are also immature, impatient, and impetuous; traits that make you a danger to yourself and others."

I know what he's referring to—the Ab El Malik case. This past spring, I almost died on a pet sitting assignment. A sweet little dog named Max walked me straight into the middle of a plot to kill a powerful international businessman, Sheik Mohammed Ab El Malik. I got into some pretty crazy situations, including almost getting bitten by a venomous snake. But I made it out alive, and so did the Sheik. Surely that counts for something?

"I know I've made some impulsive moves, sir. But—"

"*However,* you have handled yourself well under duress. And your bravery matches your, shall we say... occasional lack of judgment?"

I can take that. I let out my breath, relieved he didn't say stupidity.

"I'll do better. I promise, sir."

"It's simply a matter of tempering enthusiasm with reason, Miss Stack. Do you understand?"

"Yes. Absolutely."

While I'm not sure it's always possible, I do grasp the concept of "think before you act." And I need to keep this meeting on the right track.

"Very well. That's settled. As far as placement goes"—he strums the desk with his fingers—"your choice of assignment should be someplace interesting but out of immediate harm's way. Somewhere you can sharpen your skills while practicing the art of patience."

The first hurdle is over. He's agreed to accept me into the internship program. Now I have to sell him on Bell River.

"I've got it." His eyes light up. "A bustling coroner's office."

Ew, gross, and not what I had in mind.

"Actually, Professor, I have an idea."

"Oh, do you?" He raises one wiry black eyebrow as if I've got a lot of nerve. "Do tell."

I take a deep breath. Here goes. I place the folder containing my proposal and initial research on his desk.

"I was thinking about the Bell River Police Department. They have a Student Enrichment Program that aligns with your internship parameters."

The hint of a smile passes his lips. He's not surprised by my suggestion. "Go on. Why Bell River, specifically?"

"Well, BRPD is a small department, so I'd have the opportunity to learn different aspects of day-to-day investigations. As you know, the crime rate is high in the county. I want to look into that from a sociological perspective. And I could stay with my mother and save on costs."

"And...?"

He's going to make me say it.

"And with access, maybe I can poke around... um, I mean research my brother's case?"

"That would be very unorthodox, but perhaps you could." The corners of his mouth turn up in an almost imperceptible smile. "However, I don't imagine you'll be very well-received by the Bell River PD. Have you considered that?"

"Yes. But a new detective is running the department, Cecilia Myers. I've never met her, but she may be more open. I'm not looking for a welcoming committee Professor, just a way in."

"And what do you hope to uncover?" There's a glint in Wolfson's eye. He loves the prospect of an investigation.

"I'm not sure. But Cole Braedon supplied me with new evidence before he took off last spring, a lab report never presented at Tyler's trial. I plan to start there."

I met the mysterious Cole Braedon after stumbling onto the plot to kill Sheik Ab El Malik. He claimed to be working under-cover for a government agency, but his story had serious holes, leaving me with more questions than answers. Before he took off, he sent me the lab report.

Wolfson shakes his head. "What is the second rule, Miss Stack?"

He is referring to number two on the list of five "Golden Rules" hanging on his classroom wall. We were required to memorize each rule during our first week of school. Number two reads: *Trust no one: Consider the Source. Listen to all leads but always be wary of second-hand information and biased sources.*

"It's true. I'm not sure of Braedon's motives or his real identity. But it's the only lead I've got." I take a chance and add, *"Please, sir?"*

Wolfson leans back in his chair, steeples his fingers, and considers my request. It feels like the world has stopped as I wait for this great man to decide my brother's fate. Finally, he comes to a decision.

"Very well. Bell River it is."

I exhale in a rush, "Thank you!"

"*If* Bell River PD will have you."

My heart sinks. He's right. There's no guarantee my application will be accepted, and Wolfson can't send me to Bell River unless the head detective of the BRPD agrees.

"Maybe you could call Detective Myers? Put in a good word?" I know I'm pushing it. But an endorsement from Wolfson could make all the difference.

"Perhaps." He shrugs his shoulders.

I know that's all I can expect for now.

"Thank you, sir." I stand up to leave, but he stops me.

"Miss Stack, whether or not arrangements can be made, I feel I must advise you... with this predicament you find your family in, as with all challenges in life, you must learn to control your emotions. Keep a cool head. Follow every lead. Remember rule number one. *Slow and Steady Solves the Case.*"

I recite the rest from memory, "*Unless lives are in imminent danger, take your time, be smart, find the proof.*"

"Precisely." Wolfson waves a hand toward the door, indicating our time together is over. "I'll notify Detective Myers of my endorsement. But remember, the final decision is hers and hers alone."

"Thank you, Professor." I cross my fingers; at least I have a chance.

As I step out of Wolfson's office, my phone buzzes.

Speak of the devil. It's a text from Tyler's public defender, Marcus Caton.

Marcus: *Just got word. Tyler's in solitary. 15 days.*

My mood deflates. What now?

Me: *What for? Is he all right?*
Marcus: *Fighting. He's OK. Just banged up. Don't worry.*

Don't worry. How can I not? My brother *is* in imminent danger every day he remains in prison.

Chapter 4
Serve & Volley

Rick Muraro's law office in Brooklyn is in an old Italian neighborhood called Cobble Hill that has become popular with young, upwardly mobile families. Walking along the sidewalk, I can see why. The streets are quaint and surprisingly quiet. Birds chirp in the trees while parents push baby carriages and chat with neighbors. I pass several restaurants, a chic wine store, a chain drugstore, and an old-fashioned watch repair on my way to the address on Court Street. The office is on the ground floor of a red brick building sandwiched between an Italian grocer and a nail salon. Above the metal security door, a black and white sign reads:

Muraro and Hill
Attorneys at Law

The doorbell buzzes loudly, and the heavy metal door clicks open almost immediately. Inside, the waiting room is small and sparsely furnished. A heavily made-up receptionist with big hair looks up at me from behind a tidy desk.

"Can I help you?"

"I'm Jenna Stack. I have an appointment at nine?"

"Take a seat." She waves long zebra-painted fingernails in the direction of a stiff vinyl couch, then picks up a corded phone to announce my arrival.

I can tell right away the conversation is not going well. The likelihood of getting in to see the boss looks less than assured.

"No. I didn't schedule it." The receptionist whispers emphatically. "But it's on your calendar. And she's *here*." Her charm bracelet rattles as she covers the receiver. "Did you say you were referred?"

"Yes, my grandma passed. I'm not accustomed to my new situation. I heard about your office from... neighbors." I catch myself before blowing my cover by saying Natalie's name. "I was told Mr. Muraro does estate planning. Wills and trusts, that sort of thing? I need some advice."

"She needs help with an inheritance," the receptionist says into the phone. "Fine." She hangs up and taps her nails on the desk. "There was a mix-up. If you hang tight, Mr. Muraro will see you shortly."

"Thank you." I don't have to fake how relieved I am. I have no backup plan for serving Rick the Temporary Custody Order. One way or another, I need to see him.

Miss Zebra Nails returns to her work, and I pass the time practicing one of Wolfson's favorite exercises, "observations." The challenge is deducing details about a person based on their behavior, mannerisms. and appearance.

Pretending to scroll through my phone, I discreetly evaluate the receptionist. Her hair, makeup, and fingernails are flashy, designed to attract attention. But she's wearing a conservative high-neck sweater, preventing anyone standing at her desk from sneaking a peek down her cleavage. Smart girl. She keeps glancing between her computer screen and a closed interior door while tapping her black and white nails on her desk. I'm trying to determine if she's anxious or just impatient when the doorbell rings.

The receptionist looks up at a small video screen tucked above the front door. A middle-aged man in a rumpled suit stares into the security camera. She purses her bright red lips and exhales loudly, a sure sign she's annoyed. Then she takes her time pushing a button on her desk to release the lock. Miss Zebra Nails definitely has some attitude.

The new arrival clamors through the front door. He's pretty short, no taller than five-foot-four, with wild, collar-length hair and a bald spot on top. His clothes are ill-fitting and unkempt. But he's wearing brand new, expensive sneakers. He slaps a piece of paper down on the receptionist's desk.

"Jack," she sighs, "You realize you can email an invoice?"

"Yep," Jack barks. "But then I wouldn't get to see you, now would I, Josephine?" His voice is loud and gruff, and he has a strong New York accent.

Josephine rolls her heavily mascaraed eyes.

"I also gotta get cash for expenses. I ain't—"

"I know. I know. You ain't gonna go out of pocket." She mimics his accent, but he doesn't seem to mind.

Josephine picks up the phone, hits an extension, and announces, "Jack needs cash."

"Thanks, doll." He winks. "You're the best."

Jack steps aside and notices me for the first time, "Well, hello there, little lady."

Making a show of pretending to look up from my phone, I smile politely. He winks at me as if we've just shared a magical moment.

This guy is certainly a character but also a bit of a puzzle. He clearly has a business relationship with the law firm. But I seriously doubt he's a lawyer. He isn't at all concerned about his appearance. But he is willing to invest in comfortable shoes. Then it hits me. I bet Jack is the private investigator Natalie mentioned.

An attractive dark-skinned woman, neatly dressed in a charcoal gray pantsuit, emerges from an inner door carrying a small, zippered pouch in one hand.

"Becky! How's it hanging?" Jack says.

"It's Rebecca, and fine, thank you," she replies, all business. "What do you need?"

"A grand should cover it."

Rebecca pulls a wad of bills, a small notebook, and one of those tiny golf pencils from the pouch.

"For which case?" she asks, pencil poised for note-taking.

"Something special for the boss," Jack non-answers.

"Which boss?"

"You're kidding, right?"

Rebecca shakes her head. "One thousand dollars petty cash to Jack Russell for case number 'something special,' allegedly approved by Rick." She makes a note and hands him the cash. "Josephine?"

"A grand to Jack. Okay'd by Rick. Witnessed," the receptionist calls back.

"Ladies." Jack stuffs the cash in his pocket and tips an imaginary hat.

Then the small, aggressive man who shares his name with a breed of small, yappy dogs heads out the front door.

Rebecca watches him leave as she zips up the pouch.

"That guy..." she starts, but Josephine inclines her head toward me.

"Oh. Sorry." Rebecca seems surprised.

"This is Jenna Stack," Josephine says. "She's local. Her grandmother passed. She's waiting on Rick."

"Stack?" Rebecca looks me up and down. Her intelligent brown eyes pause on the large envelope in my lap. "I don't recognize the name."

My heart stops. She's suspicious. I scramble for a reason she doesn't recognize my last name; adopted name, married name, witness protection? Luckily the inner door opens again and a neatly dressed man steps into the waiting area.

"Hi, Paul," Rebecca and Josephine chime in unison.

So, this is Paul. I watch his cheeks flush as he tugs at his jacket. He's not bad looking. Just a bit awkward.

"Cappuccino? Pastry?" He offers.

Josephine shakes her head. "You know you're supposed to send me out for that kind of stuff."

Paul shrugs. "I don't mind. It's nice to get out."

He hands her a slip of paper. She writes down her order and then looks at Rebecca.

"I'm fine. Thanks."

"How about you, Miss Stack?" Josephine offers. "Espresso? Cappuccino?"

I shake my head just as the intercom buzzes and a male voice shouts, "Send her in!"

"Sound like he's ready for you." Rebecca glances at the envelope in my hand again and grins. "Why don't I show you the way?"

Rebecca escorts me into the inner offices. A cheap, wooden door opens, and a man steps into the cramped hallway. I assume this is Rick Muraro because as soon as he appears, Rebecca strides away quickly.

"Miss Stack, is it?" He flashes a brief, artificial smile; all teeth, no warmth. "I'm Rick Muraro."

Rick isn't much taller than me, but what he lacks in height, he makes up for in polish. His wavy brown hair is shiny, carefully styled, and unnaturally dark, probably dyed to stave off the grays. His deep-set eyes are framed by carefully maintained eyebrows. His suit fits impeccably, and his stiff shoes are polished to a high gloss. Unlike Jack, the investigator, this guy cares a lot about his appearance and does not select his footwear for comfort.

"Thank you for seeing me." I extend my hand to shake, but he ignores the gesture.

"Crazy morning. Go ahead in. I'll be right with you." And he's off down the hall.

Classic move. Rick Muraro is setting the tone for our relationship. I'm the poor, little rich girl who needs lots of expensive advice and paperwork. He's the busy, necessary lawyer squeezing me into his hectic schedule. Lucky me.

I'm pretty sure that technically, I could "drop serve" him at this point; leave the papers on his desk and go. But I promised Natalie I'd ask Rick about dropping off the dogs, so I wait.

Looking around Rick's office, I'm struck by how different the vibe is from everything else I've seen so far at Muraro and Hill. The room is filled with heavy, dark furniture and expensive-looking bric-a-brac.

Two walls are completely covered with photos. Above his desk are carefully arranged pictures of Rick in gold frames: Rick bungee jumping, Rick parasailing, Rick drinking champagne with a statuesque beauty on a yacht. There are also the expected photos of Rick shaking hands with important politicians and clients. It's a visual power statement—a photographic pat on the back.

The perpendicular wall is a different story. The space is covered in framed photos spanning decades. There's a series of school pictures: Rick playing basketball, posing in a tux with a prom date, wearing a cap and gown at graduation. In the corner are Muraro family weddings and celebrations, black and white photos of long-gone relatives in their Sunday best, smiling at the camera. I recognize a young Rick, probably around ten years old, standing in front of the law office with a man in a shiny sharkskin suit. They're both wearing Mets caps and smiling broadly.

No photos of Natalie on either wall. She's been erased from his history.

Rick's office door opens, startling me. Without saying a word or making eye contact, he slowly removes his jacket, carefully hangs it on a coat rack, and gently smooths the fabric. Finally, he turns his attention to me. I wonder how many times a day he pulls that power move?

"These old photos are wonderful." I smile.

"Yes, well. This used to be my father's office. The old neighborhood clients expect to see them." Rick points to a masculine-looking club chair, "Please, have a seat."

"Thank you." My heart beats rapidly as I perch on the edge of the chair.

"I'm sorry to hear about your recent loss." Rick's words are kind enough, but there's something insincere in his delivery like he's said them too many times or would rather be someplace else. "But I'm sure we can help ease your mind."

The intercom buzzes, and a flash of anger crosses his face. He picks up the phone and, in a condescending tone, scolds, "I told you I did not—" Then changes his attitude to all business. "Fine. Yes. Tell him I'll be there at noon."

Rick turns his attention back to me, smiles serenely, and holds his hand out. "Now then. Let's see what you've brought."

I realize he thinks the manila envelope I'm clutching is my grandmother's will. I pass it to him and hold my breath as he carefully unhooks the metal fastener, slides out the papers, and begins to review the contents. His eyes narrow, his lips clench, and beads of sweat appear along his hairline.

"What the—" He glares at me, eyes black with rage.

I try to keep calm as I recite the speech I prepared.

"I'm sorry to have misled you, Mr. Muraro. But you've been served. That is a Temporary Custody Order for the dogs Olive and Pepper."

He stands up, slams his hands on the desk, and looms over me.

"How dare you come to my place of business and disrupt my busy morning with this crap!"

I can feel my fight or flight response kick in, the adrenaline racing through my veins. You could say I'm more of a fighter, so I cross my arms and wait for his temper tantrum to pass.

"Mr. Muraro, we need to—"

He waves the papers at me. "Not only is this bullshit ridiculous, I'll quash it in court!" He crumbles the pages and drops them into a gold mesh wastepaper basket.

There's a timid knock on the office door, and Paul Hill sticks his head in, "Everything okay here, buddy?"

Paul looks at me, concerned. I give him a quick nod and slight smile, hoping to indicate that I'm all right but glad he interrupted.

"No, *buddy*, everything is not okay. This *person* just served me —in my own office!"

A look of surprise registers on Paul's face, but he quickly recovers. "That's unfortunate, but—"

"How did this happen?" Rick demands. "How did you get on my calendar in the first place, you little sneak?"

"Now, Rick, she's just doing her job," Paul says calmly.

"Don't use that patronizing tone with me!"

I feel bad knowing Paul is the one who made my appointment, but I don't want to stick around to find out what happens next. I have one more piece of business with Rick Muraro. Then I'm out of here.

"*Mr. Muraro.*" I try to sound as calm and professional as possible. "I'm sorry, but you've been served. You can take whatever legal steps you feel necessary. But in the meanwhile, I'd be happy to relay a message about when Natalie can expect the dogs."

"Get out of here!" He screams at his law partner, and little flecks of spit fly out of his mouth.

Paul starts to back out of the doorway. I hope he isn't going to leave me alone with this maniac.

"I'll be right outside, Miss Stack," he says in a reassuring voice.

A chilling stillness falls over the room as Rick turns his attention back to me. "You think you're helping her, don't you? Well, you're mistaken. Go ahead, take those whining mutts off my hands. But tell Natalie this will be the last time she sees them." He wipes his mouth with the back of his hand. "You tell her I'll spend any amount of money to make sure she loses them forever. Understand me? I'd rather send them across the rainbow bridge with my bare hands than let her win."

What kind of person threatens to kill a dog with a gleam in his eyes?

"I'll give her that message, Mr. Muraro. When can she expect the dogs?" I refuse to argue with this psycho, but I will not stand down.

"I'm not a taxi service. You can pick them up for her."

"Me?"

"You don't know?" He grins at the surprised look on my face. "I have a restraining order against Natalie. Pick those bitches up tonight, or they're going out on the street." He pauses for effect. "Or worse."

I have no doubt he means every vile word. No wonder Natalie is scared of this man. He's out of control.

"Fine. I'll pick the dogs up. But it will have to be after eight."

Rick scribbles his address on the back of a business card and tosses it at me. "Be there by nine. Not a minute later."

"I'll be there."

"And don't bother me. The dogs will be in their carrier outside. I'll be watching on the security camera."

I shove his business card in my pocket and head out the door. Paul Hill is waiting for me in the narrow hallway. He puts a hand under my arm and whispers, "I'm so sorry about that." As we shuffle along, a loud, guttural scream erupts from Rick's office, followed by an explosive crash. Paul hustles me past Josephine, who does not look up, and opens the front door.

"Sorry, Mr. Hill." I smile apologetically.

"Tell Natalie not to worry. Everything will be fine." He smiles nervously.

Two blocks later, I'm still replaying the scene in my head. I was never in any real danger, but it was frightening and weirdly exhilarating. I glance at the card Rick gave me. The address is on the west side of Manhattan, in the 80s. That's a fancy neighborhood for a small-time lawyer.

I text Natalie.

Me: *It's done. Picking pups up from Rick at 9 p.m. tonight.*
Natalie: *You're an angel. Bring their carrier too?*
Me*: Sure. I'll bring them straight to you.*
Natalie: *Thank you so much! I can't wait to see my babies!*
Me: *Glad I could help.*
Natalie: *And be careful!*

Chapter 5
Day Shifting

My second job, actually my first job, is bartending at a rock and roll club on the Lower East Side called Cellos. The cheerful blue and white awning and turquoise-painted brick create a welcoming exterior. On a crisp, clear day like today, we keep the large front windows open to let in fresh air and light. But even under the best circumstances, the bar's interior is significantly less upbeat than the facade. Even though the bouncers haven't arrived yet, the glass door is ajar.

Inside, the familiar aroma of stale beer and greasy fries fills the room. Past the scarred wooden tables and worn leatherette booths is a long wooden bar with bottles of alcohol stacked on shelves. Slowly, my eyes adjust to the dim light.

Bartending at Cellos is a great gig. The tips are decent, the hours flexible, and my coworkers are friendly. The food is also cheap and delicious, which comes in handy on my limited budget. I'm fantasizing about one of Cello's legendary burgers when Sharon, the manager, pops up from behind the bar.

Sharon is a knockout with long, shiny blonde hair, big blue

eyes, and a voluptuous figure. Today she's wearing a KISS T-shirt slashed and styled into a low-cut tank top with a thick silver glitter belt.

"Hey, stranger." She glances at the clock above the door. "First, you disappear for days. And now you're right on time. You're a mystery, Jenna Stack."

"I try."

"To be punctual or mysterious?"

"Both." I step behind the bar and toss my backpack in the utility closet while Sharon checks her makeup in the mirror. Her skintight jeans are tucked into six-inch vinyl platform boots.

"How do you stand in those things?" I marvel.

"Not as well as I'd like. I'm trying them out for *Glam Night*."

Last year Sharon figured out that she could boost her already excellent tips by coordinating her outfits with the evening's lineup. I thoroughly approve of the practice since bartenders pool tips at Cellos.

"Guess who stopped in for lunch?" she says coyly.

"Who?"

"That cute cop, Denning." She pulls a bag of limes out from under the bar and hands them to me.

"What did he want?" I start cutting the fruit into neat quarters as Sharon wipes down the bar.

"Said he was working a crime scene nearby and was craving a burger. But I think he had a craving for you." She snaps a bar towel at me.

"Ew. Gross!"

"Oh, come on, he's not so bad. He's kind of"—she puts a hand on her forehead in a fake swoon—"dreamy."

"You think so?"

"Sure. Like he's all earnest and by the book, but deep down, he's tormented by the responsibility of protecting our fair city." She leans against the bar and smiles with a faraway look.

"What? Do you know something I don't?" I say as I slice the citrus.

"I bet he's got a dark side."

"I seriously doubt he's that deep."

"Whatever you say." She shrugs. "But you really should start dating again."

Ever since I broke up with Liam six months ago, everyone has tried to set me up with just about anyone, all the time.

"I told you I'm not ready yet. And I won't be looking for someone like Denning when I am. He's way too full of himself. Not to mention he's a cop."

"A hungry, sexy cop." Sharon lets out a little roar and paws the air.

I met John Denning last spring during the Ab El Malik case. Most of our interactions involved Denning scolding me and trying to get me to butt out and behave like a good little citizen, even when my life was in danger. Of course, I did not comply.

"You could do a lot worse, J. And he was asking about you."

"I'm sure he was just being polite." After we cracked the Ab El Malik case, Denning admitted I have good instincts and even encouraged me to continue my criminology studies. But we haven't exactly stayed in touch.

"I dunno. He seemed pretty interested to me. He even asked about Tyler."

"Well, that was nice." People don't know how to act when you have an incarcerated loved one. Some never mention their name again, like the person doesn't exist. So I always appreciate it when anyone asks about my brother.

"Maybe he can help in some way. Ever thought of that?"

"I doubt it. The Bell River police put Tyler in prison. It seems unlikely a cop, any cop, would want to help me prove his innocence." I move a pile of quartered limes into a stainless-steel receptacle.

"Well, he *is* quite the charmer." Sharon smiles.

"If you're so into Denning, why not go for him yourself?"

"I do enjoy flirting with him."

"You certainly do." The only time I've ever seen Denning blush is when Sharon is laying it on thick.

"Sadly, not *enough* dark side for this girl."

"Suit yourself. Just stop trying to push him on me."

"Oh! Speaking of visitors"—Sharon tilts her head toward a back booth—"see if your sidekick needs anything. I think he's been waiting for you."

Sitting alone, hunched over a laptop, with his stringy black hair tucked behind his ears is Nadir ibn Rashid ibn Asad Al Farhan or, as he likes to be called, but nobody ever does, *Naughty*, munching on a mound of fries.

Wolfson introduced me to the skinny computer whiz kid last spring, and he just stuck. Not only is hanging out with Nadir like having your own personal, not-so-legal search engine, but he's also trustworthy and loyal. He's been a regular in my life, and at the bar, ever since.

"Naughty!" Every once in a while, I acquiesce and use his "nickname" just to see his face light up. I cross the room and slide into the booth next to him. There are several photos of Cole Braedon open on his monitor.

"Oooh, find anything new?" I say, examining the photos. Cole's intense, green-eyed stare pulls me in. Why does he always look like he's up to something?

"So far, it's stuff we already know. Braedon has multiple identities, an FBI agent, a dead Canadian, a Krov gang member..." Nadir zooms in on one of Cole's hands. "Those tattoos are from White Swan prison."

"So, he must be Russian or Ukrainian. Anything else jump out at you?"

"Just that no one ever gets outta White Swan, J. It's a hell hole."

"So, how did Cole?"

"Heavy help. Maybe the Russians or Americans. Or someone else. Just not sure who... yet."

"You'll keep looking?"

"Try to stop me." He grins.

"What about the evidence he sent?" I grab a fry off of Nadir's plate. It's cold and a little soggy.

"That report's legit. I hacked the lab."

"Any files we haven't seen?" I try not to let Nadir see how impressed I am. It'll just go to his head.

"Not in the database. But there's bound to be evidence and records, all kinds of stuff, in *physical storage*. You'd have to go to Bell River IRL to access it."

"I'm working on that. Listen, there's something else I need. What can you tell me about this guy?" I slap Rick Muraro's business card on the table.

Nadir finishes the fries and pushes the plate away. He quickly types the printed information from Rick's card into his laptop.

I flip the card over. "That's the home address."

"Posh," he says and continues typing. "Is that all you have on this guy?"

"Well, he's got one hell of a temper."

Nadir gets to work, fingers flying across the keyboard like a concert pianist. Screens of information flash by in a blur. Where does he find this stuff?

"Okay"—Nadir cracks his knuckles—"graduated from CUNY

law school, took over his practice from an M. F. Muraro, Esquire. He was arrested twice for disorderly contact. Charges were dropped both times. He's got a few properties, a cabin upstate, and a condo in Florida. He owns a high-end Mercedes SUV and a Ducati motorcycle. That's pretty dope. Married to one Natalie Swanson Muraro."

"That's my client." I'm disappointed. It's not much more than I already know and certainly not surprising. "Is that everything?"

"That's the easy stuff. Need more?"

"Yeah, could you dig a little deeper?"

"Gimme a few days? I've got a monster assignment due this week."

"Of course." I sometimes forget Nadir is still in college.

"And refill my root beer?" He lifts his empty glass sheepishly.

"My pleasure. Want some fresh fries?"

His eyes light up. "Thanks, J."

I grab his glass and head to the bar. If only everyone in my life was as easy to negotiate with as Nadir.

Chapter 6
An Occasional Lack of Judgment

By the time the Lyft arrives, I'm running late. I don't want to think about what Rick will do to the dogs if I miss his deadline. The car smells faintly of marijuana, and the driver bobs his head and sings along to rap music. He weaves through traffic, heading from the Lower East Side to the Upper West.

I don't question his choice of route. Instead, I avoid making conversation entirely for fear of distracting him and check my messages. Nothing urgent, just the usual pet dramas and school notifications. *Delete-scroll-delete.* Luckily, 1st Avenue is less crowded than I expected. We should make it uptown with time to spare.

At 14th Street, a bus wrapped in an advertisement for a gruesome Halloween zombie show crosses in front of us. The leering, eyeless face stares at me for a moment before pulling over to let passengers off. My nerves tighten as we whip past the 40s and the street numbers get higher with each block.

I imagine Natalie anxiously waiting for her puppies and steel myself for a confrontation with her ex. There was something about Rick Muraro. The combination of rage and arrogance was unnerving. I just want to get this task over quickly and get home. Finally, we make a left on 85th street. Within minutes, the tall buildings disappear. We pass through the treelined beauty of Central Park at night and emerge on the West Side of Manhattan. The sky above is dark and cloudy, threatening rain. Please let me deliver the dogs and get home before it starts pouring.

We turn onto an expensive residential street lined with elegant brownstones. Rick Muraro's law firm must bring in a lot of money to afford a neighborhood like this. The car abruptly stops near the end of the block.

"We're here, lady," the driver says and starts texting on his phone.

One of the streetlamps is out, creating a pool of shadow. I squint to read the address. This is the place, all right. The house is dark, and the street is quiet. Most of the buildings have iron railings with stairs leading up from the sidewalk to the front door. The landing isn't big enough for a pet carrier. I check my phone. *8:53 p.m.* Did Rick give me the wrong address out of spite? Then I notice a waxy yellow porch lamp casting a dim light underneath the stairs, and a small patio with a gate.

"Can you wait for me a minute? I'm just picking something up. I can be your next ride."

The driver pauses for a beat. "All right. But make it quick. I don't get paid to wait."

I walk through the little wrought iron gate into the patio. No dogs. Just a small metal table and a pair of garden chairs next to a patch of fake grass. The porch light barely cuts through the darkness. A brisk gust of wind chills me. There's a hollow metallic thud. I peer under the table and find a small dog kennel with a neatly coiled leash on top. A second leash lies on the concrete floor. Inside the plastic carrier are two fluffy white dogs napping quietly. Thank goodness!

"Hey there, you two," I whisper gently to wake them up, then pull a couple of dog treats from my pocket and slide them through the bars. "I'm going to take you to your momma now. Sound good?"

Olive and Pepper munch on their treats and lick my fingers.

Now, where's the security camera Rick mentioned? I plan to wave into the lens and get the hell out of here. Above the door is a small camera pointed straight down at the floor. That's weird. The angle is too steep. Besides, don't these things usually have red indicator lights to show they're on? This one is entirely black.

"Just one more minute!" I call out to the driver.

Is this a separate apartment or connected to the main house above? I knock lightly. The hinge creaks as the door swings open a crack.

"Hello? Is anyone home?" The porch lamp casts a small circle of light into the foyer. Inside, the place is dark and still with a faint, unpleasant odor I can't quite place. I examine the doorknob. There are scratches around the keyway, a telltale sign the lock's been picked—the hair on my neck bristles.

Something is not right here.

At street level, a horn honks and tires squeal, the sound of my ride taking off. Damn it. I'm on my own. Olive and Pepper whimper in their carrier, restless.

"I know, girls," I whisper. "I want to get out of here too."

Something is wrong. I strain to hear a sound, but there's only silence. I should lock the door and leave. Instead, I thread my keys through my fingers and make a sharp fist before stepping into the dark hallway. There's a small sitting room to my right filled with gym equipment and a spiral staircase in the corner leading to the main residence upstairs.

"Mr. Muraro? It's Jenna Stack," I call out loudly. "The door was open—"

The house is absolutely dark, except for a seam of dim blue light streaming from underneath a crack at the end of the hallway. I check each room as I go. There's an empty bathroom. I peek behind the shower curtain. Nothing. Not even shampoo or soap. Then a closet filled top to bottom with legal boxes. Outside the last door, I pause and listen. Silence.

"Mr. Muraro? Are you in there?"

My mind flashes back to my evaluation. What did Wolfson say about my occasional lack of judgment being dangerous? I hope this isn't one of those times. Slowly, I open the door. Two enormous computer monitors glow with ghostly blue light in the dim room. Rick Muraro leans on a desk, wearing headphones. Relief washes over me. He's fallen asleep at his computer. I clear my throat loudly. No effect. As my eyes adjust to the light, my pulse quickens.

In the center of Rick's back is a large, wet circle. A spray of blood covers the monitor and keyboard. Black marks surround the bloody hole in his back. I recognize the scattered pattern. We spent an entire quarter studying gunshot wounds and residue at U of M. I rush to his side and shake him.

"Mr. Muraro! Are you—"

He's not moving. No pulse. His skin is cold, and he's not breathing. Rick Muraro's not sleeping. He's been shot. *Murdered.*

My stomach lurches. I'm in the middle of a crime scene. Holy crap! My heart hammers, filling my ears with a rushing sound. Is the murderer still here? I strain to listen. Nothing but silence.

I start to call 911 but change my mind. Once Rick Muraro's dead body is discovered, there will be forensic squads and news crews. I'll be detained, and no doubt Natalie will be questioned too.

So, I call the only cop I know—Detective John Denning. We're not exactly friends, but at least I get how he operates. The phone rings four times before he finally picks up.

"Stack?" He sounds surprised to hear from me.

"Yes," I whisper, afraid I might not be alone. "Listen, Denning. I found a body. He's been shot."

"Paramedics?" He gets right down to business.

"No need. I'll text you the address."

"I'll call it in. Wait outside."

"Okay." I text my location and take a deep breath to calm my heart. There's a little time before Denning arrives. Won't hurt to look around, as long as I don't disturb anything.

The cool light of the monitors washes over the room. At first glance, everything is in order. Papers are stacked neatly on the desk. The only sign of a struggle is Rick's rumpled clothing. This doesn't look like a robbery... and a random psycho is too farfetched. So how did Rick Muraro end up dead?

Next to his body lies a round mirror with a pile of white powder and silver straw. Speed or cocaine? No wonder the guy was so amped. Rick's face has a ghastly expression of surprise. White dust rings his nostrils. Pressed into his ears are Bluetooth earbuds with mics. Did he even hear whoever shot him? I pull my sleeve over my hand and tap the space bar on the keyboard. The screen saver dissolves, and several windows appear on the monitor. There's a map with a route leading to Massena, New York. Three days on the calendar are crossed out and labeled *Travel*. There's also an open document.

I'm picking up Milania the day after tomorrow—
Goddammit! You? No! You can't do this to me!
It's not what you think! No, no, no—

I mull over Rick Muraro's last words. He was picking up a woman named Milania in upstate New York. He must have been using dictation when he was interrupted. Someone walked into the room—someone he knew. He pleaded for them to stop. So why was he shot in the back? Did they order him to turn back around? What did he mean by, *It's not what you think.*

Denning will be here any minute. Using my phone, I snap photos of the computer screens, the drugs, Rick's body, and the letter. It's morbid, but this place will soon be swarming with cops and technicians. I want a record of how I found the scene. I notice a familiar photo from Rick's office on the desk. A young Rick is standing with an older man wearing matching New York Mets baseball caps.

Who is that guy? Rick's father? An uncle? I snap a picture. In the trashcan, there's a gift bag. The paper is thick and glossy with a logo of a mask—half white, half black—the legend reads Facèré Boutique. It probably means nothing but I snap a photo anyway.

A loud wailing shatters my concentration. Sirens. I rush back through the hallway, check on the dogs, and step onto the sidewalk.

A black Dodge Charger with red and blue flashing lights pulls up and double parks. Detective John Denning steps out, wearing jeans and a casual jacket. I'm reminded why Sharon turns into a puddle of hormones whenever he's around. Whether sitting on a bar stool or managing a crime scene, John Denning embodies the ideal Hollywood casting call for a "sexy, confident police detective." He's six feet tall with short, tousled hair but not the kind that's been styled to look messy. More like he's just too busy solving crimes to bother. I'm pretty sure he's in his mid-thirties, but it's hard to tell. The lines on his forehead and around his piercing blue eyes give him a rugged, world-weary toughness. He's also smart and slightly cynical but not above turning on the charm to get what he wants.

"Stack?" He snaps a finger in front of my face. "Are you in shock? Do you need a doctor?"

"No. Sorry." How embarrassing! "Just thinking—"

"About what? The fact you're at yet another crime scene? I can't wait to hear your excuse this time." His tone is impatient, like he's talking to a poorly behaved child.

"That's not fair. It's been months."

But he's already looking at the brownstone, adding things up.

"Wait here." Denning pulls a pair of black latex gloves from his pocket and disappears inside the building. After a few minutes, he returns, peels the gloves off, and shoves them into a plastic baggie. As casual as he might look, Denning always plays by the rules.

"You were right. Who's the dead man?"

"A guy named Rick Muraro."

"You knew him?"

"Sort of..." I stomp my feet. It's freezing out here.

"Hold that thought." Denning walks over to his radio and mumbles a bunch of codes. Then he returns to where I'm standing, shivering in the cold air.

He looks at me curiously. "You realize most people if they're lucky, never find themselves calling the police to report a dead body. And they certainly don't have a Manhattan detective on speed dial."

"Are you sorry I called?" My voice cracks. The adrenaline is starting to dissipate, and my feelings are a little hurt. You'd think he'd appreciate me tossing him a nice juicy murder to solve.

"Of course not." Denning's tone softens. "And I'm glad to see you're all right. But you realize how crazy this is, right? You're like a magnet for danger. Why are you here, anyway?"

"I was just doing someone a favor."

He furrows his brow. "A pretty dangerous favor if you ask me."

Before I can explain further, a police cruiser pulls up.

"Settle in, Miss Stack." Denning shakes his head as he walks away to greet his colleagues. "You're going to be here a while."

Chapter 7
Night Maneuvers

Denning wasn't kidding about a long night. The front of the Muraro brownstone is blocked off with crime scene tape, and I've been trapped on the wrong side of the yellow line for over two hours now. The rain never materialized, but the temperature dipped, making me wish I had a coat.

The moment the flashing lights arrived on the scene, the neighbors started to stream out of their front doors. Now, the street looks like a block party with casually dressed, wealthy New Yorkers chatting and sipping from coffee mugs or wine glasses while texting on their phones. Undoubtedly, they're gossiping with friends and updating the Citizen app with images and speculation. They try to act blasé, like the police blocking off their street is an everyday occurrence. I guess posting photos of a murder scene makes them feel like everything is under control. But take away their fancy clothes and multi-million-dollar homes, and they could be a group of nosy neighbors anywhere.

Denning has assigned a methodical detective named Lopez to interview me. He stands in front of me, wearing a sharp crewcut, neatly trimmed mustache, and crisply pressed suit. Everything about him screams uptight as he writes my answers down in a notebook before repeating the same questions. I'm starting to doubt his competence. I've answered everything he's asked more than once—but he still won't let up.

I understand the police are doing their job, but I'm exhausted and starting to lose patience. I texted Natalie to say I was running late—but did not mention the murder. Now I'm worried she'll see the news before I can tell her in person that her ex is dead. Then there's poor Olive and Pepper locked in their travel crate. They must be hungry and scared.

"I'm just trying to understand." Lopez drills on. "Tell me one more time why you went inside a dark, strange house by yourself?"

I'm reminded of television crime shows where the shrewd detective plays dumb to trick the target into revealing crucial information. Now I'm wondering; is Lopez slow or crafty? I can't tell.

"I told you. The door was open. I sensed something was wrong."

It's not that I don't want to be helpful, but I've learned through my brother's experience never to offer information to cops unless directly asked.

"Please be more specific, Ms. Stack. What time was that?"

There you go, Lopez. That's better.

"I arrived shortly before nine p.m. to pick up the dogs."

"And Mr. Muraro was expecting you?"

"Yes, but when I got here, a few things were off. The door was ajar, the lock had been tampered with, and the camera wasn't working. That's when I realized something was wrong, so I went inside."

Lopez writes carefully in his notebook. Then he looks at me with a blank stare. "What do you mean tampered with?"

"The keyway was scratched. Usually, that means the lock has been picked."

"How do you know what a picked lock looks like?"

"I'm studying criminology at U of M."

He looks up from his notes. "Wolfson?"

WTH? Does everyone in law enforcement know Wolfson?

"Listen, Detective Lopez. I've already told you everything. I found the body. I called Denning. That's it."

My phone buzzes in my hand. It's Natalie texting.

Natalie: *I'm starting to worry. Are you OK? Are my babies OK?*

Detective Lopez doesn't stop me, so I text her back quickly.

Me: *Yes. Dogs are fine. Be there as soon as I can.*

I stuff my phone in my pocket. I need to get out of here.

"And who was that?" Denning has finally rejoined us.

"Natalie Swanson. Rick Muraro's wife, actually estranged wife." The minute the words slip out of my mouth, I realize I've offered too much information. Something about Denning changes; his expression hardens, and his posture grows rigid.

"Mmm hmm," Lopez says, taking notes, unfazed by my revelation. "Did you know she's studying at U of M with Wolfson?"

"Yes, I know." Denning narrows his eyes, fixing me in an icy gaze. "Thanks for your help, Lopez. I'll finish with the *witness*."

"Are you sure?" Lopez looks disappointed.

"I'm sure. See you back at the station." Denning tosses the

officer one of his reassuring smiles. In response, Lopez tucks his notebook away in his jacket and walks toward a waiting squad car.

Once his colleague is out of earshot, Denning hits me with direct questions. Too bad Lopez isn't here to see how it's really done.

"So the victim was *married*? When did the wife move out?"

"I have no idea. Look, Natalie's worried about her dogs. And I am too. Olive and Pepper have been locked in that crate for hours."

"So you're here for the dogs?"

"Yes, I'm on a—"

"Pet sitting job?"

"Exactly. There's something I should tell you. I saw Rick earlier today." No point hiding anything. Denning will find out. The guy is like a bloodhound.

"The murder victim?" A vein on his temple begins to bulge. He looks at me with a new intensity.

I take a deep breath and try to frame the situation in a casual voice. "I served Rick a Temporary Custody Order for the dogs. He freaked out—"

"You served papers on this guy?" Denning stares at me in shock before his brows knit together. But there's something behind his eyes. Am I sensing a sliver of concern? I must be imagining things.

"I tried to tell you earlier, but you strolled off to play king of the crime scene and left me with Dopey Lopez."

Oh God, did I say that out loud? Yes, Jenna. You did.

Denning's face turns red, but he manages to keep his cool. "I'm sorry you've been so terribly inconvenienced by the murder *you* discovered. But I'm here now. So please continue. You served Rick Muraro papers. Here? At the murder scene?"

"No, at his office, in Brooklyn."

"For the wife?"

"Yes, because he backed her into a corner."

"What kind of corner?"

"She was afraid of him, so I volunteered."

Denning bites his lip. "Where's the wife now?"

"At her apartment, waiting for me to bring the dogs."

"Does she know what's happened here?"

"I haven't told her yet. But she's going to see this"—I gesture to the circus of people on the street—"on the news, online, somewhere."

Denning runs his hand through his tousled hair and shakes his head. "Seriously Jenna, what on earth have you gotten yourself into now?"

I guess I'm not imagining things. He is concerned. The idea throws me off. Suddenly, I feel a flush of confusing emotions. I'm about to answer his rhetorical question when a scream, more like a wail, interrupts our conversation.

Several yards away on the sidewalk, a tall, dark-haired woman in a stunning black evening dress and sky-high heels has collapsed into the arms of a young female officer. The woman is sobbing. The officer's expression is panicked like she's never consoled anyone in her life. Detective Lopez is standing next to them, scribbling away in his notepad. This must be Elena Solaris, Rick Muraro's glamorous girlfriend.

"What the?—Wait here," Denning orders and walks away quickly.

"Hey Denning," I call after him, "the dogs need to do their business. Can I let them out?"

"Go ahead," he shouts back.

Relieved, I walk over to the crate, gather the leashes, and sit cross-legged on the ground. Two sets of eager little dog eyes stare out at me. I start to unlatch the grate. Olive and Pepper whimper. Poor things.

"Now, let me just get these clips on," I reach in. "Stay…"

To my surprise, the dogs don't try to rush out.

Clipping on their leads, my hand sinks into piles of fur. They feel like two fluffy, warm piles of white cotton balls. I hope neither of them had an accident, but first things first. I walk the dogs over the fake grass. As I suspected, they immediately get down to their business. Both dogs pee, then step off of their "yard." One of them hands me her paw, which I shake. The other turns in a little circle before tilting her head curiously as she sits down.

"Wow. You are very good girls."

I check their tags. They look almost exactly alike. The one who shook my hand is slightly bigger with a purple collar. Her tag reads *Olive*.

"Hello Olive." I scratch her head, and she licks my hand. "That makes you in the pretty pink collar, Pepper." They seem clean and dry, but I want to check the carrier to be sure there's no mess. "Can you two wait here for a minute?"

I feed them each a treat and loop the ends of their leashes under one of the metal chair legs to be safe. Then I pull the carrier out from under the table.

I'm patting my hand around the inside of the kennel, looking for any sign of dampness, when I feel something hard under the pad. Strange.

I lift the cushion and catch a glimpse of metal. I pull the pad out entirely and set it on the ground. The lights from the squad cars flicker, illuminating the inside of the crate. Crammed in the back corner is what looks like a gun—but like no gun I've ever seen. The barrel is black, but the handle is white, decorated with a silver and gold design. I wonder if it's even real. Maybe it's a dog toy, someone's terrible idea of a joke.

I resist the urge to pick up the strange object.

"Detective Denning?" I call loudly.

He glances up and cocks his head. I signal him to come over.

He waves his hand dismissively, indicating he's busy.

"*John*," I use his first name, hoping he'll recognize how unusual that is and realize I'm serious, "I think you better come here. *Right now!*"

~

Denning approaches, brow furrowed, police lights flashing behind him. The wind whips his hair as he rubs his temples in concentration. Sharon's description of him pops into my head—what was it? Serious about the job but tortured by the responsibility.

As soon as he's within earshot, I point at the crate. "In there."

Denning looks at the dogs and the open crate, raising an eyebrow.

"This better be good, Stack."

"You'll need gloves." I wrap my arms around my ribs. It's cold out and getting colder. Without a word, Denning pulls a fresh pair of gloves out of his pocket, slips them on, and crouches down to look inside the carrier.

I sit on one of the metal chairs and pull both dogs on my lap. Fatigue has set in, and holding their poofy little bodies is warm and comforting.

"You're kidding me." Denning shakes his head in disbelief as he removes the gun gently. He holds the weapon up and examines the make and model. The shiny, decorative barrel catches the light. It's unusual, almost beautiful; a feminine-looking gun.

"Is that thing real?" I cradle the dogs, and they lick my face.

"Very." Denning turns the gun over carefully, examining the details. He points to a logo on the handle. "A limited run Beretta— one I've never seen before. You didn't touch it, did you?"

"Of course not." I'm insulted he'd ask.

He sniffs the end of the barrel, examines the trigger, then the firing pin. Then he tilts the gun to catch the light.

"What are you looking for?" My mind flashes to the unsettling image of Rick slumped over his desk. I push the thought away.

"Powder around the chamber. This gun has been fired recently."

It dawns on me that Olive and Pepper were sitting on top of a loaded gun for hours. I squeeze them tighter, grateful they weren't hurt.

"So that's the murder weapon?"

"Probably," Denning waves over a crime scene tech dressed in white plastic. The tech takes possession of the gun and carefully bags the evidence. "Check the chamber against the bullet in Muraro's torso. Bring the crate too." The technician waves over a colleague, and they start photographing the plastic carrier and cataloging evidence.

"How long will that take?"

"If I fast-track the case? A few days. In the meanwhile, we'll try to trace the gun to its owner."

"It looks expensive. Sort of like a collector's piece."

"Should make it easier to track." Denning is deep in thought, mouth curled up at the corners. I've seen that look before. "You were supposed to bring the dogs back to your client, the estranged wife. Correct?"

"Well, yes. But—"

"Did she specifically tell you to bring the crate?"

It's obvious where he's headed, and I don't like it.

"Listen, Detective. Natalie didn't do this."

"Oh, we're back to Detective, are we? A minute ago, it was John." He looks at me with those steady, clear blue eyes. Blood rushes to my cheeks.

"I was trying to get your attention—" I manage to say.

Denning steps closer. He's a head taller than me, at least. My breath catches in my throat as he focuses on me with laser intensity.

"Listen, Jenna. You still have a lot to learn."

There he goes again. Condescending. Arrogant. I glare at him, but he's already moved on to the next task. He opens his passenger door and whistles sharply. Olive and Pepper obediently hop off my lap and race to the car.

"Come on, Stack," he says. "Time to introduce me to Mrs. Muraro."

Chapter 8
A Chilly Dilemma

Olive and Pepper are standing on my lap, sniffing the night air, their little tongues flapping, enjoying the car ride. I've cracked the window, but I'm too nervous to lower the glass any more. Not until I know these two white fluff balls a bit better. Meanwhile, Denning has barely said a word. I'm unsure if he's deep in thought or annoyed with me. Despite his moodiness, he drives efficiently, accelerating through the turns, attention focused on the traffic ahead like a fighter preparing his strategy. I try a little small talk.

"So, it's been a while. How are you?"

"Cold. Shut the window," he commands while keeping his eyes fixed on the road.

"Come on, Denning. It's not that bad. The dogs like the air." I kiss the top of Olive's fluffy little head, or is it Pepper?

"They're dogs. I'm a person. It's my car."

Okay, I guess he is officially mad. Why? What the hell did I do?

"You can manage. We're practically there." I turn toward the window. In truth, I'm a little chilly myself, but I don't like his tone. Besides, what's the big deal? Let the dogs live a little.

"Why are you always so difficult, Jenna?" He clenches his jaw and grips the steering wheel tighter.

Jeez. Has he always been this uptight?

"Fine, I'll shut the window." My voice rises louder than intended as I fumble to find the button on the armrest.

"No. It's okay. Leave it." He glances over, his tone softening. "What kind of dogs are those anyway?"

"I have no idea." I could offer that they look a little like Bichon Frises with longer hair. But what am I, the dog-breed police?

"Well, they're ridiculous," he grumbles, a hint of a smile appearing.

"Ridiculously cute, if you ask me." Ugh, I can't stop disagreeing with him, even when he's trying to lighten the mood. What is it about this guy that drives me so crazy?

Denning's knuckles tense on the steering wheel again.

"Listen, I don't want you interfering when we get there. Do you understand?"

There's that tone again; older brother mixed with a hint of a school principal. My blood pressure ticks up ever so slightly.

"Natalie is a client. I'm delivering her dogs as requested. That's hardly interfering."

"This is serious, Jenna. A murder has been committed. I'm sure even *you* can comprehend why Natalie is a suspect."

"Even *I* can comprehend? What's that supposed to mean?" I may not know as much as Denning, but give me some credit. I know more about crime and the justice system than the average person.

"You know what I mean." His tone is condescending. "You're not a cop." He weaves expertly through traffic as we zero in on Natalie's neighborhood. Even arguing with me doesn't throw this guy's reflexes off.

"I'm telling you, there's no way Natalie murdered someone."

"How can you be so sure?"

I can't stop challenging him, and he can't give me an ounce of credit. This conversation is going nowhere. I take a deep breath, trying to control my temper.

"I'm not stupid, *Detective*. I have an undergraduate degree in psychology."

"Okay then. Please enlighten me. What was your impression of Rick Muraro?"

"I only met the guy once, but he was hot-headed."

"How many times have you met Natalie?"

Damn it! He's got me. The fact I've only met her *once* will sound ridiculous. I ignore the question.

"My gut, and my education, tell me she's innocent."

"Would you care to elaborate?"

I look down at the dogs. Pepper is still enjoying the breeze. Olive has curled up on the floor between my feet and is napping.

"Well, for starters, murderers lack empathy. Natalie is sweet and caring. She loves her pets. There's no way she shot her ex in the back."

Denning shakes his head, exasperated.

"You know how many times I've heard someone isn't capable of murder? And guess what, Jenna? Most of the time, it turns out, not only are they capable of murder—they *did* it!"

"And sometimes they *didn't*!" My voice rises with frustration. I'm tired of arguing with him. Why does he have this effect on me?

Silence fills the car. I resist the urge to speak for a whole city block.

He breaks first. "I don't understand how you can be so naive, Jenna. The world is a nasty place. You should know that by now."

I'm surprised by his words. I'm not the most optimistic person, but that's a pretty bleak worldview. I pivot in my seat to face him.

"Do you really believe that?"

"I do." He stares straight ahead, his conviction chilling.

"But there are *some* good people?"

"Very few." The scene through the car's windshield seems to illustrate Denning's point. A man in a tattered coat shakes his fist at the traffic while a couple faces off in the street, yelling at each other.

"Well, I have faith in the inherent decency of humanity. And Natalie is one of the good people." Pepper licks my face as if she understands I'm defending her human. I ruffle her ears.

"We'll see." He shakes his head as if I'm a child incapable of understanding a difficult concept.

"Why are you so closed-minded?"

"I'm being realistic. There's a difference."

"What about other leads? Wasn't Rick going to meet someone, *Milania*?"

"So you read the computer monitor? That figures," Denning says tightly. "We're looking into her. According to the girlfriend, Rick went upstate to his fishing cabin regularly—alone. Maybe the place was a hook-up shack."

"Ew. Gross." The thought of angry Rick Muraro hooking up in a shack with some random woman is repulsive.

Denning smiles. "You really are naive."

Jerk! If he'd witnessed Rick Muraro's temper tantrum this morning, he'd be grossed out too. "I'm just glad you're considering other suspects."

"Of course we are. But as you know, other suspects rarely pan out."

"What's that supposed to mean?" I bristle. Suddenly it feels like we're not talking about Natalie anymore.

"Aren't you trying to dig up an alternate suspect in your brother's case?"

I glare at Denning. He looks straight ahead, eyes fixed, mouth set in a thin line. Lights flicker through the windshield. My anger evaporates, replaced by something colder.

"Are you saying Tyler's case is a waste of time?"

He shrugs. "It might be."

This is why I never asked for his help. If a cop is supposed to be as cynical as possible and doubt every explanation, Denning certainly excels at his job.

"Tyler's innocent. Someone else killed Joe Vitner. So yes, I'm still trying to dig up an alternate suspect."

He drums his fingers on the steering wheel.

"All right. All right. It's just—"

"Just what?" My blood is boiling.

"Well, your brother was found guilty in a court of law—"

"You don't know—"

"Let me finish, Jenna. I think you're wasting your time. But if you're *right,* if Tyler was framed, looking for answers could be dangerous."

Denning glances at me and there's genuine concern in his eyes. Or is it pity? Somehow, his expression is worse than the argument. How can I jab him with a snappy comeback when he's looking at me that way?

"I'm not afraid—" I manage.

"I know you're not. That's what worries me."

Silence fills the car again. This time I have nothing left to say. I lower my window a few more inches, letting a gust of brisk wind inside. Passive aggressive, I know, but I can't help myself. Denning makes a wide turn onto Natalie's street and pulls up in front of her building. The flash of television screens shines through the drawn curtains of the apartments on the block. Olive wakes up, and the dogs start to whimper excitedly.

"That's right, girls. We're here." As I open the door, Denning stops me.

"Listen, Jenna. I brought you with me as a courtesy."

"And to put your suspect at ease." I cross my arms. We can play this game all night as far as I'm concerned.

"Maybe a little. But I'm serious. I'll ask the questions. Understand?"

As we get out of the car, Denning puts his hand out for their leashes. "I can deliver the dogs myself, Jenna. You're free to head home."

"Fine. I'll keep quiet." I hand him Olive's lead and keep Pepper. I'm not leaving Natalie alone with this guy.

"Now, let's see what we can find out."

Chapter 9
Running Interference

The sidewalk on 46th Street is quiet. It's well past midnight, and the street is dark. I should be home, but here I am with Detective Bitter Table-of-One. The night air cuts through my thin sweater as Denning and I wait for Natalie to answer her buzzer. He takes off his coat and offers it to me. As tempted as I am, I ignore him. I'd rather catch a cold.

"Suit yourself." He slips the coat back on and buzzes again.

Come on, Natalie. What's taking so long? There's a crackle of static.

"Yes?" Natalie's voice floats through the speaker. She sounds disoriented.

"It's Jenna. Are you okay?"

"Yes. I... fell asleep."

Denning cocks an eyebrow. I know what he's thinking. A cold-blooded killer sleeps the soundest.

"I have two sweet dogs, excited to see their mom."

"Oh my gosh! I'll buzz you—"

"Natalie?" I add quickly. "There's someone with me."

"Not...?"

"No, not Rick. I'll explain everything. Just let us in."

There's a loud electronic buzz. Denning yanks the door open and heads up the stairs briskly. My muscles are cold and stiff, and I'm out of breath when we reach the top. Standing in the doorway, Natalie looks tiny and frail in a set of plaid oversized men's pajamas. The deep look of concern on her face disappears when she sees Olive and Pepper.

"My babies!" she squeals, scooping them in her arms and inside the apartment. The dogs ride along, tails wagging, licking her face and sniffing her hair.

The small space is a little less cluttered than yesterday. The moving boxes have been unpacked and folded against the wall. There's an open box marked *O & P*. Two dog beds are on the floor, one pink and one purple, with Olive and Pepper embroidered in gold. Food and water bowls and a few toys litter the kitchen.

It's obvious Natalie has been home all evening, unpacking. I toss an "I told you so" look at Denning, but he ignores me.

"What happened? I was so worried!" She sets the dogs down, strokes the fur on their heads, and pulls a baggie of treats out of the open box. "Good girls," she coos. They look at her with big brown eyes as they gobble up their biscuits.

Denning takes in the cramped apartment. I can practically read his mind. Nobody goes from a luxurious three-story brownstone to a four-hundred-square-foot walk-up without some bad feelings.

"Ms. Swanson, can we sit down?" He gets right to business.

Natalie glances at Denning, then me.

At this point, nothing will soften the blow.

"Oh, of course. I didn't mean to be rude. I'm just so happy to see my girls. You're a friend of Jenna's?" Natalie sits on the couch, and the dogs immediately jump into her lap. I sit next to her, and Denning casually takes a chair across from us. Once he faces

Natalie, his expression morphs, he tilts his head, smiles gently, and looks at her with kind eyes.

"Ms. Swanson, I'm a police detective." He flashes his badge.

"Oh." Her eyes widen with surprise.

"You're also known as Natalie Muraro?"

"Yes, I am." She glances at me, unsure of what's happening.

"And you're still married to Rick Muraro?" Denning pulls a small pad and pen from his coat pocket.

"We're separated. That's why I use my maiden name."

"I'm sorry to inform you." He cuts right to it. "But your husband is dead."

Natalie sits bolt upright, a confused look on her face.

"Dead? *Rick?*" She looks to me for confirmation, lip trembling. "Jenna?"

"It's true, Natalie. I didn't want to tell you over the phone."

Denning leans forward, his steely blue eyes focusing on her intently. "Do you need us to call someone for you?"

"No, I'm fine." Natalie fiddles with a button on her pajamas nervously. "What happened? Was there an accident?"

I want to jump in and tell her the whole story, from arriving at Rick's brownstone to finding his lifeless body, but I keep my mouth shut. Denning warned me not to interrupt, and I'll have plenty of time to tell her later.

"No, Mrs. Muraro, your husband was shot," Denning says bluntly, scanning Natalie's face for her reaction.

A sheen of sweat appears on her forehead, and the color drains from her face. "Shot?" she parrots Denning. "When? By who?"

"Tonight. And that's what I'm trying to find out."

Natalie swallows hard. She looks faint.

"I'm so sorry." I put a hand on her shoulder. I go to the small kitchen and get her a glass of water. She accepts it and takes a long drink but still looks pallid.

Denning waits, feigning concern. But I can see he's on the hunt, probing, analyzing her reactions and movement. He's already used some emotionally charged words and phrases, mentioned her marital status, and he keeps addressing her as Mrs. Muraro. Now he's going to gather her version of events. If she makes a misstatement, he'll use it against her. He flips open his notebook and clicks his pen ceremoniously. This is it.

"Can I ask where you've been tonight?"

Natalie looks at me, clearly nervous. Anyone would be.

"I was here. I've been here since five." She twists her fingers anxiously as he jots down her response.

"Was anyone with you? Did anyone call you?" Denning's body language is relaxed, but his questions are targeted.

Natalie takes another sip of water, hand unsteady. "No, I was alone. Jenna texted once, around nine-forty. Then I tried her—closer to eleven?"

I nod in agreement, more for Natalie's benefit. Denning already knows I texted her.

"So there's no one to confirm your whereabouts? What were you doing here?" He casually walks to the window and glances outside. No doubt checking for other routes in and out of the building.

"I was getting the house ready for the girls." She gestures to the dog beds and food bowls. The danger of her situation hasn't fully hit her yet.

"Mrs. Muraro, do you own a weapon?" Denning pushes.

Natalie is taken aback by the bluntness of his question. Her mouth falls open, and her eyes go wide with fear.

"Well, I—"

Denning knows he's pushing the line, bullying her, digging for information without a lawyer present.

"Don't answer that!" I blurt out. "You need a lawyer."

Denning shoots me a warning look. "Stay out of this, Jenna!"

Natalie looks pale and unsteady. "I—I think I should s-speak to a lawyer." She glances at me, and I nod, encouraging her to stay strong.

Denning crosses his arms. The interview is over, and he's *fuming*.

"Fine. But you'll need to make a formal statement. Tomorrow, I'll expect you at the precinct with your lawyer." He glares at me, and his eyes are flinty.

Natalie is frozen in place. Olive licks her face, but she doesn't respond. She takes a deep, shuddering breath.

"It's okay, Natalie. It's just a statement."

But even as I'm saying the words, the look in Denning's eyes tells me it's not okay. Natalie has no real alibi—he's elevated her from a person of interest to his number one suspect. Denning's expression makes me nervous as he slides his card across the coffee table.

"Here's the address. Let's say four p.m.?"

Natalie's eyes well with tears. She's falling apart.

I put my hand on her shoulder and shake her gently. "Natalie?"

Her eyes come back into focus. "Will you come with me, Jenna? *Please?*"

Denning scowls at me, silently telling me that I'm not needed or welcome as far as he's concerned.

I pat Natalie's limp hand. "Of course I will."

Chapter 10
The Obvious Suspect

Denning stands up and zips his jacket, jaw tight. I doubt the outside temperature will be as chilly as the mood between us.

"Come on, I'll take you home." He opens Natalie's front door.

"No thanks. I think I'll stay." I cross my arms defiantly.

Denning narrows his eyes and takes a breath like he's about to argue. Then he leans in closer until I feel the heat between us.

"Fine. But watch your step, Stack. You know the only thing worse than interfering with an active investigation?"

"No. What?"

"Interfering with one of *my* active investigations. Lawyer or no lawyer. If your client is guilty, she's going down." Denning storms out.

The door shuts and I turn to Natalie. She looks up with sad eyes, red-rimmed and damp from tears. I grab a box of Kleenex on the counter and sit down next to her. She pulls a handful of tissue out of the box.

"I don't even know why I'm crying"—she sniffs and blows her nose delicately—"Rick was such a jerk."

"I'm sure you loved him at one time." I barely know Natalie, but I can't imagine her falling for the man I met yesterday.

"I did. At first." Natalie looks up from behind her tissue.

She still doesn't know how serious the situation has become.

"Natalie, you're in trouble. That cop is trying to poke holes in your alibi."

"Alibi? What do you mean?"

"He thinks you shot Rick."

The color drains from her face, and her lip trembles.

"*Me?* But that's crazy. Why me?"

"Because you're the obvious suspect." I take her hand and lead her into the living room. "Now, tell me everything you know about Rick; his life, business, associates." I sit on the couch, and Natalie sinks down beside me.

"I don't know anything, just a feeling."

"What kind of feeling?"

"That Rick was involved in something bad."

"What exactly?"

"Honestly, Jenna, I'm not sure. You know who his father is, right?"

There's fear in Natalie's eyes. I remember Nadir mentioning that Rick took the law firm over from M. F. Muraro, but the name doesn't ring a bell.

"No, who?"

"Have you heard of Manuel Muraro? Around the neighborhood, they used to call him Manny the Rock?"

"No, should I?"

"Maybe we need a drink." Natalie retrieves glasses and a bottle of red wine from the kitchen. The dogs settle on the couch between us. Natalie collects her thoughts. Finally, she begins.

"When I met Rick, he was finishing law school. It sounds cheesy. But he was so charming. He swept me off my feet." She smiles wistfully and pours the wine. "I met his family. They were a big, loving, loud *famiglia*. Totally different from the way I grew up. His dad, Manny, was nosy, but in a good way. You knew he cared. I felt so happy and loved like I belonged."

"That sounds nice," I encourage her.

"Then we got married, and things were wonderful until...." Natalie looks down, ashamed.

"Go on. I'm listening." Wolfson taught us a technique called *Active Listening* to encourage the interviewee to share details that could be important. Right now, the only way to help Natalie is to find out everything she knows.

Natalie swallows hard. "Well, Rick confided his dad was a wiseguy."

I try not to spill my drink. "You mean the Mafia?"

"Yes, exactly. Manny was a made man."

"I thought he was a neighborhood lawyer?"

"Most of his cases were defending minor players and legal filings. Rick said not to worry." Natalie bites her lip nervously.

This must be why Denning asked how much I knew about Rick Muraro. Did he already know about the Mob angle?

"That must have been tough."

"The first few years were fine. Rick had a temper and a few strange clients, but nothing scary. Then he inherited the practice from Manny. Suddenly, more money was coming in—*a lot* more. He bought the brownstone with cash and kept a roll of bills in his pocket. When I asked where it all came from, he got angry. Of course, I had my suspicions."

Natalie finishes her glass of wine and pours another. She's rattled. The memories are obviously upsetting.

"How bad did things get?" I prod gently.

"Well, he started to disappear on *business trips*. He was short-tempered, even paranoid. One day he demanded I quit my job as a translator—to mind the house. And stupid me—I did. Then things got worse. He complained when friends called and never wanted me to go out. I felt so scared and alone."

"It's not your fault. That's abusive behavior. He was isolating you."

"When I said I needed company, he bought me Olive and Pepper." She looks at the dogs sadly. "I mistakenly asked him why we were buying purebreds when so many shelter dogs need homes —that's when he *hit* me."

"Oh my God, I'm so sorry."

"He said no wife of his was going to walk a common dog around the neighborhood." Natalie scratches Pepper's belly. The little dog rolls on her back. "It's not your fault you're fancy. I love you anyway." She fights back the tears.

"When did you finally break up?"

"Not right away. I was scared of what he'd do... and didn't want to lose my family. Manny was always so kind to me, sweet even. He called me his *piccolo tesoro*. His little treasure. It's hard to believe Manny was into anything shady. But Rick? Toward the end, I was terrified. I complained when I learned about his girl-friend, but part of me was relieved when he met Elena. I just wanted out. I didn't even ask for money, just my little bolos."

"Bolos?"

"Short for Bolognese. That's their breed." She ruffles Olive's fluffy ear.

"Like the meat sauce?"

Natalie smiles. "I know. Silly, right?"

I scroll through my phone and find the picture I took at the crime scene; young Rick and an older man wearing Mets caps.

"Is this Manny the Rock?"

"That's him." She smiles sadly. "Did Rick have that on his desk?"

"Yes, he did." I text the photo to Nadir.

Me: *Rick Muraro was murdered. Check out his father?*
Manuel Muraro, aka Manny the Rock. Mob connection?
Nadir: *On it.*

"This whole thing is so crazy," Natalie says.

I squeeze her hand. "I better go. And you need some rest."

"Jenna? What happens tomorrow?" Natalie looks scared.

"Tell the truth. But first, talk to a lawyer."

"I was thinking of asking Paul Hill. Would that be a conflict?"

"He's your friend, right?"

"I hope so." She looks down shyly.

"Do you trust him?"

Natalie's cheeks flush pink. "Yes. He's not like Rick at all."

"Then call him right now." I sling my bag over one shoulder. "Tell him everything and ask him to meet us tomorrow."

As I head to the door, Natalie grabs my sleeve. She's scared, and I don't blame her. Denning played hardball tonight. I know he has reasons to be cynical, but tonight his pessimism blinded him to the obvious—Natalie is out of her depth.

"Jenna? I didn't kill Rick. I hate violence, and I despise guns. You believe me, don't you?"

"I do. And Denning will too. After tomorrow, this will all be over."

Chapter 11
Fuzzy End of the Lollipop

The last time I was at the First Precinct Detective Division was late at night. The waiting area, filled with shabby furniture and peeling paint, is even more dismal under the harsh fluorescence of daylight.

Across the room, Natalie Swanson sits in a chair, looking sick and disoriented. Paul Hill stands beside her, gently patting her back. I turn my hands up in a questioning gesture as I approach them.

"They asked Natalie to identify Rick's body," Paul says. "As you can imagine, it was quite a shock."

"They couldn't find anyone else to ID him?" My fists clench involuntarily at the idea of putting Natalie through that kind of unnecessary trauma.

"I offered, but the lead detective on the case, Denning, insisted. No doubt a strategic move designed to rattle her." Paul looks at Natalie with concern. "As you can see, his plan is working."

"Denning can be a real jerk." I shake my head angrily. "He's also smart and good at his job. I wouldn't put it past him to pull something like that."

"Well, if he's good at his job and *honest*, there's nothing to worry about."

Natalie lifts her head. "What do you mean, Paul?"

"You didn't kill Rick, and anyone with half a brain can see that fact. Plenty of people hated the guy. That doesn't make them murder suspects. Once you give your statement, I'm sure your part in this tragedy will be over."

"Do you really think so?" Natalie looks up at Paul hopefully. "I just want to put this all behind me."

Detective Lopez appears wearing a short sleeve shirt and crisply pressed jeans. He looks uptight and uncomfortable, even in casual wear.

"Follow me." He escorts us through a maze of busy cubicles.

Denning stands up as our group approaches his desk. He ignores me completely and speaks directly to Natalie.

"Thank you for coming, Ms. Swanson. Why don't we talk in a room?"

"Is that really necessary?" Paul asks warily.

"Of course not." Denning shrugs and looks around at his crowded workspace. "But we'll all be much more comfortable."

Natalie glances at Paul for guidance. I'm about to interject that I don't think it's a good idea, but he responds before I have a chance.

"Fine, Detective." Paul places a protective hand on Natalie's shoulder. "Let's get this over with so my client can go home."

I start to follow, but Denning blocks my path. "And where do you think you're going, *Ms. Stack*?" There's a hint of amusement in his tone.

"If you remember, *Detective Denning*, Natalie asked me here."

"Well, your friend seems to have representation."

"Yes, but—" The words dry up in my throat. He's so aggravating. I don't know enough about Paul's experience to feel comfortable leaving them alone with Denning, but I can't exactly say that out loud.

"Do you doubt Mr. Hill's ability to advise Ms. Swanson?" A smirk crosses Denning's lips.

My face flushes with anger. He knew exactly what I was thinking.

"Of course not!"

"It's okay, Jenna," Natalie whispers.

I consider my options, but the truth is I have none. This is Denning's turf, and he clearly doesn't want me in the room when he questions Natalie. Despite his stupid tactic, I refuse to leave the precinct without her.

"Fine. I'll wait for you right here, Natalie. I have some reading to do for school anyway."

I sit down in the guest chair next to Denning's workspace. The government-issued desk is exactly as I remember from the last time I was here; covered in scribbled notes, a beat-up old computer, a banker's light, and a pile of ragged file folders. Detective Lopez sits directly across, buried in a stack of papers.

"Keep an eye on our guest, Lopez." Denning drops his cell phone on the detective's desk. "If my call comes through, come get me." Then he shuffles Paul and Natalie into an interrogation room.

I dive into the assigned chapter in my *Psychology of Criminal Behavior* textbook. It's dense reading and takes some concentration. I'm just getting to how the Central Eight Criminogenic Risk Factors relate to recidivism when I'm startled by a loud buzzing.

"Denning's phone," Lopez shouts into the device. He pauses a moment and adds, "Thank you for your help. Can you send that to this number?"

Lopez stares at the screen for a second before smiling. He gets up, phone in hand, walks briskly to the interrogation room and knocks.

After a few seconds, the door opens. Denning leans against the frame and scans his phone. Then he walks to the table and passes the device to Paul Hill. Paul looks at the screen for a moment before his posture deflates, his shoulders sag, and his mouth drops at the corners.

Gently but firmly, Denning pulls Natalie to her feet. "You have the right to remain silent. Anything you say can and will be used against you...."

"What?" Natalie gasps.

Paul stares motionless at the unfolding scene. What did Denning show him? Why isn't Paul doing anything?

I race across the squad room.

"What's happening? What the hell are you doing?" I try to step between Denning and Natalie, but his eyes and face have hardened.

"My job." Denning clicks the handcuffs on Natalie's delicate wrists. "Ms. Swanson, you are under arrest for murder."

"But I wasn't there," Natalie pleads. There's a look of shock and horror on her face. Tears fill her eyes and spill down her cheeks.

"My God, Denning. She's not a killer—" My voice shakes with anger.

"No one asked you," he snaps. "Lopez? Take Ms. Swanson to a holding cell."

Lopez looms over Natalie and pulls her toward the door.

"Paul?" Natalie's voice is barely a whisper.

Anger and confusion threaten to overwhelm me. Everything is spiraling out of control as Natalie is led away by Lopez.

Paul Hill snaps out of his trance and bolts to his feet.

"I'm going to get you out, Natalie," he calls after her. "Just hang on, okay?" His hands ball into fists of frustration.

"What the hell is going on, Paul? What happened?"

"According to the detective, the murder weapon belongs to Natalie," Paul says, frantically packing his briefcase.

His words hit me like a shockwave. That fancy gun in the dog carrier?

"How can that be?" I manage to say. "I thought Natalie hated guns?"

"I don't know how, but Denning has everything he needs to tie Natalie to the murder weapon." Paul takes a few deep breaths. I can't tell if he's thinking or trying to stave off a panic attack, but his lack of action worries me.

"What are you going to *do*, Paul?" The tone of my voice snaps him out of his fear. He looks at me with determination in his eyes.

"First I need to convince the judge to grant bail and get her out of lock-up."

"You mean she's going into the general jail population?"

He nods, and I feel sick. The thought of sweet, innocent Natalie sitting in a cell waiting for a trial is insane. I've been down this road with Tyler, and things did not end well. Paul is right. His priority is getting an arraignment set and convincing the judge to grant bail.

"Listen, I need to start the paperwork." Paul shuts his briefcase. "Pick up the dogs, will you? And try to find out what that detective knows, or thinks he knows." Paul glares at Denning, who has returned to his desk as if nothing has happened. His smug expression enrages me.

"Don't worry. I'll find out what's going on."

"Thanks." Paul pushes past Denning's desk. "You'll be hearing from me, Detective," he announces formally, then races out.

I walk over to the desk and sit in Denning's guest chair. Don't blow up, I tell myself. Stay calm. Focus. I wait but he ignores me and calmly flips through a report. I'll need to push to get him talking.

"How could you?" I lean in and glare at him, imagining my eyes burning a hole in his temple.

Finally, he closes the file and folds his hands. Then looks at me with a cool, measured expression.

"I get no pleasure from this, Jenna," he says calmly. "I understand you like Natalie and believe she's innocent. But the situation does not look good."

"Thanks to you!" The words burst out of me. So much for keeping calm.

"This isn't personal. I'm just following the evidence—and the law." His composure is maddening.

"By arresting an innocent woman for *murder*?"

"Listen, we have all the evidence we need. That gun you found? It's a rare and expensive, limited edition engraved Beretta 92FS with a pearl handle."

"So? That doesn't mean—"

"Please, let me finish. We spoke to a gun dealer who remembers selling that exact Beretta to the Muraros. The husband wanted protection for his wife because he was out of town a lot. The dealer remembered the sale because a collector's edition Beretta is an expensive gun for home protection when any gun would do."

Natalie's comment about Rick buying her the dogs flashes in my mind. No wife of his was going to walk a *common* dog around the neighborhood. I guess no wife of his was going to use a *common* gun to shoot an intruder.

"So, he bought her a gun. That doesn't mean she knows how to use the damned thing."

"True. But we found this in the house." Denning pulls a photograph out of a folder and tosses it on top of the files.

The photo shows Rick with his arms around Natalie, teaching her how to aim the Berretta. On the wall behind them, a sign reads *The Pistol Palace.*

"See that?" He taps the photo. "That's a shooting range the Muraros visited after they took possession of the weapon. The owner keeps all of his security footage. It took a while, but he dug this up and sent a copy to me."

Denning opens his phone and turns the screen to me. The video shows Rick teaching Natalie how to shoot. She beams with pride after each shot, and he praises her for doing well. The time stamp reads one year ago. This is what they were all looking at, the final piece of circumstantial evidence that convinced Denning Natalie is the killer.

"But..." My words evaporate as I stare at the damning video. Even I have to admit that the evidence is piling up.

"Face it, Jenna. We've got motive and opportunity—a messy divorce with a lot of money at stake and a weak alibi. We have a gun with a partial print at the crime scene and proof it was purchased for the suspect. We have video evidence of the suspect using the gun registered in her name and a shell casing found at the scene. All that's left is for ballistics to confirm a match."

My mind is spinning, flashing on all of the circumstantial evidence that convicted my brother of murder, and grasping for any way to shift Denning's focus away from Natalie. "What about the autopsy?"

"We don't have the results yet, but it sure looks like Natalie's gun was fired into Rick Muraro's back."

"That still doesn't prove she was the shooter. Don't you think it's strange she used a rare gun, registered in her *name*, to commit a murder?"

Denning shrugs, unfazed by my logic. "I've seen it all. Maybe it was a crime of passion. She wasn't in her right mind."

"But shooting Rick when I was on the way to pick up the dogs? That's just plain stupid."

Denning folds his hands on his desk and looks at me with a tolerant expression. "Did it ever occur to you that maybe she planned it that way?"

"Planned to commit murder when I was due to arrive any second? That's crazy."

"Or genius. Think about it, Jenna. Natalie hid the gun in the carrier because she knew you would bring the dogs to her *and* become her alibi. She takes the pups on a stroll and tosses the murder weapon in the East River. By the time Rick's body is discovered, no more gun."

I admit the evidence looks bad, and I can practically see the wheels turning in Denning's head as he puts the pieces of his theory together.

"What about the scratch marks on the door lock?"

"That could have happened anytime. Those basement doors are a favorite entry point for would-be burglars."

"But the door was open."

"Simple. She panicked and didn't shut the door properly."

"What is it, Denning? Is Natalie a criminal mastermind or a frenzied impulse killer?" I can feel my blood pressure rising.

"Natalie's plan was solid. Her only flaw was that she didn't count on you being so nosy. All the evidence points to one thing. Natalie killed Rick."

"Maybe that's what the real murderer wants you to think."

"Not everything is a conspiracy, Jenna," Denning says condescendingly. "NYPD should be thanking you. You're the reason we caught her."

Infuriated, I stand up. Nothing is going to change his mind but cold, hard facts. I sling my backpack over one shoulder and turn to walk out.

"I have to pick up Olive and Pepper now."

"I'll let the team know to expect you."

Team? I stop in my tracks and face him. "What team?"

"The one searching Natalie's apartment." Denning starts dialing.

No wonder he's so smug. Video or no video, he planned to arrest Natalie for murder today. He executed a search warrant while Natalie was at the station.

I turn around, barely able to contain my anger.

"You were never going to give her a chance, were you? You wait. I'm going to prove you wrong."

"No, Jenna. You're not. This is police business. You're going to stay out of this case. Understand?"

Damn him! If he thinks I'm staying out of this case, he's not just a jerk; he's a fool.

"You're making a big mistake, *detective*. You'll see."

Chapter 12
Doc Forbin

After three tries and forty-five minutes, I find a Lyft driver willing to transport the dogs. When we arrive at Natalie's building, the block is crawling with police cars. An after-work crowd has gathered, ogling the scene from across the street. Undeterred by the chaos, my driver pulls up behind a double-parked forensics van, puts the car in park, and looks over his shoulder at me expectantly.

"You gonna be all right, Miss?" he says.

"Sure, I'll just be a minute." I scan the crowd and spot a policewoman holding Olive and Pepper's leads on the sidewalk. I hop out of the Lyft and wave. "I'm Jenna Stack. Denning called you?"

"Took you long enough. Picking up poop is not in my job description." She hands me the leashes with disgust and marches back toward the brownstone.

Cops are weaving in and out of the building, collecting evidence, labeling plastic bags, and sealing boxes. I wonder how long Denning had this whole thing planned? I wrangle the two overly excited bolos into the back seat. The minute I close the door, the driver loops around smoothly.

"I got a Pomeranian named Cocoa," he says. "She's my little angel."

The dogs pant frantically as I stroke their furry bodies and try to calm them. After a few minutes, Olive curls up on the floor, and Pepper settles on my lap to look out the window.

But I can't relax. I'm still fuming. The video at the gun range makes Natalie look guilty as hell, but the evidence is circumstantial. And even though Natalie has no real alibi, my instinct tells me she's innocent. Now Natalie is sitting in a jail cell and desperately needs my help. If Denning won't look for answers, I will, so I text Nadir.

Me: *I know you're busy but I really need your help.*
Nadir: *Wassup?*
Me: *Long story. Can you meet me in thirty minutes? Dave's place. I'll order pizza.*
Nadir: *On my way.*

The Lyft driver drops me off, and I take his card. A driver who'll transport dogs is like gold in this town. The bolos take tiny, mincing steps to the elevator and sit quietly as we travel up to Dave's floor. As the door opens, I'm hit with the smell of melted cheese and spicy tomato sauce. The pizza guy beat me home. Luckily someone let him into the building, and he's standing in front of the door. I thank him for waiting, let the dogs in, and brace myself for a long night. I'm hungry and exhausted, but now is not the time to rest.

Being in a new place with new scents, including pizza, has set off the normally well-behaved Olive and Pepper. They're alternating between balancing on their hind legs, begging for food, and running laps around the apartment. I almost feel bad about breaking Dave's "no dogs in the apartment" rule. But my current mess can be traced directly to that envelope he had me deliver. So basically, this is *his* fault. I put the pizza into the oven to stay warm.

Just as the dogs quiet down, there's a knock at the door. Through the peephole, I see Nadir in the hallway holding up a six-pack of Mountain Dew.

"Security's for shit in this place, J. Some clown just let me walk right in."

I open the door, and Nadir glides inside, computer bag slung over one shoulder. Olive and Pepper go berserk, jumping and yapping excitedly.

"Bolos!" he exclaims, patting them on their fluffy white heads. "Ciao cagnolini." In addition to being a computer genius, Nadir speaks about a dozen languages, which comes in handy when he's snooping around online. I don't bother to ask how he knows the dogs' breed.

"Sorry, they're a little upset. Their human, Natalie, just got arrested for her ex's murder."

"Wait? Your client got tagged for the Muraro murder?"

"Yep, and she's innocent, Nadir. It's a nightmare."

"No doubt." Nadir sets his bag down on Dave's desk.

"So I need that deeper dive *tonight*. Anything you can find about Rick Muraro, his girlfriend Elena Solaris, the law firm, Manny the Rock, Natalie, or a mystery woman named Milania. All of it."

Nadir sets up his laptop and grumbles about the speed of the network. But within seconds, his fingers are flying.

Once I feed the dogs and get pizza on plates, I focus on my actual job running Tails of the City. First, I arrange for Gary to pick up Olive and Pepper. He loves boarding little dogs and has playpens and toys. Then I catch up on emails and text out assignments. One hour and several slices later, Nadir is ready to review what he's uncovered.

"Okay," Nadir says. The puppy party on the couch perks up at the sound of his voice. "Who do you want to start with?"

I throw up my hands. "Dealer's choice."

"All right then. First off, the law firm. Manny, the Rock, used to represent some heavy wiseguys back in the day. But since Rick took over, things look pretty tame."

"Are you sure?" That's not the impression Natalie gave me.

"I checked out Paul Hill and the employees, Rebecca and Josephine. Nothing stands out. I found some other businesses in Brooklyn, so I checked Rick's accounts. At first glance, they're legit, almost vanilla, but dig a little deeper, and things start to look off."

"What do you mean by off?" I lean in, intrigued.

"Well, for one thing, he's partnered up with some notorious characters."

"What kind of characters?"

"The kind that are into hiding assets. There's a shell corporation formed out of state, possible money laundering, that sorta thing. Nothing solid. Just looks mad shady."

"Sounds promising. Is it the kind of thing the police will find?"

"Shouldn't be too hard—if they look."

"What if they don't?" Which is what I'm afraid of. "Is there anything I can tell them?" Nadir's methods aren't always above board, and I would never want to get him in trouble.

"Let's hope they dig this stuff up on their own."

I take that as a no and move on. "What about Rick's girlfriend?"

"Looks like she comes from money. She was born in Colombia. Boarding school in Switzerland. Came into New York on a student visa, and now the law firm is sponsoring her, which I'm guessing is a stretch?"

"Unless she's a secret paralegal." I doubt Rick's glamorous girlfriend clocks in at the firm.

"So either Elena Solaris is clean," Nadir adds, "or she's dirty enough to cover her tracks."

"And Milania? What about her?" I'm starting to feel desperate.

"Can't find any Milania—last name, first name, or business name—connected to Rick Muraro."

I dread asking my next question, but a good investigator is thorough.

"What about Natalie?"

Nadir leans back with his hands clasped behind his head.

"Aside from crap taste in husbands, your pal appears to be clean. Grew up in North Carolina. Straight A student. Went to Cornell on a scholarship. Graduated Summa Cum Laude. Speaks a few of the Romance languages. Used to work at the UN as a translator. Cute dogs." He smiles at Olive and Pepper, who seem to follow his every word. "No record. No tickets. No history of anything sketchy. Nothing at all."

Relief washes over me. "So my instincts were right about her."

"Looks like it."

"Crossing Natalie off the suspect list permanently." I make an imaginary check mark in the air.

"And that brings us back around to Rick's old man."

"Manny the Rock? I thought he was dead?"

"Says who?"

"Natalie. She told me Rick inherited the law firm."

"Well, he's definitely not dead. Just indisposed." I can tell from Nadir's grin he's been saving this juicy piece of information for last.

"What do you mean?"

"Dude's in prison. Manuel Muraro, aka Manny the Rock, is serving twenty on a murder charge with a dash of racketeering and extortion. It seems he got caught up in an investigation, and his Mob buddies let him take the fall."

"Really? Natalie said he was a wiseguy. But murder? Are you sure?"

"Yup. And his list of known associates is epic. I don't think he's consigliere level. But he's in the Mob for sure. He got nabbed a coupla years ago."

"Right around the time Rick took over the practice?"

"Exactly. There's more than one way to inherit. And I checked the prison records. Rick has never visited his father. Not once."

"That's weird."

"Ice cold if you ask me."

"Where *is* Manny?"

"Uh…" Nadir steels himself. "He's at Eastmoor."

Eastmoor Correctional Facility? The information shocks me, and I have to force myself not to visibly cringe. So these are the kind of people locked up at Eastmoor? Hardened criminals and mobsters. Until this moment, the idea was only half-formed, far away. Now, I can't ignore the ugly truth—Manny the Rock, a Mob lawyer and a murderer, is in the same prison as my little brother.

"Sorry, J—"

"It's not your fault." I pull Olive on my lap and squeeze her tight.

"Hey, J?" Nadir has a sly smile. "Want me to put the Doc on 'em?"

Doc Forbin is the name of a program Nadir wrote that can monitor a person's credit cards and other types of activity online. He named it after the scientist who created an all-knowing computer in a 1970s science fiction movie called *Colossus: The Forbin Project.*

"On who exactly?"

"All of 'em." There's a wicked look in his eyes. "The law firm staff, the girlfriend. Just to see if anything crazy pops up."

"Fine, but only for the credit cards and unusual activity. No snooping."

"Me, snoop?" He turns back to his laptop and, with a mischievous grin on his face, starts typing furiously.

My phone buzzes, snapping me out of my thoughts. It's Paul Hill.

Paul: *Can you meet me at the office tomorrow? 9 a.m.?*

Maybe he's got some good news?

Me: *I'll be there.*

Chapter 13
The New Boss

The waiting room at Muraro and Hill is empty. When I walk inside, I notice a little shrine to Rick Muraro on one side of the room decorated with his picture, a bouquet of white roses, and a black ribbon. Josephine, the receptionist, is dressed in a black suit with black manicured nails set with rhinestones. Based on my interaction with Rick, I'm a little surprised by the display of grief. Although Natalie said he could be charming.

"Sorry for your loss," I say gently.

"They're in the conference room." Josephine points to an interior door. No hello. No have a seat and someone will be with you. Her eyes look a little puffy under her doll-like lashes. "Second door on the right."

The conference room is large but spartan, with a single wooden table and eight faux leather chairs. Paul Hill and Rebecca are inside.

Paul paces back and forth, talking excitedly on his phone. His briefcase is open on the table, with loose papers and files spilling out. Crumpled notes litter the floor. I count four empty Starbucks cups in his immediate vicinity. No wonder he's anxious. He's strung out on caffeine.

"Yes, I'm still holding!" Paul snaps in frustration.

I wonder how much experience he's had with criminal cases. He seems in over his head. On the other hand, Rebecca sits at the conference table with a legal pad and pen, calmly making notes. She notices me standing in the doorway.

"Jenna Stack? Please come in. We didn't formally meet the other day. I'm Rebecca Stone." We exchange a handshake.

"Have a seat." She gestures to a chair. "Paul is working on getting the arraignment scheduled as quickly as possible."

I take a seat.

Across the table, Paul suddenly stops pacing.

"Fine, yes." He hangs up and notices me for the first time. Dark circles have formed under his eyes, and his expression is tormented. He leans his forearms on the back of a chair and collects himself. "I tried to file for an emergency arraignment, but no luck. The police are stalling."

"I'll get started on the writ of habeas corpus," Rebecca says.

"What can I do?" I'm not sure why Paul asked me here today, but I'm willing to do anything I can to help.

"We're trying to piece together what happened that night," Paul says. "We're hoping you can fill in some blanks. When you were at the crime scene, did you see anything odd? Something that stood out?"

"I took pictures." I slide my phone across the table.

Paul and Rebecca glance at each other in surprise before she picks up the phone and scrolls through the crime scene photos. Paul peers over her shoulder.

"My God," Rebecca says. "You were smart to make a record."

"As you can see, the place looked like someone broke in. The weirdest thing was the note Rick dictated. He was planning to meet someone named Milania—"

"Rick never mentioned her." Paul stares at the photo of Rick's body. "Why was he shot in the back if he recognized the murderer?"

"Exactly what I thought. He would have been facing his killer."

"I wouldn't put an affair past him," Rebecca adds and slides the phone back. "Could Milania be involved?"

"Maybe, the cops can't seem to find her."

"What else?" Paul leans on the chair back, thinking. "What about... I don't know... any impressions or feelings?"

"Just that Rick was into some bad things. I mean, doing drugs, taking trips to meet strange women, and no offense, but that expensive brownstone and this office don't exactly line up."

"Agreed," Paul says. "I've thought the same thing for some time, but we've never seen evidence of illegal dealings."

"Have you checked his accounts? What about Rick's father? I know he's in prison and connected. Could Rick have pissed off the Mob somehow?"

"Natalie said you were studying to be a detective." Rebecca smiles. "But I seriously doubt Manny is involved."

"They haven't spoken in years," Paul adds. "The only reason Rick keeps Manny's photos up in his office is to fool our older clients into thinking he cares."

"What about Elena?" I strum my fingers on the table, thinking.

Rebecca laughs. "Elena? All that woman does is shop, exercise, and schedule beauty procedures; not to mention Rick was her ticket to citizenship. Elena's best life was Rick alive, well, and divorced from Natalie."

"What about enemies? Rick must have made a few?"

"He wasn't well-liked, but *enemy* is a strong word," Paul says.

"Maybe Jack will turn up a clue," Rebecca says.

"If he ever shows up." Paul rubs his eyes. He looks stressed, and Rebecca notices.

"Why don't you take off, Paul? You've got enough to do." She smiles sympathetically. "I'll wait for Jack."

"Good idea." Paul seems relieved as he shuts his briefcase without bothering to straighten the contents. "I've got calls to make and favors to pull in if we're going to get Natalie out of lockup."

The minute he's gone, Rebecca stands and starts cleaning up, pushing in chairs, and tossing papers. I join in, stacking empty coffee cups.

"Has Paul ever handled a criminal case?" I try to be as delicate as possible, but honestly, I'm worried.

Rebecca looks at me with sharp eyes.

"Not on his own. But he's helped Rick with a few. He's a good lawyer, and he cares about Natalie. And he's not alone. I'll be doing some of the work."

"Sorry. I didn't mean to be rude."

"It's okay." Her face softens. "I didn't mean to snap. We're all on edge."

"How did Paul get mixed up with Rick anyway? They seem like such unlikely partners."

"They knew each other from law school. When Rick took over the firm, he asked Paul to partner. Paul was thrilled, of course. He's smart and a hard worker. But I'm sure you noticed he lacks confidence. Rick was charming, self-assured, and had a client list and family contacts. It seemed like a perfect fit."

"What about you? How did you end up here?"

"I started as a paralegal in a work-study program for CUNY Law. I'm waiting for my bar results now. I was planning to quit as soon as I know I've passed." Rebecca leans a hip against the table. "But now that Rick's gone, who knows."

"Was Rick that bad?"

"Oh, he was a world-class asshole, that's for sure. Condescending. Volatile. Manipulative. But I can handle that. It was the strange invoices, weird expenses, and secret clients that creeped me out. As you pointed out, this place doesn't add up. But I have a feeling that might change now."

A chill runs down my spine. If Rick's nefarious business dealings endangered the law firm, Paul would have a solid motive to want him dead. I'm glad Nadir is monitoring the firm's associates with his Doc Forbin program. Like Wolfson's rule number two warns: *Trust no one.*

The phone on the conference room table buzzes, and Rebecca hits an intercom button. "Yes?"

"Jack's on his way in," Josephine says.

Jack walks into the conference room, hands thrust deep in his jacket pockets, shoulders hunched, ready with a line.

"Jeez, Paul. Can't a guy take a day off to mourn his buddy?"

"Paul's not here." Rebecca bristles. "You're here because Natalie's been arrested for Rick's murder."

"Really?" Jack looks surprised. "Sweet little Natalie? She always seemed like such a mouse." He nods at me and plops down in an empty chair. It groans under the weight of his small, rotund body.

"Paul is defending her. And you, Jack"—Rebecca crosses her arms—"are heading the investigation."

Jack smirks. "With Passive Pauly on the case, she's gonna need me."

As abrasive as Jack Russell is, he could be right. Paul seems concerned with Natalie, but what if hiring Jack to investigate is just a performance? For all I know, Jack Russell is Natalie's best option.

"That's *not* funny," Rebecca snaps. "And Natalie is innocent, Jack. Aren't you interested in finding out who killed your friend?"

"Okay, okay. But I'm on the clock, right?"

As much as I don't trust Paul, I can't believe the nerve of this guy. His friend's been murdered, and all he cares about is getting paid?

"Yes, Jack. Paul's authorized as many billable hours as necessary." Rebecca taps the intercom. "Josephine. Jack is pre-approved for billable hours."

"Yes, ma'am."

"I'll get right on it." Jack runs a hand through his thinning hair.

An idea pops into my head. Up until now, Jack has barely acknowledged me, and he doesn't seem like someone I particularly want to spend time with investigating a case. But tagging along with him could be a great way to gather information. Other than keeping Tails of the City on track, I don't have any commitments today. What have I got to lose?

"Would you mind if I come with you?" I ask sweetly.

"Aren't you the dog nanny?"

He's got me there. "I'm also studying criminology at U of M." I've found flattery goes a long way with macho personalities, so I add, "Maybe I could observe? Learn something from a professional?"

"Is Wolfson still there?"

Good old Wolfson. You never know what door he'll open.

"Yes, he's my advising professor. I'm sure he'd love the idea of me following a real investigator on an important case." I force a wide-eyed, hopeful expression onto my face.

"I like it." Jack smiles. "Teach the girl rookie how it's done. It'll be my good deed for the week."

He sure is full of himself. I can think of several unkind retorts, but I put those aside in the interest of the case and try to sound grateful.

"Really? Thanks so much! Where do we begin?"

"In cases like this, you always start with the wife or girlfriend. Since the wife is our client, let's go see Elena."

Chapter 14

White Knuckle Ride

From the outside, Jack's car is a nondescript, slate blue four-door sedan, perfect for surveillance. Most people wouldn't notice it and certainly wouldn't guess the owner's profession. But the inside is something else entirely—a private investigator's command post. As I open the door, I'm hit with the pungent aroma of cigar smoke and fast food. The passenger seat is littered with candy bar wrappers, and the dashboard is plastered with sticky notes. There's a small cooler behind the passenger seat, probably for food and drinks on stakeouts. A dark blanket covers a lumpy mass, shaped vaguely like a human being, across the back seat. Jack guns the engine and unlocks my door. I hop inside, buckle up, and roll down the window.

"Get ready to see how it's done." He pulls away from the curb abruptly, maneuvering the sedan through traffic, almost side-swiping a red BMW. By the time we turn onto the Brooklyn-Queens Expressway, my knuckles are white from gripping the sides of the seat, and my stomach is queasy. I'm grateful to have the rush of fresh air on my face.

"Isn't that a yellow light—"

"First off, you're gonna need a car." Jack suddenly speeds up and changes lanes. "Single most important tool in your arsenal."

"Ah—" I'm pretty sure he means weapon in my arsenal or tool in my toolbox, but I get the point, and I'm not about to correct him.

"You listenin'? I got gems to share, and I'm not gonna repeat myself."

"Yep. I need a car." I'm not sure I agree. But this is a fact-finding excursion, and I want to stay on his good side.

"But be careful with the GPS. You never, ever want to use traceable technology to find someplace you shouldn'ta been."

"That's smart." I have to admit, that's a solid piece of advice.

"Plus, ya know, the government uses 'em to track us."

That part, I doubt. But who knows? "Okay, no traceable tech. Got it."

Jack merges onto the Brooklyn Bridge. The East River and downtown New York come into view. Sunlight reflects off the buildings and casts a dazzling glow off the glass and metal structures.

"Look at that. Don't cha just love it?"

I smile. "Yes, I do." The Manhattan skyline always takes my breath away from any angle, any time of day.

"Let's see, what else. Oh, here's a good one. What do you do if you're on a case and a real cop shows up?"

"Clam up." I've never used the phrase clam up in my life, but this seems like the time for it.

"That's right!" Jack wags a finger in my direction, pleased.

I'm weirdly proud my answer went over so well. Jack is defi-nitely a character, but he's growing on me.

"And always ID yourself as a *Private* Investigator. In your case, *Private* Investigator Stack. I got dragged downtown once cuz I wouldn't cooperate with the wrong cop. He tried to get me for impersonating an officer."

"What was the case?"

"A guy I knew wanted me to retrieve a personal item from an associate's residence. Unfortunately, said associate was dead at the time."

"Murdered?" This is turning into one of the weirdest car rides ever.

"Yeah. By my client. The stinking rat was trying to frame me for it. But the joke was on him. I was passing the time at *The Slap and Tickle* just minutes beforehand. Plenty of witnesses cuz I'm a real good tipper. Which brings us to the next lesson."

He maneuvers deftly through the streets of Chinatown, avoiding a group of tourists and a delivery cyclist balancing food bags from his handlebars.

"You gotta assume the client is lying to you about something. That's a big mistake dicks make, trusting their clients. Remember this one. They only ever tell you what they want you to know."

"Isn't that awfully cynical?" My voice jumps an octave as Jack blows through another yellow light.

"Maybe, but that piece of advice is gonna help you solve and survive, which is the name of the game. Whoever hired you *wants* something, and you are their means to get that thing. Period."

He abruptly swerves to avoid a bag of garbage in the street. I hold onto the car's grab handle for dear life.

"Of course, you know about trash. It's public domain. Always have your garbage-picking gear. You wanna look for receipts, shredded documents, or scribbled notes. You wouldn't believe what I've found written on envelopes—Social Security numbers, lock combos, and phone numbers. That stuff is pure gold."

He leans over and pops open the glove box. What is that weird cologne he's wearing? It smells like furniture polish.

"Shouldn't you be writing this stuff down? Like I said, I ain't gonna repeat myself." The small compartment contains tools: screwdrivers, tiny wire cutters, and even a compass. Mixed into the clutter are at least a dozen pens, a few business cards, and three or four small flip-top notebooks.

"Go ahead. Take a notepad and one of my cards while you're at it."

I grab a pad and tuck his card inside. Then I quickly jot down his tips and repeat each item aloud.

Need a car (nothing flashy)
GPS Bad (Govt?) / No traceable tech
Clients lie, trust no one
Dumpster diving (be prepared)
If cops show, ID yourself as PI

"I think that's everything," I say, pen ready for the next pearl of wisdom.

"That's good, real good!" Jack grins, turning onto West Broadway, taking us out of bustling Chinatown and into fashionable SoHo. "That's quite a memory you got there."

"Wolfson keeps us on our toes," I say and hang onto my seatbelt as he pulls up in front of a stately brick and glass building, busy with activity.

"I don't like these guys much either." Jack points to a valet approaching the car. "Sneaky way to get into a person's car. But parking's no-go around here. We'd spend more time looking than we'll be inside. Gotta take the chance. But write this down—*Avoid valets*."

A uniformed attendant opens my door while another takes Jack's keys and hands him a ticket. He looks back at the valet suspiciously as we head for the glass doors.

"So whad'ya think?" Jack smooths his hair and hikes up his pants.

I'm not sure if he's asking about his lessons, the ride over, or the hotel, but it's a safe bet he means the nuggets of detective wisdom he's been dishing out.

"I guess you've been at this awhile," I say.

"Twenty years of working my ass off. That's another thing; there's not much money in this racket. Make sure you get paid."

"Have you worked for Muraro and Hill for twenty years?"

"Yep. I knew Manny back in the day. Great guy."

Jack checks his reflection in the glass doors before they swing open on a bustling lobby.

"Fancy," I marvel, taking in stylish room.

"You think this is posh. Just wait 'til you meet Rick's main squeeze. She's a real class act."

Chapter 15
The Suite Life

The hotel lobby is bustling with the rich, chic, and fabulous. A woman with a heavy French accent checks her luggage for a day of shopping before her evening flight. An overly tan, blond man taps his passport, demanding an early check-in. His girlfriend hides behind her phone and dark sunglasses, while more sophisticated people ignore her. Every table at the interior patio cafe is occupied with business deals being made or couples planning their city excursions. Harried servers deliver avocado toast and kale salads. Jack couldn't be more out of place as I trail him to the elevators. And he couldn't care less.

This guy is growing on me.

Thankfully, we're alone in the elevator, allowing me to ask about Rick's girlfriend. As Jack presses the button to the top floor, I lean against the wood paneling.

"Is Elena tall and trim with dark hair?"

"Her and about a million others," Jack says, checking his scratched Timex watch. "Who wants to know?"

"I think I saw her outside the house the night Rick was killed."

"Wait—" Jack looks at me, confused. "You were at Rick's house?"

"Didn't Paul Hill tell you?" I'm surprised the office detective doesn't have all the facts.

"Passive Pauly? How he got through law school is beyond me. What the hell were you doing at the crime scene?"

"Picking up the dogs for Natalie. I'm the one who found Rick."

Jack's eyes flare with interest.

"Well, that must have been a shocker. You give a statement?"

"Yes. Lopez and Denning both grilled me."

"Okay. I'm gonna need you to go through it all with me. But for now, finish the part about Elena. You saw her outside? Was that before or after you found Rick?"

"After. She came home while forensics was still in the house. She seemed pretty upset. Kind of fell apart."

"Yeah, well. Wouldn't you? Boyfriend shot dead like that. Pretty upsetting stuff." The elevator door opens. We find Elena's room halfway down the hall. Jack knocks loudly and calls out. "Elena? It's Jack. I'm looking into this... thing. Gotta ask ya some questions." He turns to me. "Keep quiet and just watch. Got it?"

It's the second time a man has told me to shut my mouth this week, which is getting old. But it's his party, and I might learn something.

"Sure, I got it."

Elena opens the door. Aside from being barefoot, she looks like she's on her way to a trendy luncheon. She's nearly six feet tall with long, shiny hair and olive skin. Her eyes are bloodshot, and her makeup is heavy but flawless. She wears skinny white jeans and a low-cut patterned blouse, accessorized with gold hoop earrings, a large gold medallion around her neck, and several brightly colored bangles. She gestures us into the room with inch-long mauve nails.

"Jack, come in." Her voice is weak and hoarse.

We enter a large, bright sitting area with sleek modern furniture. There's no bed, but there are two doors, undoubtedly leading to a bedroom and bath. This is an expensive suite in an upscale hotel. There are worse places a person could mourn.

"Elena Solaris, this is Jenna Stack. She found Rick when she was picking up those dogs."

"I remember seeing you." Elena extends a limp hand which I take and shake lightly. "The night Rick was mur—" The final word catches in her throat.

"I'm so sorry for your loss."

"Yeah," Jack chimes in. "It's a real tough break, Elena. Rick was a great guy. A real prince."

Elena slumps down in a chair. She removes her heavy bracelets and tosses them onto the glass coffee table. Then she absentmindedly plays with the medallion around her neck. At first, I'm dazzled by the enormous pear-shaped diamond ring on her left hand, but a flash of sunlight draws my attention to her necklace. It looks like a large gold cameo of a Catholic saint, but the central figure is a cloaked skeleton holding a scythe surrounded by a burst of tiny diamonds. It's expensive and exquisitely made but a bit morbid.

"Excuse this." She gestures to her outfit. "I thought getting dressed would make me feel better. Now I feel ridiculous."

Elena peels first one, then the other, false eyelash off deftly, and sticks them to the top of the coffee table next to the discarded bangles. Tears start to flow, and Jack hands her a tissue from a nearby box.

"Well, you look real nice, Elena."

She smiles meekly. "Thanks. I feel awful. Did you know they wouldn't even let me see him? They had *her* identify him. He loved *me*."

"That's rough," Jack says and sits on the small sofa across from the despondent woman. I take his lead and seat myself next to him. Like any good interviewer, he waits for her to continue talking. She sits quietly, dabbing away tears before taking a deep, shuddering breath.

"I can't imagine my life without him. The whole thing is so unfair. How could *she* do that?"

"Who do you mean?" Jack prods her gently.

"Why *Natalie,* of course. She took Rick away from me. Why do you think he left her? She was after his money. And she knew he would fight her."

"What makes you think that?" Jack says. He knows what he's doing—acting sympathetic, drawing her to reveal more. But Elena and Natalie's stories don't match. One of them is lying.

"We were going to get married," Elena continues. "Just as soon as that"—she flutters her hand, shooing a thought away—"divorce was behind him."

"I know. He loved you a lot, Elena. Talked about you all the time. And you know he was my pal. It's a real tragedy."

Elena nods. Mascara-drenched tears fall into her lap.

"Listen, Elena. I don't wanna take up your time. Just dotting the I's and crossing the T's. Understand?" Elena doesn't know Jack is technically working on Natalie's behalf, and he doesn't offer the information. Some people might see that as devious. But it's the best way to get honest answers and the best approach for the case. I'm impressed.

"Of course, Jack." She looks at him, eyes damp. "What can I do to help?"

"I know it's tough, Elena, but could you walk me through what happened that night? One more time, and we'll get out of your hair?"

"But I already spoke to the police—"

"I know. I just gotta double check."

Elena takes a sip of water and clears her throat.

"I last saw my Rick early in the evening." For the first time, I notice the trace of an accent; rich and lilting, almost musical. I understand why Natalie felt so intimidated by Elena. Even distraught, she's mesmerizing.

"What time was that?" Jack presses.

"It hadn't been dark for long. Maybe seven o'clock? He said he was going to do some work in his downstairs office. I went to a party at my friend Mimi's boutique. He doesn't, I mean, he didn't, like that kind of thing anyway. When I left him, he was fine. But when I got back—"

Elena starts crying again, softly. Jack hands her the box of tissues.

"What's the shop called?"

"Facèré Boutique. It's over on Columbus."

The minute Elena says the name of the boutique, I remember the bag at the crime scene; the half-black, half-white mask logo. So this is Elena's alibi? I must admit; a party is an excellent alibi— plenty of witnesses.

"How long were you at the party?" Jacks says.

"A couple of hours. It was such a nice night. I walked home. Maybe if I'd taken a taxi, Rick would still be alive."

Elena sniffs, plucking a fresh tissue from the box.

"Or you'd be dead too," Jack says matter-of-factly.

"Oh." Elena's eyes open wide at the thought.

"Elena, I gotta ask. What about the drugs? You know there was coke at the scene?"

"I know." She looks down at the crumpled tissue in her hand. "He, *we*, dabbled a little. Just for fun."

"It was more than a little, hon," Jack says.

"Sometimes, Rick, he used the *cocaína* to stay awake. You know, if he was working late."

"Where did he get it?"

"I don't know. He had a guy. A college kid, I think? But what does that have to do with Natalie killing my Rick?" Elena's voice rises. She's on the brink of breaking down again.

"Just one more question. Did Rick have any enemies? Could someone else have killed him?"

Elena looks Jack directly in the eye and states calmly through tears. "No. No enemies. Natalie killed my Rick. And I hope she spends the rest of her life in prison."

Outside, the hotel entrance is busy. New arrivals pile out of yellow cabs and long black limousines. Departing guests wait impatiently for their transportation to arrive. Frazzled bellhops load designer luggage on and off of rolling racks. Rick Muraro is dead, and Natalie is in jail. But life carries on as usual for the well-heeled New York traveler. As we wait for Jack's car to arrive, he pulls out his phone.

"And what do we do with alibis, baby cop?"

"That's easy." I smile confidently. "We try to poke holes in them."

"You got it." He looks something up, then dials a number.

"Can I talk to the manager, please?"

He covers the phone with his hand. "Watch this."

"Hey. Yeah. I'm one of the investigators on the Rick Muraro case. Was a Miss Elena Solaris at your establishment the night before last? Mmm hmm. What time was that? Thanks. You've been a big help."

He hangs up and grins in my direction.

"Did you see that? I didn't actually say I was a cop. I just let the little lady think what she wanted."

Jack certainly knows all the tricks. Misdirection is a great technique.

"So what did she say?"

"Alibi holds up. Elena arrived around seven-thirty and left after ten."

"And that's it? You believe her?"

"Manager says plenty of people saw Elena there." He shrugs nonchalantly. "Maybe Natalie *did* kill Rick."

"I can't believe that."

"Never trust the client, kid. They'll break your heart every time."

The valet pulls up with Jack's car. He hands him a crumpled bill and snatches the keys from his hand. Then he turns to me. "Wanna lift?"

"No. One of my dog walking assignments is nearby," I lie. "But thanks for letting me tag along. I learned a lot."

"Anytime, kid." Jack climbs in his blue sedan and drives off leaving a noxious blast of gasoline fumes. Now it's my turn to do some checking.

Stepping away from the busy hotel entrance, I pull out my phone and google Facèrè Boutique. According to the Yelp listing, the shop is brand new and only has three reviews. The owner Mimi is a "genius," the selection is "upscale and exclusive," and the grand opening party was just two days ago—the night of Rick's murder.

Wait? How did a bag from the Facèrè Boutique end up in Rick's home office *before* Elena got home from the grand opening night party? Especially if the shop only opened that very same night? The timeline doesn't hold up.

Did I just poke a hole in Elena's alibi?

Chapter 16
Facèré Boutique

Wolfson encourages us to follow our instincts, and mine are pointing me toward the Facèré Boutique. To help get into character, I swing by Dave's and change into a red floral Diane von Furstenberg wrap dress, purchased at a thrift store in Bell River last Christmas. Red isn't really my color, but the designer dress was surprisingly cheap and has a stylish, classic vibe. Wolfson stresses the importance of maintaining a "varied wardrobe" to suit any sleuthing occasion. After layering on a dark cardigan sweater, black tights, and flat equestrian-style boots, I'm reasonably confident I'll blend in with the clientele at any high-end shop.

Despite the cloudless day, the air is crisp as I exit the subway at 81st Street. I stop to peel off my sweater and watch some dogs play in a park. We're close to Rick's brownstone. I wonder if Natalie ever brought Olive and Pepper here to play. After patting a few floppy heads, I collect my thoughts and head toward Columbus Avenue. It took me two minutes online to realize Facèré Boutique had just opened. Did Denning already check this place out? And what about Jack? Why was he so quick to accept Elena's alibi? He's a good investigator. Maybe he's just too close to the case. The only thing I know for sure is that if neither one of them is going to dig any deeper, I will.

The front of Facèré Boutique is floor-to-ceiling glass windows covered with an opaque reflective film. It seems strange for a business trying to attract customers to stay hidden. But who knows? Maybe that's part of the mystique? I recognize the subtle stencil etched on the glass door—the only indication that I'm in the right place—the half-white, half-black mask matches the logo on the bag I saw at the crime scene.

I pull the heavy door open. The shop is cool with subdued lighting. Despite the chill, perspiration beads on my forehead. The place is upscale, with only a few select items on the clothing racks. Practically everything is silk or leather, with a few elaborate sequined pieces.

The stark white walls are decorated with ornate carnival masks of colorful feathers and sparkling jewels. Exquisitely crafted and stunningly beautiful, they look like works of art, not souvenirs. Suddenly, I feel dowdy and cheap in my thrift store dress. To make matters worse, I'm the only customer.

A woman around my age, but worlds apart, stands next to a pair of glass display cases. She's dressed to perfection in a low-cut, sleeveless white jumpsuit that accentuates her trim figure and bronze skin.

"Welcome." She clicks across the shiny floor on silver stiletto heels. "I'm Camilla. How may I help you?"

There is no way this glamazon will believe I'm a customer.

"What a fabulous store," I manage to spit out, trying to buy myself time to rethink my approach. "Is it yours?"

"I wish. Facèré belongs to my aunt." Camilla strokes her glossy, chestnut hair and blinks her long lashes as she evaluates me.

"Those masks are amazing."

"Aren't they? Aunt Mimi loves Carnival. She's collected dozens on her travels. If you're interested, I can get a price list."

"Oh no. Thank you. I was just admiring them."

"I see. Then, can I help you find something?" Camilla arches an eyebrow as if she suspects I'm wasting her time. I need to find a way to ask about the opening night party. An idea strikes me.

"Yes, but not for *me*. My *employer* sent me."

"Oh, of course." Camila nods knowingly, signaling that she's accustomed to dealing with the lowly assistants of New York's wealthy elite. "Please. Have a look around. Let me know if you have any questions."

Strolling around the store, I pretend to evaluate the offerings. I have to hide my shock. Four hundred dollars for a blouse! Twelve hundred for a dress! Are they serious? I end my tour in front of the matching glass display cases. Unlike the sparsely stocked clothing racks, the cabinets are packed with a selection of jewelry designs, ranging from understated to over the top. A stunning hammered gold choker inlaid with sparkling blue stones catches my eye. I wonder if the metal masterpiece costs more or less than the average New Yorker's rent.

"That's unusual. May I see that necklace?"

"Oh yes." Camilla perks up at the possibility of a sale. "Wonderful choice. It's by a brilliant local designer called Estrada."

She pulls out the choker and hands the piece to me. It's lighter and more delicate than I expected. A tiny price sticker reads $3,500.

"May I?" I hold up my phone.

"Of course. But it's difficult to see the artistry in a photo, and we have a very lenient return policy."

Camilla knows what she's doing. I'm sure most rich people don't bother with returns. She's gently pushing me to make the purchase knowing that once that choker leaves the store, it's probably gone for good.

"Estrada's very hot right now," Camilla continues her pitch. "We had several other pieces. But they all sold."

And *here's* my opportunity.

"Wow. So quickly? Didn't you open a few days ago? I hear the party was wonderful."

"Oh, it was." Camilla's face lights up at the memory. "But that was just our *official* opening. We've had private showings for clientele all month."

That's interesting. If Elena is friends with the boutique owner, she could have visited, and brought a shopping bag home, a dozen times before Rick was murdered. So was she at the party? And when? Time for some name-dropping.

"Do you have anything like this in silver?" I turn the piece in my hands.

"We're expecting more Estrada pieces next week. I could arrange for a private viewing?"

"Oh, that's very kind. I'll let my boss know. A friend of hers, Elena Solaris, told us about the store. I think she was at your opening?"

"Elena? Oh yes, she was here all night. She's been very supportive."

There goes another theory up in smoke. Elena was at the party, just like she claimed, and Jack confirmed. So far, her alibi is tight as a drum.

I hand the necklace back to Camilla. As she opens the case, a small pendant on a chain slips out of her cleavage. The glittering gold medallion catches my eye; a skeleton draped in a cloak, surrounded by a smattering of tiny diamonds. It's much smaller than the medallion I saw around Elena's neck, but I'm sure it's the same ghoulish design.

"That's lovely." I feign appreciation of the creepy bauble.

For a split second, Camilla's serene smile dissolves. Then she recovers her composure. Did I strike a nerve?

"Thank you." She locks the jewelry case.

"Does it have some significance?"

"Not really. Sort of protection charm. Aunt Mimi gave it to me." She tucks the necklace back into her top.

"I didn't mean to pry. It's just that Elena has one too." I decide to push a little further. "My boss told me what happened to her husband. It's so terrible."

Camilla's perfect smile disappears completely, and her shoulders slump.

"I wasn't sure if you knew. Yes, it's just awful. She was here, with us, the night it happened." Camilla makes the sign of the cross over her heart.

Now I feel bad. Camilla's confirmed Elena's alibi and explained the existence of the bag. But I've upset her in the process. Time to get out of here as quickly and gracefully as possible.

"Elena's lucky to have such good friends—"

"One minute." Camilla click-clacks over to a small desk at the back of the store and returns with a business card. "Just let me know if there's anything I can do. Really. We're *delighted* to accommodate."

"Thanks for your time." I take the card printed with the Facèré Boutique name, logo, address, contact information, and social media handles.

That gives me an idea. Outside, I open Instagram and type in #FacereBoutique. Bingo! There's a tumble of images from the opening night party. Scrolling through, I see candid photos of Camilla, Elena, and a woman I assume to be Mimi, chatting. They appear to be having a good time. In another shot, Mimi and Elena toast with champagne flutes. Elena's smile dazzles the camera. A chic leopard print scarf is tied jauntily around her slim shoulders. I'm struck by how happy she looks, not a care in the world. Soon her life would be shattered. The photos check out. With her alibi confirmed, I mentally cross Elena off the suspect list.

Up ahead is the subway. Commuters hurry to catch their trains home or meet friends for after-work drinks. Locals walk their dogs. A couple dressed in the latest fashion step out of a limo and float past a backdrop of glass and steel; the city's transition to evening has begun.

The Facèré Boutique is a dead end, so now what? What's my next move?

My phone rings. The words *Department of Corrections* flash across the screen. I pick up the call.

"Tyler?"

"No, Jenna, it's Natalie." Her voice is barely a whisper and slightly muffled. "Paul put some money in an account for me."

Behind her, I can hear a commotion, some banging, and voices raised. Then, what sounds like a fight breaks out in the background.

"Shut your mouth, bitch!" a loud voice booms. "What'd you call me?"

"Biiiiitch!" shouts a shriller voice. "That's mine, goddammit!"

Then there's a thud, like a body thrown against a wall.

"Natalie, are you okay?"

"Oh my God, please, Jenna! You've got to get me out of here!"

Chapter 17
Ouroboros

The stone steps in front of the University of Manhattan feel steep today. I was up half the night worrying about Natalie after our phone call. I've learned a lot from Tyler over the years, so I was able to give her some pointers on how to avoid trouble. I hope she's okay. The truth is, I feel guilty. I'm the one who called Denning and found the gun registered to Natalie. She might not be in this situation if it weren't for me. There's got to be a way to fix things, but right now, I'm late for an important seminar: *Blood Evidence Testing and Techniques*. The rumor is that the splatter demonstration is to die for, and I need the credits. Who knows, maybe it'll help shake something loose in my investigation.

U of M has one of the top criminology departments in the country, and there are always a ton of workshops and demonstrations. The instructors are exciting, and I get to see the theories and forensics I'm studying in action. Also, Wolfson says workshop attendance adds weight to his final evaluation. So I sign up for as many different seminars as possible.

My favorite demo so far this semester was *Covert Entry*

Training. The half-crazed military type leading the class seemed on the razor's edge of criminality himself. Watching him work was amazing. He broke down the major lock types and explained how to spring everything from a combination lock to a deadbolt. That's how I recognized the scratch marks on Rick Muraro's doorknob and why I now carry a lock-picking kit in my bag.

Today's class is being held in the large Frances Glessner Lee auditorium. I'm dismayed to find every seat taken. Then a hand waves at me from the fifth row. *Yes!* My classmates Cody and Sam saved me a seat.

Cody's a beefy former high-school football star on his way to becoming a third-generation New York City cop. Sam is a shy, skinny science nerd. They've been buddies since childhood. They were a bit standoffish at first but warmed up to me over time. Now we're school friends and study pals.

"Did I miss anything?" I whisper as I take my seat.

"No, you're good," Cody says.

"The sharks were circling your seat," Sam says, distracted by a pretty coed across the room. "What do you think she's majoring in?"

"With your luck, Forensic Entomology," I say, trying not to laugh.

"Ooh baby," Cody says in a high girlish voice. "Tell me all about the maggot development in the corpse—"

The lights blink, and today's presenter steps up to the front of the room. Ms. Davidoff is tall with horn-rim glasses, severe bangs, and a ghostly complexion. She writes her name on a chalkboard and turns to the audience.

"Okay. Let's get started." Her clear, commanding voice has a New England accent. She points to two dark wooden boards leaning against the wall. "Although you can't see it now, these boards are covered in blood spatter. One has been cleaned with bleach; the other is just the spatter. Ready?"

The students murmur as Davidoff uses a remote control to switch off the lights. "First, I'm going to apply luminol to the uncontaminated spatter."

She spritzes the chemical across the board, and a faint blue glow appears.

The class responds with a collective, "Ahhhhh."

"And here's what happens when a criminal tries to destroy blood evidence with bleach." Davidoff sprays the second board.

This time the chemical reaction is spectacular. Blue light flashes brightly, almost crackling across the surface before fading.

"Whoa," Cody says. "Not too subtle."

"So that's what we call a hot reaction." Davidoff switches the lights back on. "Now, if we have latent or old blood, luminol may not be enough. Forensics will probably move to fluorescein, which, as you know, is more sensitive. Right?"

Another murmur travels through the audience, signaling Davidoff to continue. She moves the boards aside, revealing a fresh panel underneath.

"Before we move on, can anyone tell me how we identify the difference between passive blood drops and projected blood drops?" She scans the crowd. "Anyone? Passive versus projected?"

For a second, I control myself.

I'm sure Sam knows the answer too, but he rarely speaks up in class. When no one takes the initiative, I can't resist and shoot up my hand. It feels good to have the answer to anything right now.

Cody groans and whispers, "Here we go."

Davidoff points at me. "Yes?"

"A passive drop will have a round circumference due to the force of gravity. The angle of impact will distort a projected drop's shape."

"Very good." Davidoff smiles. "What other factors—"

A door at the front of the auditorium opens. A young student steps inside and crosses over to hand Davidoff a note. She opens the paper and reads it aloud.

"Jenna Stack?"

I raise my hand again, this time more slowly.

"Oh, it's you. Professor Wolfson wants to see you in his office."

"Now?"

"Right away," Davidoff says.

"Uh oh," Sam mumbles, sinking in his seat.

My stomach lurches. What now?

"Don't worry about Miss Know-It-All," Cody says. "She'll be fine."

"You're just jealous of my GPA." I stand up and grab my backpack.

"She's got you there." Sam offers me a fist bump. I tap his knuckles lightly, trying not to disturb the demonstration further. Then I head for Wolfson's office, anxious to learn my fate.

Classical music blares behind Professor Wolfson's closed office door, not the light, soothing kind, but a bombastic symphony. "Ride of the Valkyries"? It's doubtful he'll hear me, but I knock anyway.

There's no answer, just a crashing crescendo of horns.

Cracking the door open, I peek inside. Two massive Bluetooth speakers dominate one corner of his office. The soaring strings and operatic voices grate on my raw nerves. But the music seems to have the opposite effect on Wolfson. He's leaning back in his chair, rubber-soled loafers propped up on the desk, eyes closed, wearing a serene expression. Afraid to startle him, I clear my throat.

"Professor Wolfson? Sir?"

Wolfson slowly opens his eyes, and his tranquil expression morphs into a sly smile, exposing a row of crooked teeth. Suddenly, I feel like a mouse that has accidentally wandered into a snake's lair.

"Miss Stack? Do come in. Take a seat."

Wolfson hits a key on his computer to stop the music and gestures to the chair I occupied earlier in the week.

"I hope I'm not interrupting," I say.

"Beautiful day, isn't it?" He stares at me calmly as if waiting for an explanation for my sudden appearance in his office.

"Yes, sir." When he doesn't speak, I soldier on. "You wanted to see me?"

"Indeed, I do." He claps his hands together. "I thought you might like an update on your internship."

I've been so caught up in the Rick Muraro murder case I'd forgotten about my internship proposal. I hold my breath hoping it's good news.

"I informed Cecelia Myers of my confidence in your ability. She indicated that your application is under consideration. You should have an answer soon."

Not exactly a news flash. Although I'm grateful to hear my inquiry wasn't met with a flat-out no.

"That's great, Professor. Thanks for vouching for me."

"Certainly." He turns his attention to straightening a stack of folders.

I wait for a beat, but he seems to have lost interest in the conversation. He didn't call me out of the blood demo for that update. Did he?

"Was there anything else, Sir?"

"No. No. Nothing in particular. But, as long as you're here…."

Wolfson is acting even stranger than usual. What is he up to?

"Yes?" I fold my hands.

"Anything intriguing happening"—he gestures toward his office door—"out there?"

"Davidoff's blood demo is pretty interesting."

Maybe he'll take the hint and let me go, or at least get to the point quickly so I can catch the rest of the lecture.

"Oh yes. Fascinating stuff. But what about *you*?"

"Me?"

"Yes, *you*. Any new developments?"

I'm unsure where he's going with this question, so I start with something simple and not exactly new.

"Well, I did uncover a curious fact. It's looking less and less like Cole Braedon is a government agent. Did you know that?"

"I had my suspicions." He nods. "What makes you say that?"

"Well, he seems to have been to prison in Russia for one thing —White Swan."

"An infamous place. You're still trying to track Mr. Braedon down, I see?"

Trying being the operative word since the guy's alias is a dead Canadian. "Do you have any ideas about his real identity, Professor?"

"There are so many possibilities. Both the CIA and FBI use freelancers and informants. The line between who you might consider the good guys and the criminals can get quite blurred. Which brings us to the other reason I wanted to see you."

Aha! I knew it! Wolfson is up to something. He takes a long pause for effect, and I must admit the trick works. My curiosity is beyond piqued. Knowing he's testing my patience, I hold my tongue and wait for him to continue.

"I got a call from a friend in law enforcement about you."

Uh oh.

"Let me guess. John Denning?"

"Indeed." Wolfson leans in and whispers conspiratorially, "I hear you discovered a body?"

Denning probably called to ask Wolfson to tell me to butt out of the case.

"Yes, I did. But—"

He raises a hand to quiet me. "And someone you know has been arrested for murder?" His attitude seems more curious than scolding.

"Yes, sir. One of my pet sitting clients, Natalie Swanson. But she's innocent. No matter what Denning tells you."

"Ah, a mystery." He folds his bony hands on his desk. "Please do start at the beginning."

Slowly, I reveal the entire story in detail; meeting Natalie, serving the papers to her ex, picking up the dogs, finding the gun, and even the part about Facèrè Boutique. Wolfson listens attentively with a contented look on his face. It's as if murder and mayhem calm his spirit. When I'm done, he takes a deep breath.

"Well, it looks like your Pandora instinct has been ignited again. May I presume you are determined to help Ms. Swanson?"

"Absolutely—I am."

"And you feel strongly that Detective Denning, who you know is an intelligent, experienced, and dedicated officer, has drawn the wrong conclusion?"

I'm sensing a trap. Is he going to tell me to back off?

"Yes, sir. I don't mean any disrespect, but I believe Denning is wrong. A woman's future is at stake. I can't look the other way."

"Bravo!" Wolfson claps his hands and smiles broadly. "And what fun! I'll tell you what I'm going to do for you, Ms. Stack. I'll inform the dean that I've permitted you a short"—he flutters his fingers mischievously—"leave of absence to do extra credit prep work for your upcoming internship. That should free up some time for your investigation. Do you think you can keep this our little secret? And, of course, stay current with your studies?"

For a moment, I marvel at the turn of events.

"Miss Stack?"

"Why, yes, sir. Thank you!"

"Very good. Please rely on your instincts, utilize your resources, and remember what I've taught you. If you're right and this woman is innocent, I'm confident you can help her. If you're wrong, then that, in itself, will be a valuable lesson. Don't you think?" He raises an eyebrow.

"I do, sir." I resist the temptation to elaborate, afraid he'll change his mind if I say the wrong thing.

"Excellent. I have one more thing for you." His eyes glitter with delight. "It's a word."

"A word?"

"A special word, a *password*, to guide you on your quest for the truth."

"My quest?"

What on earth is he talking about?

"I want you to contact a pathologist named Arvin Rand," Wolfson continues. "He's assigned to Rick Muraro's autopsy, which I know has been placed on rush status. I recommend you seek his counsel immediately."

"Wait a minute, Professor. I never told you Rick Muraro's name. You already knew everything and let me go on like that?"

"I wanted to be sure you were determined before offering my help." He smiles wickedly. "When you see Doctor Rand, you will give him the word—"

"The password?"

"Yes. Tell him, *Ouroboros.*"

"Like the serpent that eats its tail?"

"Precisely."

"And then what?"

"Then"—the professor clasps his hand together—"you'll see."

"I'll see?" Pretty obscure, but Wolfson's name opens doors. If he tells me repeating some random word to a stranger might help prove Natalie's innocence, then that's what I'll do.

"Indeed. And you might consider what else the serpent can show you, Miss Stack."

Now I'm stumped. I recall from a Symbols and Iconography course that the Ouroboros has something to do with eternity.

"The circle of life? Like, nothing ever really dies?"

"Simpler." He tilts his head. "Think about it. There is no beginning and no end for the Ouroboros. Why? Because the two are…?" he prompts me.

"Connected?"

"Very good. Perhaps you should go back to the beginning to find the end. When and where did the events *start* that led to your client's arrest?"

"Monday night, the night of the murder. At Rick Muraro's house."

Is he actually encouraging me to return to the crime scene?

Wolfson leans in and looks directly into my eyes. "Well then. Perhaps you should start over from there."

Chapter 18
Sidewalk Incantations

The Manhattan Criminal Courts Building at 100 Centre Street is an imposing limestone and granite complex occupying an entire block. Two enormous pillars flank the front steps. I walk into the expansive lobby and line up for the metal detector behind an agitated woman and her middle-aged lawyer.

It was easy enough for Nadir to access Dr. Arvin Rand's schedule. He should be finishing up testifying in a felony murder trial any minute. Even easier was finding a photo of Rand on LinkedIn. He's a handsome African American gentleman with close-cut hair and glasses. I have no idea about his stature.

As I clear security and fish my phone out of the little plastic tub, I scan the lobby for any sign of Dr. Rand. Nothing. A text pops up from Paul Hill.

Paul: *Natalie denied bail.*

The hackles rise on the back of my neck. I'd bet money

Denning insisted the prosecutor push for no bail. How could he? Natalie's not a danger to anyone, and she's not a flight risk.

Out of the corner of my eye, I glimpse a tall, trim, dashing man with wire-rim glasses racing past me. I'm so angry thinking about giving Denning a piece of my mind that I almost miss Dr. Rand. He disappears through the lobby doors. When I catch up with him, he's on the steps.

"Doctor Rand!"

He stops and looks me over with a discerning eye.

"I'm sorry, but I'm in quite a hurry." His tone is soft-spoken but professional as he checks his watch. No doubt he's accustomed to being stopped by family members and lawyers connected to his cases.

"I just had a few questions about the Muraro murder?"

Rand stiffens. *Murder* might not have been the best choice of words.

"Are you family?" he asks cautiously.

"Well, no. But I was referred—"

"I do not discuss active cases under any circumstances. I don't care who gave you my name." His delivery is fast and clipped. "How did you know where to find me?"

The question throws me off. Rand doesn't wait for an answer but continues down the stairs. I trot behind him, working my way up to mentioning Wolfson, trying to avoid the whole cloak and dagger code-word routine. Damn it, why won't he slow down? Once he reaches the sidewalk, I'll lose him in the crowd.

Okay then, you asked for it. Here goes.

"*Ouroboros!*" I feel ridiculous like I should be waving a wand in the air.

Dr. Arvin Rand stops in his tracks, pauses for a few seconds, and turns back to me. My code word incantation worked! I join him on the bottom step and wait for his response. People bustle around us, heading to appointments and court appearances.

"Go on. You were saying?"

"The Rick Muraro case."

"You were referred by?"

"Professor Karl Wolfson. The University of Manhattan."

"Very well. But I'm expected back at my office. You'll have to ride along." Rand crosses to the curb, whistles loudly, and a cab screeches to a halt in the street. I follow him into the back seat. Now that I have the doctor's attention, I'm unsure where to start. When I don't speak up, he prompts me.

"Am I correct in assuming you attend the university, Miss...?"

"Jenna Stack. Yes." I offer my hand awkwardly.

Rand ignores it and presses on. "Are you an exceptional student, or is your situation extraordinary?"

"Excuse me?"

"Those are the only circumstances under which Karl Wolfson would make this introduction."

"Well, a woman has been falsely accused of murder."

"That is far from extraordinary." He narrows his eyes and leans in. "Unless, of course, she's you?"

"No, she's a... friend." Even though I barcly know Natalie, I now think of her as a friend, someone I want to protect.

"And we're speaking of the Richard Muraro case?"

"Yes, shot in the back."

"I'm still waiting on test results, but I admit, so far, something feels"—he rubs his fingers together—"off to me."

"Yes!" My spirits lift with hope. "Me too. Why do *you* think so?"

"The suspicion is the estranged wife shot the deceased in the back while he worked in his home office. Correct?"

"That's the theory."

"Spousal murders are most often emotionally driven. They're

messy, violent." Rand pauses to adjust his glasses. "I am not a police officer, but I understand crime scenes, and this one lacked the element of... spontaneity."

"Yes! I agree." Finally, a reasonable person is connected to the case.

"I also found the fact Mr. Muraro was shot in the back rather odd."

"Because of the dictation?" I burst out, barely containing my excitement.

"Precisely. Mr. Muraro seemed to know his killer. So why was he shot from the back? You were at the crime scene, Miss Stack?"

"Yes, sir. And that's exactly what I thought too."

"I'm starting to see why Wolfson sent you." He looks at me with a thoughtful expression.

The cab slows down and pulls over mid-block next to a court-yard. There's a small park on the left and a concrete and glass building on the right. A sign reads *Office of the Chief Medical Examiner*. Rand pays the driver and steps out of the cab. For the first time in a long time, I feel encouraged. With this man on the case, Natalie might have a chance.

"Why don't you come inside? I can show you what I have so far."

The doctor has a twinkle in his eye. I think he's enjoying having a student around to mentor.

"Thank you. That would be wonderful."

Rand leads me along a cement path to the building's main entrance. Standing under the metal awning is a familiar figure scrolling through his phone.

"John!" Dr. Rand raises a hand.

"Arv—" Detective John Denning looks up, and his friendly expression twists into a scowl.

"Oh, this is excellent timing," Rand says. "Detective Denning, this is—"

"*Jenna Stack*," Denning says my name with disdain.

"You two have met?" Rand says, amused.

"What are you doing here?" Denning folds his arms. "With him?"

"Small world?"

"Don't test me, Stack. I warned you not to interfere." The vein in Denning's forehead is pulsing. He's mad, and he's going to ruin everything.

Denning turns to Rand. "Let me guess, *Wolfson?*"

"Indeed." Rand smiles unfazed.

"This is an active investigation, Doctor. You know better than to—"

"Relax, detective. I'm simply showing my old friend Wolfson a courtesy, discussing forensics with a future colleague."

Being called a future colleague by a respected medical examiner boosts my confidence. Rather than slink off, which I should probably do, I stand my ground next to the doctor.

"So you invited her into your office?" Denning insists.

"I thought she might benefit from some hands-on learning." Rand gestures for me to follow him.

"I appreciate your confidence in me, Doctor Rand." I flash a triumphant smile as I step behind the medical examiner.

Denning stands with his hands on his hips, dumbfounded.

"You too, John." Rand smiles. "Let's all take a look together."

Dr. Rand's office waiting area is painted industrial green. There are two yellow plastic chairs and a stiff vinyl couch. Someone took care to add a potted plant and a framed poster from a Van Gogh exhibition at the Met. But the room still feels sad and depressing.

"I need to check on a few things." Rand slides open an opaque plastic window screen and retrieves a clipboard and pen. "Miss Stack? Please sign this Non-Disclosure Agreement." He hands me the NDA and glances at Denning. "I'll be right back. Play nice."

Denning sits down on a chair and pulls out his phone.

Grateful for something to do other than talk to him, I take my time reading the NDA before adding my signature. Denning glares at me occasionally over the top of his screen. I resist the urge to make eye contact until Rand returns.

"Thank you for waiting. Follow me." Rand leads us down a narrow, starkly lit hallway, passing locked doors and metal cabinets. The smell of disinfectant grows stronger as we move deeper into the building. It's a lonely place, as if we're moving into the underworld. The hair stands up on the back of my neck.

Denning leans in from behind me. "First time, Stack?"

"Not technically," I say curtly without turning. "I did a semester of forensic biology. I know what to expect."

"Well, the real thing is a little more intense." His breath rushes in my ear. "Good luck." I can hear the smile in his voice. He's enjoying my discomfort. Just ahead is a set of industrial metal doors. My stomach tightens. I've seen dead bodies before, but never *after* an autopsy. Not yet.

"Okay, suit up," Rand says. He opens a locker and hands us paper masks, gowns, caps, and plastic glasses. We dress, and Arvin Rand looks us over and nods before opening the door. The large room looks like the autopsy suites I've seen on television; cold and stark with shiny metallic surfaces, ample drawers for bodies, and sharp medical instruments. There's a harsh antiseptic smell mixed with something more unsettling—the scent of death.

A metal table in the middle of the room is covered in a white sheet with a distinct "person" shape underneath. Rand pulls back the fabric to reveal the upper half of Rick Muraro's body.

My stomach does a turn. Denning watches my reaction. I'll be damned if I give him the satisfaction of seeing me freak out. Muraro's skin looks gray and waxy. His chest has a large Y incision indicating he's already been autopsied. I'm relieved Dr. Rand won't be cutting into Rick's body in front of us. But still, seeing a man I met when he was alive, lying cold and dead in this clinical setting is an alarming display.

"Let's start with the toxicology." Rand picks up a clipboard and finds the correct page. "There was a startling amount of cocaine and methamphetamine in the victim's system. Based on the condition of his nasal passages, he was a long-time user."

"That's no surprise, Doc." Denning shifts his weight impatiently. "There was a pile of coke at the scene."

Rand shoots Denning a pointed look as if to say he should know better than interrupting. I knew I liked this guy.

"You have the results on the bullet?" Rand continues.

"Yes," Denning answers, chastised. "The slug pulled out of Muraro's body came from the wife's gun."

"Are you sure?" I say, horrified.

"The ballistics are conclusive," Denning says, avoiding my eyes. "Our expert will testify to that fact."

My heart sinks. Natalie's future looks a lot dimmer if there's hard physical evidence linking her gun to Rick Muraro's murder.

"*And yet*, things are not always as they seem," Rand says, leafing to another page on his clipboard. "This is where the case gets interesting."

"Interesting? How so, Arv?" Denning clenches his jaw.

I'm anxious for Dr. Rand to get to the point, but I'm also fascinated by their interaction. I've never seen John Denning tread so carefully around someone. Arvin Rand has him on best behavior.

"Well, to start with—Rick Muraro did *not* die from a gunshot wound." Rand looks up over his glasses and smiles mischievously.

Denning's face twists up like someone just asked him to complete a complicated math problem without a calculator. I'm equally dumbfounded. Rand must have known the gunshot wound wasn't Rick's cause of death during our cab ride, but waited to reveal that critical fact. A flair for the dramatic? No wonder he gets along with Wolfson!

"You've got me, Doc." Denning tosses his hands in the air. "Then what the hell killed him?"

"A massive coronary, most likely brought on by the injection of a powerful drug cocktail." Rand pushes his glasses up his nose. "We found a needle mark in his neck." He walks to the corpse and points to a pin prick just behind Muraro's right ear.

"Someone gave Rick a hot shot?" Denning says, examining the puncture.

"In street vernacular, yes. The location of the injection site is inconsistent with self-administration. As you can see, there are finger-sized bruises on his arms, suggesting he was grabbed roughly and injected with a large dose of cocaine and opioids. His heart, weakened by years of drug use and who knows what else, gave out."

"But there was fresh blood at the scene. Corpses don't bleed, Doc." Denning examines the marks on the corpse.

"But dying men do, Detective. He was alive when he was shot in the back—but the bullet didn't kill him. Remove the gunshot, and Rick Muraro still would have died of a heart attack."

For a moment, Denning is quiet, mulling over the new evidence.

"So there were two people at the crime scene?" I say, starting to understand. "Whoever injected Rick and the shooter?"

"That's for Detective Denning to determine," Rand says.

"Either one person injected and then shot Mr. Muraro, or two people assaulted him, one after the other."

"Which explains the position of Rick's body and the dictation," I whisper, amazed. "Rick was shouting at someone not to inject him *before* he was shot in the back."

"But why shoot a dying man in the back?" Denning asks, more to himself than the room.

"To be sure he was dead?" Rand suggests.

"Or to set Natalie up by using her gun," I point out.

"We can't rule that out," Denning admits.

Rand gently pulls the sheet over Rick's head.

"I told you this case was interesting."

Chapter 19
Solve & Survive

Our footsteps echo against the cold, scuffed linoleum floor and down the empty corridors as we leave Arvin Rand's office. Denning puts a finger to his lips, signaling me to keep quiet. His attitude seems a bit dramatic, but I'm buoyed by the news that the gunshot didn't kill Rick. Following his lead, we maintain radio silence in the elevator and the lobby. I guess Arvin Rand freaked him out. By the time we reach the sidewalk, I'm practically bursting at the seams.

"May I speak now, Detective Mysterioso?" The temperature has dropped a few degrees since we entered the building. Trash and dead leaves scatter across the cement.

Denning looks around to make sure no one is within earshot.

"We need to be careful, but yeah, go ahead."

"You must admit things are looking a lot better for Natalie." I fold my hands across my chest triumphantly.

"Jenna, I never had it out for Natalie. I'm just trying to get to the truth."

"And the truth is she's innocent."

"Of murder, maybe. With this new evidence, it looks that way. But I'm still not convinced Natalie wasn't involved. Or at the least, shot a dying man." He glances around again. Why is he acting so paranoid? "This case is getting more complicated, not less."

"Or somebody is trying to frame Natalie. If that's the case, she doesn't belong in custody. You saw her, Denning. She's not exactly a tough cookie."

"Tough cookie? What are you a gun moll?"

"You know what I mean." I feel myself blush.

"Yeah, actually, I do," he admits. "Lock-up is a rough place for your average citizen."

"So you'll drop the charges?"

"I'm not ready to do that. *Yet*." I can practically see his mind working, running through the angles. "Besides, if you're right, and someone is trying to set Natalie up, I'm not sure she'd be any safer on the street."

My good mood darkens instantly. Now I understand why he's so on edge. We have no idea what this new evidence means—or who's involved.

"So if you release her, the real killer might think you're considering other suspects?"

"Exactly. They could escalate their plans for framing Natalie or hurt her or even kill her to cover their tracks. Not to mention put up their guard."

"I see." A stab of dread hits me. Everything Denning says confirms my fears. If we don't solve this case, Natalie may not survive.

"Right now, whoever murdered Rick, if *they* even exist"—Denning makes air quotes with his finger—"is an unknown suspect, and our Unsub thinks they're in the clear."

"Meaning they'll be less careful and easier to catch."

"Exactly. Even if I was convinced she was set up, and I'm not, it's better for everyone if Natalie remains the prime suspect."

"Which means leaving an innocent woman in prison."

"I'm sorry, Jenna, I am." Denning's clear blue eyes cloud with concern. "I can have her removed from the general population. That will make being inside a little easier. But I don't think releasing her is in anyone's best interest, particularly Natalie's. Understand?"

I know he's right, even if it's hard to hear.

"Promise me you'll find the killer?"

Denning looks at me with a sober expression. "Nothing will stop me."

There's something about Denning. Even though he drives me crazy sometimes, he's always told me the truth. I believe him.

"So what now?"

"Now we take a closer look from every angle." He shoves his hands in his pockets. "We review the evidence, reinterview witnesses, whatever it takes."

"What about Rick's dad? Did you know he has Mafia connections?"

"Of course, Jenna. Everyone knows Manny the Rock is a wiseguy."

"Well, he must have enemies. What if somebody wanted revenge on Manny?"

"Maybe." Denning shakes his head. "But they call him Manny the Rock for a reason. He's reliable. He doesn't let his friends down. And he doesn't snitch. Nobody even knows if Manny was really guilty. He just shut up and copped a plea. Didn't say a word to anyone about anything. There isn't a single soul in his world who would lay a finger on Manny's kid without approval."

"Natalie said Rick didn't get along with his dad. Maybe Manny was involved?"

Denning shakes his head. "It's a pretty big leap from being pissed off at your kid to having him murdered while you sit in prison with an air-tight alibi."

We stand in silence for a moment. Denning's expression is stormy as he runs through the case in his head. Sharon's comment about being tortured by his responsibilities comes to mind.

"Well, Elena's alibi checks out," I offer, trying to get the brainstorming session back on track.

Denning narrows his eyes. "As the detective on the case, *I* know that fact. But how do *you*?"

Oh crap, I've said too much.

"Um, I rode along with the law firm's detective to Elena's hotel room."

"Of course you did," he says with a pained expression. "Look, I can't stop you from investigating this case, but I can warn you. There's a killer out there, Jenna. This isn't a game." His face softens as he looks at me.

"What about Milania? Tell me you're trying to find her?"

"Lopez is looking. So far, we've got nothing."

"And the people in Rick's office? Paul Hill could have a motive?"

"We're checking all their alibis, Jenna. Don't worry. Tomorrow I'm going back to the crime scene, and I promise you, I will go over the place with a fine-toothed comb. Do you think you could stay out of trouble while I'm there?"

"Come on, Denning. You have to admit I can be helpful sometimes."

"Maybe. But we don't know what, or who, we're dealing with here."

As we reach his car, Denning opens the door for me. I slip into the passenger seat. He leans over and pulls the seatbelt slowly across my lap before snapping the catch shut. Physically, there's something imposing about him.

"I can take care of myself," I say nervously.

"Can you? Because if anyone tries to hurt you…I swear I'll…." His words trail off, but his eyes hold mine with an intensity that makes me blush—a current of electricity races through my limbs.

Did Detective John Denning just flirt with me?

He closes my door and flashes a rare smile. As much as I want to ponder the mysteries of John Denning's "almost, but not quite" declaration of feeling protective of me, something more pressing draws my attention. Now that I know Denning will be at the Muraro house tomorrow, I have only one chance to check out the crime scene—*tonight*. I hope he sticks to his plan because if he sees me there, he might have a coronary.

Chapter 20
Duck & Cover

The streets of New York are never empty. But they get pretty quiet on a residential block in a swanky uptown neighborhood. Waiting in the shadows on Rick Muraro's street, there's a good view of the houses. People arrive home after work and lock doors for the night. Finally, there's only one guy left, a neighbor walking a chubby pug down the sidewalk.

Finally, he disappears into a house two doors down. As soon as the coast is clear, I jog down the road dressed in dark leggings, a long-sleeved shirt, and running shoes. A casual observer might think I'm out for a late-night run, but inside my fanny pack are the tools needed to enter the Muraro house; a mini flashlight, lock-pick kit, and latex gloves.

A loud scraping noise behind me makes me jump. Before I can gather the courage to turn around, a teenager on a skateboard whooshes past.

"On your left!" he yells, barely missing me.

Maybe this is a bad idea? Denning warned me to back off and that things could get dangerous. But tonight is my last chance to review the crime scene. The night of the murder was chaotic and upsetting. If I revisit the crime scene with a cooler head, there might be fresh clues—the kind Denning could bag, tag, and hide from me tomorrow.

The front of the house is quiet and lightless, crisscrossed by yellow crime scene tape. Before I lose my nerve, I slip under the tape and through Rick's small patio gate. The basement-level door is hidden from the street. I pull on the gloves. The door is outfitted with a basic knob lock on the handle and a more complicated deadbolt above. Since the Covert Entry Training Seminar, Cody, Sam, and I have been practicing lock picking, primarily for fun but also because we know the skill might come in handy.

I pull out my tools and work on the bottom lock first. With the torque wrench, I apply light pressure and insert a Bogota rake into the lock. It takes some time, but I feel the key pins line up with the driver pin. Once the plug starts rotating, I delicately increase the pressure and close my eyes, nuancing the pick. Almost there. Sharp clicks announce my success. I feel a tingle of satisfaction in my fingers. I turn the knob, and to my surprise, the door opens. The last person in the house must not have had keys. They just locked the bottom lock and pulled the door shut.

Inside, the house is stuffy and warm. The unmistakable, coppery odor of human blood hangs in the air. Turning on the lights could alert a neighbor to my presence, so I flick on my mini flashlight. The house is quiet, and the long, darkened hallway seems to go on forever. The tiny circle of light leads me deeper into the house. The floor creaks and my heart pounds.

The only illumination in the back office creeps through French doors that open onto a small, enclosed patio out back. It's so quiet I can hear myself breathing as the flashlight beam passes over the scene. At first glance, the office looks similar to the night of the murder, minus one dead body. My eyes adjust and I notice the forensic team has left traces of fingerprint powder and a blood stain on the floor. The trashcan is emptied, and the bag from Facèré Boutique is gone. The crime scene techs probably took the contents of the basket for processing. The keyboard, computer monitors, photo of Rick and Manny, and pile of drugs have also been removed. The desk drawers are practically empty: a stapler, some sticky notes, a box of pens. But at the back of a bottom drawer, I find some Canadian coins. I take photos of the open drawers with my phone. Then examine the pictures on the wall, something I didn't have time to do the night of Rick's murder.

A small, framed photo catches my eye. It's of Rick and my new pal, Jack the PI, dressed in fishing gear, standing in front of a large, modern-looking cabin, almost like a fancy chalet. I take pictures using my low-light camera app, so there's no flash. I'm engrossed in my task when I hear a soft, crunching noise outside. I freeze, and the possibilities race through my mind. A neighborhood cat? A cop on patrol? Rick's killer?

I nearly jump out of my skin when my phone buzzes, announcing an incoming call. The caller ID reads: "Federal Bureau of—" with the rest cut off.

FBI? What the?

"Hello?" I whisper, cupping the mouthpiece.

"Jenna. Get out of there."

The voice is unmistakable.

"Cole? What—"

"No time to explain. Just get *out* of that house."

"But—"

"Get down! Now!"

A shot rings out. One of the pictures on the wall above me shatters, and fragments of glass shower over my head. I crouch down, clutching my phone, my heart racing.

"Holy shit!" I hiss, breathing hard.

"Listen to me, Jenna!" Cole shouts. "Go out the French doors and over the neighbor's fence!"

"But—" *Isn't that the direction the shot came from?*

"Just do it!"

There's broken glass everywhere. I crawl on my stomach, across the floor, inching toward the patio door. Another shot rings out as I turn the handle. Splinters of wood hit my hand.

"Goddamnit!" I say under my breath and flatten myself against the floor, cheek to the ground. Paralyzed by fear, I stare at the dark shadows under the furniture. A small, spotted cat is curled up under Rick's desk, just beyond my reach. What the hell? Has that cat been there this whole time? It must be so scared. I scoot along the cold wood floor and stretch my fingers, trying to reach the frightened animal. Just as I touch the cat's back, it collapses into a pile of fabric. My brain kicks in—that's not an animal at all. My mind is playing tricks on me. It's just a piece of leopard-print fabric, like a scarf or a wrap, that got kicked under the desk and forgotten.

"Jenna! What are you doing in there? You need to move!" Cole's voice bellows from my phone, snapping me out of my confusion. "Get out of there. GO!"

I take a deep breath for courage and crawl back to where the last bullet hit. Then I shove open the door and hurl myself through the opening. Another shot rings out as I tumble onto a small deck and down three wooden steps to a concrete slab. Huddled behind the stairs, I listen for Cole's voice intently, aware that he's my only lifeline.

"Cole? What is going on?"

"Wait there. Don't move until I tell you...."

My right leg is throbbing. Expecting a gunshot wound, I reach down and find my leggings are torn at the knee. I'm relieved there's no entry wound, just a deep, bloody scrape.

"Pay attention! Look, due west. See that fence? On the other side is the neighbor's yard, then a park. When I say go, you need to scale that fence."

I'm trying to get my bearings and figure out which way is west.

"Jenna? Are you there? Did you hear me?"

"Yes," I whisper. "I'm just trying to figure out—"

"GO—NOW!"

The grass churns under my feet as I race toward a vine-choked fence. Halfway up the chain links, a shot pings off the metal. Leaves scatter as I scramble the rest of the way and drop into a neighbor's yard.

Lights flick on in an upstairs window, and a figure peers down at me. For a moment, I think it's the shooter and freeze. But the silhouette is holding a phone, not a gun, *probably calling 911.* There's a throbbing pain every time my knee bends. I've got to keep moving. I check the gate, but the damned thing is locked. *Really?* Across the small yard, a patio table butts up against—guess what? Another fence. This one is made of wood. Ignoring the pain, I run and climb.

The pointed top knocks the wind out of me, and splinters dig into my hands. Wood explodes an inch from my cheek as another bullet flies.

Bastard! With my last bit of strength, I clear the pickets and land hard on a wet, grassy mound. I quickly checked my extremities—nothing is broken, just bruised and beat up. Time to get out of here.

Across the grass is a wrought iron fence, and beyond that, the sidewalk and freedom. With my luck, the gate is probably locked, but there's only one way to find out. I'm tiptoeing slowly across the grass when a dark figure appears on the sidewalk. The shooter?

I slip back into the shadows. The figure looks through the

fence's bars, jiggles the handle, and swings the gate open. My heart beats so fast that I can barely catch my breath.

A man, around six feet tall, steps into the park. Shadows obscure his face. He scans the area. There's a glint of light on metal. He's holding a gun. Slowly I draw my legs into my chest, trying to make myself as small as possible—a leaf cracks under my foot. The figure stops. I hold my breath, terrified of what will come next.

I'm curled into a ball in the corner of the little park, with my heart racing in my chest, hiding from a gun-toting stalker. Eyes closed, I can hear footsteps coming closer. No use trying to hide. To make it out of here alive, I'll have to fight. I learned a move in Krav Maga called the slap disarm—hitting the gun and arm simultaneously in opposing directions, using torque to dislodge the weapon. I've never had occasion to try it out in real life. Now might be the time.

Come on, Jenna, don't think—do it. The dark figure is less than ten feet away, moving cautiously, gun held out, hunting. He inches toward my hiding place. *Come on, you psycho, just a little closer.* When he's a foot away, I leap up and slam the gun with one hand and his arm with the other.

"Ow!" he cries.

Like magic, the gun flies out of his hand. But in a move I've never seen before, he catches the weapon in midair with his other hand and points the barrel directly at me. Our eyes meet.

"Cole?" My body floods with relief, and I throw my arms around his neck and collapse against his chest. His jaw is scratchy with stubble and he smells familiar, like cheap cologne and expensive tobacco.

Cole peels me off, pins my arms at my sides, and looks me in the eye.

"What the hell, Jenna? When did you learn Krav Maga? Do you know how dangerous that little stunt was?" He tucks the gun in his belt and checks the direction I ran from, listening.

"Sorry, I thought you were—"

"The cartel hitman? Why was he shooting at you anyway?"

"Wait? What are you talking about?"

"Are you telling me you don't know?" He shakes his head, grabs my elbow, and pulls me toward the sidewalk.

"About a hitman? Of course not!" I dig in my heels and resist, terrified of what or who might be waiting for us. "What's going on?"

"Listen, are you hurt?"

"I'm fine," I lie. My knee is stiffening, and my lungs burn, but whoever shot at me is a more significant threat.

"Then we need to move. Now!" He squeezes my arm and pulls me toward the exit. "This place is like a cage."

I look around at the high walls and fence. He's right. If the shooter finds us here, there will be no place to run.

"I have a car close by." Cole steers me through the gate and across the street. As we hurry around a corner, he peels off his black quilted jacket and turns the tan lining inside out. He hands the jacket to me. "Put it on."

"Okay, okay," I say, shoving my arm in the sleeve.

"There's a cap in the pocket."

I try to stop to get organized, but he keeps moving. I hustle to catch up. Cole pulls a wad of plastic from his front pocket and unrolls a thin navy windbreaker with a wrist flick. In one quick motion, he slips the jacket on, transforming himself into a casual New Yorker prepared for rain.

I understand what he's doing now, so I let my hair down, pull the cap on, push up my sleeves and untuck my shirt. As I shrug into the impromptu disguise, I look more like a college student and less like a runner.

"See, just a happy couple out for a stroll." Cole drapes an arm around my shoulder and finally slows down.

I slip my arm around Cole's waist and match his pace. As we walk, he scans the sidewalk for danger. Finally, my heart slows down enough to speak.

"What did you mean about a hitman—"

A figure turns onto the street at the end of the block. My body stiffens. I don't know what my pursuer looks like, but something about this man's posture, the way his head moves slightly from side to side, reminds me of Cole. He's hunting. I hold a hand in front of my mouth and whisper, "Your one o'clock."

"Good spot. Exactly what I was thinking," Cole whispers back. "Follow my lead." He casually slows to a stop at the mouth of an alley and pushes me a few steps back from the sidewalk. He puts both arms around my waist and leans over me, blocking my face with his. I resist the urge to run and focus on keeping my body pliable and my senses alert. I wrap my arms around his neck. I feel his chest rise and fall against mine and the heat of his breath in my ear. A warm tingle shoots down my spine.

"He's coming this way," Cole whispers. "If I say go, run. Head uptown, hail the first cab you see. Understand?"

I hear footsteps approaching, getting louder and slower, more methodical. Cole turns his back to the sidewalk and pushes me deeper into the alley.

"I'm so sorry, babe. I'll never disappear on you like that again." His voice is earnest and sincere with a strong New York accent. "Ya gotta forgive me."

He's playing a part, but the words feel real.

The stranger is just a few feet away from us now. I'm bracing for Cole's signal to run when brakes squeal.

"Any luck?" a man's voice booms over a loud, muscle-car engine.

"Nothing," the figure on the sidewalk responds. "Perra estúpida."

"Then come on. The boss wants to see us."

A car door slams. I start to move, but Cole holds me back for a moment. Our eyes meet. He puts a finger to my lip and holds my gaze. The fear rushes from my body, leaving a sensation of longing. I feel myself leaning into him when he abruptly lets go and steps out of the alley.

"Well, that was exciting." He smiles and runs a hand through his thick, dark hair. His knuckles are red and bruised, and his nose is sunburnt and peeling. Where has he been?

"For you, maybe!" I shudder, reeling from the roller coaster of emotions. "Now tell me, what—"

"Come on. Let's get off the street." He points to an all-night diner down the block. "You look like you could use a hot drink."

I follow Cole to the brightly lit restaurant's entrance, grateful to be alive but determined to get some answers.

Chapter 21
Sugar Rush

The diner's interior is deep and narrow with a vaguely retro theme. I keep my head down as we pass an elderly couple sharing a sandwich at the Formica counter. We make our way to a back booth. Cole positions himself with a clear view of the entrance and turns the mugs on the table right side up, signaling we want coffee. I slide in across from him. I'm about to start with my questions when a middle-aged waiter with a bored expression appears. He stands over our table with a steaming pot of coffee and fills our cups.

I pretend to look inside my zipper pouch with trembling fingers. I'm a mess—no need to draw any extra attention.

"We'll have a slice of that chocolate cake." Cole points to the pastry case. "And *two* forks."

"I'm fine." I brush a stray leaf from my hair.

"You need some carbs, trust me."

The waiter leaves to fetch a slice of cake. The smell of strong, hot coffee is somehow soothing. I pour cream into my cup and look up at Cole. His eyes are laser-focused on my right hand. I follow his gaze and a hot blush fills my cheeks. At the end of the Ab El Malik case, when Cole sent me new evidence concerning my brother, he also enclosed a gift, an Irish *Claddagh* ring. I slipped the silver band with two hands holding a crowned heart on my finger that day and never took it off. It's become a symbol for me, a reminder to never give up on Tyler. Why did Cole give me a ring? I'm not sure. We barely know each other. But I suddenly feel exposed and quickly pull my hand into my lap.

"What's going on, Cole? I've been trying to reach you for months. Now you show up out of nowhere? Today? When I'm being shot at?"

"Aren't you glad to see me, Jenna?" He grins.

"Well, yes." Under the table, I twist the ring on my finger. "But where have you been all this time?"

"You know I can't tell you that." He leans back, totally relaxed, as if the last thirty minutes had never happened.

"Were you following me?"

"No, but lucky I showed up." He sips his coffee, green eyes watching me under dark lashes.

"Then why were you at that house?"

"I was working."

"That's it? Just *working*?" I try to imitate his annoyingly laid-back tone, but the impression gets stuck in my throat, and I sound like I'm choking.

"You okay?" He slides a glass of water closer to me. "I think I have a lozenge in the car."

My frustration rises. Is he going to deflect every question? I want answers and will not let him steer me off track.

"Okay, why did that man just try to kill me?"

"I'm still trying to figure that one out."

I decide to try a different tactic. "The last time you were in town, you claimed you were an FBI agent. What's your story this time?"

"Let's just say it's complicated. Why were *you* at that house, Jenna?"

His stonewalling is infuriating. After all, I'm the one who almost got killed. Two can play this game.

"Then you were doing surveillance. Was your target the house owner or the shooter? Judging from your call, I'm going to say the shooter."

"Something like that...." He reappraises me. "I was amused to see you show up. Until that bad guy tried to snuff you." Cole's eyes flick over my shoulder. My heart flutters until I realize it's just the waiter arriving with our order. He sets an enormous piece of chocolate cake, with two forks, between us. Cole gestures for me to take the first bite, but I decline. I want answers, not dessert. He picks up a fork and digs in, going straight for an outside corner of the top layer, the spot with the most frosting.

"That's it? That's all I get? Some murdering psycho tries to kill me, and you have nothing to say?"

"Mmmm, that's good." He licks his lips, then goes back for a second and third bite. "You sure, Jenna? You're missing out."

"Fine." I help myself to a small bite just to move things along. The cake is moist and dense, and the icing is just a little bit chilled. It's delicious. Suddenly ravenous, I take a BIG bite and savor the chocolaty, comforting goodness.

"Right?" His eyes glint with satisfaction watching me devour another forkful. We get into a rhythm, alternating bites until the cake is almost gone.

"So, you were doing surveillance...." I prompt him.

"And imagine my surprise when you showed up and broke into the house. Nice job, by the way. The target responded by setting up a foldable sniper rifle on a neighbor's rooftop. That's when I warned you."

"Then why send me out the back way?"

"Because the sniper's colleague was parked out front. I wasn't sure if they were trying to kill or grab you. But your chances were better if you ran."

"He almost shot me—*twice*." I sip my coffee as my nerves slowly steady.

"You're welcome, by the way. I'd think you'd be happy. I did just save your life." Cole presses the back of his fork to the plate, picks up the last bits of cake crumbs, and licks the prongs clean.

"Oh. Right. Sorry," I stammer. "Thank you."

"My pleasure." He grins and pushes the empty plate away. "Now, you tell me. How the hell did you get mixed up with *Darius Candelas Izar*?"

"Who? I've never even heard that name."

"Well, he's heard of you."

"Listen, Cole. I understand if you can't tell me all of the details. But I almost got killed. At least tell me why this Izar person was shooting at me?"

Cole steeples his fingers over his mouth as if he's considering a complicated equation. "Look, this is strictly classified. Understand?"

"Cross my heart." I lift my hand like I'm swearing from a witness box.

"Izar wasn't shooting at you. That rain of bullets was courtesy of his first lieutenant, a hitman named Romero. He was my target. I followed Romero into the country last week." Cole's expression is matter of fact. I guess following a hitman across international borders is no big deal for this guy.

"And where does Romero come from exactly?"

"South America. Colombia to be exact. But the real question,

Jenna, is what was Romero doing at that house? And how did you manage to piss him off enough to start shooting?"

"Me? Nothing!" How is this suddenly my fault?

"Then why were you there?" Cole watches me curiously.

I take another sip of coffee. How to put this delicately? Is there even a point to being diplomatic with Cole Braedon?

I cup a hand over my mouth and whisper. "I found a dead body."

Cole's eyes widen. "A dead body? When?"

"A few days ago, at the same house. I came back to look for clues."

"Why am I not surprised?" He leans back and laughs, shoulders shaking. As soon as he finishes, he folds his hands. "So, who's the stiff?"

"A lawyer named Rick Muraro."

"*Muraro*, where have I heard that name before..." He squints his eyes, trying to recall the context.

"Manny the Rock? The Mob lawyer? That's his dad."

"Of course!" Cole says. "The wiseguy lawyer. I remember now. Still, it doesn't explain how a South American cartel and the New York Mob are mixed up."

Good point. This case just keeps getting more complicated. Rick the cokehead was involved with a cartel? And why was the hitman at his house? Was he connected to Rick's death? Covering his tracks?

"Maybe they're in business together?" I offer. "Cartel or Mob, isn't it all just organized crime?"

"Kind of. But the Izar Cartel is worse than anyone Manny the Rock normally associates with."

"What's Izar into? Drugs?"

"Drugs, yes, but also human trafficking, murder, extortion. Pretty much everything you can imagine and don't want to think about. The Izar Cartel is highly organized and ruthless and have no code of ethics."

"How did Rick get involved with an organization like that?"

"Good question… Darius Candelas Izar is brilliant, brutal, and practically untouchable. The FBI wants Izar on the ten most wanted list, but he's too well protected by powerful forces in his country and beyond. What do you know about Rick Muraro's murder?"

That's ironic. First, he won't tell me a damn thing. Now he wants to pick my brain? Maybe I should give him a taste of his medicine.

"I'm not supposed to discuss it."

"Okay, then. Let's see." Cole types into his phone at lightning speed. There's a whoosh sound, and he grins. A minute later, the phone pings. He scans the information and frowns. "Looks like one Jenna Stack attended an autopsy for Rick Muraro and signed an NDA. The cause of death was a drug cocktail administered against his will. And someone shot him in the back."

"How did you do that?" I stare at his phone like it's a snake.

Cole smiles and leans toward me.

"A hot shot? Now, *that* sounds like the cartel. So tell me, if you already knew how he was killed, why were you there looking for clues?"

"Someone is trying to frame my client for Rick's death. I thought I might turn up something useful."

"Your client? You're not working cases, are you?" Cole stares with an intensity that makes me uncomfortable.

"No, my pet sitting client, Natalie. She was married to Rick. They were separated—"

"It's usually a loved one." Cole nods. "So, she's the one who shot him?"

What is it with everyone?

"Not this time. Natalie's innocent." I try to hide my frustration. So far, I've accomplished nothing to save her. And I'm worried that another little piece of her will die every day she's locked up.

"Relax," he says, seeing right through me. "We're just talking this through. In this case, I can tell you one hundred percent there's no reason a cokehead lawyer is on the cartel's radar. Not enough to send Romero. If the cartel killed him, Rick did something to cross them. They might make an example of him."

Our waiter circles back to refill our mugs and drop the bill.

"Maybe the cartel gave Rick the hotshot?" I offer.

"It's possible, but an elaborate frame-up isn't exactly Izar's style. So the bullet in the back is strange. There might be another player involved."

"Maybe Romero was checking the crime scene too?"

"And you were in the wrong place, at the wrong time?" Cole says. "That tracks. Maybe they wanted to scare you off."

"I like that better than a sicario was sent to kill me."

"If the cartel wanted you dead, Jenna, you'd be dead."

I glare at him. "Not very reassuring, Cole."

"Sorry." He shrugs. "Sometimes I forget you're a civilian."

"If you're freelance, why did your caller ID say FBI?"

"I work with the FBI, sometimes. But in this case, I had to ensure you'd pick up the phone. Most honest citizens answer when they think law enforcement is calling." He tosses a twenty-dollar bill on the table. "I need to get back to work. Can I drop you somewhere?"

"But—"

"That's all you'll get out of me tonight, Jenna. Okay?"

It's not okay. But I don't want to push Cole away. I have more questions, not just about the Muraro case but about my brother. I don't want Cole to disappear again.

So I'd better play the long game.

The night is cool and refreshing as we step onto the street. Cole leads me to a sleek, black sedan parked in a red zone at the far end of the block. How did he get away with that? He beeps the doors open, and I sink into the passenger seat. The interior is expensive and hi-tech. Every surface is black leather or highly polished silver, and there's an enormous shiny screen on the dashboard. Even the new car smell seems foreign and unfamiliar. A parking permit sits on the dashboard, New York City's most sacred object. I examine the plaque as he slides into the driver's side.

"Clergy? Really?" I don't know why, but I'm stunned by the audacity. First, he arranges caller ID from the FBI. Then he somehow gets a sealed autopsy report in a New York minute. Now he's got a pass to park anywhere in the city?

Cole just grins. "Long story."

A story I'm pretty sure he's not going to tell me.

I buckle up and lean back in the buttery seat as Cole pulls into the traffic flow. He checks the rearview mirror and hits the gas.

"Where to?"

Chapter 22
The Many Uses of Cocoa Powder

A line of thirty people snakes down the sidewalk in front of Cellos; young New Yorkers decked out in band T-shirts, studded leather accessories, and wildly teased hair. It must be metal night. They laugh and chat as they wait to show their IDs to Wally, the bouncer. Nadir stands out front, lean and self-conscious, talking on his phone.

As we drive past, he spots me and lifts a hand to wave. Then he notices Cole behind the wheel, and the look on his face morphs into concern. I wave back to reassure him I'm fine. But am I? In the last two hours, I've been shot at and chased by a cartel hitman, and something warm is seeping over my knee. It looks like my wound has reopened.

Cole pulls up to a fire hydrant and shifts the car into park. Then he turns to me, his expression serious. "Listen, Jenna. I don't think you're a target—but stay sharp. Understand?"

"Got it." I tug off his jacket. "The cartel probably won't try and kill me. But watch out for random hitmen."

Cole's eyes cloud with worry. I guess he's not happy with my casual reaction. "I'm serious, Jenna. Say it out loud." He looks at me with a stormy intensity that makes me almost forget what we're discussing.

"Okay, I promise. No dark alleys alone. Happy?" Cole's right. I need to be more careful. At least until I figure out who murdered Rick.

"Good." He leans toward me and my pulse quickens. I lift my arm to hug him before I realize he's just going for the center console. It's too late to hide my mistake. His eyes tell me he caught my move, but at least he doesn't say anything. I do like that about Cole. He teases, but he rarely gloats. He pulls a cheap flip phone out of the compartment and holds it up.

"My number is programmed into the speed dial—I'm number one. Call if you get into trouble."

"Number one, really?"

"That's right." He smiles and hands me the phone. That makes three phones; Dave's business mobile, my iPhone, and a prepaid disposable burner. You've got to be kidding me. On the upside, I finally have a way to get in touch with Cole. Once the dust settles, I'll push him for more information on Tyler's case. Maybe he can pull some strings for me with one of his mystery employers.

I unzip my waist pack and hold the pouch open. Cole places the new phone gently inside and looks at me thoughtfully.

"One more thing, Jenna. I'm going to arrange a meeting for you with a colleague of mine. Tell him everything. He might be able to help your friend."

The thought of Natalie in jail makes my heart sick. I remember her voice on the phone last night, pleading for help. She was so scared and alone. But as desperate as I am to solve this case, the idea of meeting with a colleague of Cole Braedon's is unsettling. My mind reels at the possibilities.

"What kind of colleague?"

"FBI."

"*Real* FBI?"

"Yes, *real* FBI."

"Okay, what's his name?" I can feel myself going down the Cole Braedon rabbit hole. If Dave were here, he'd warn me to run.

"Agent Smith."

"Not very original."

"Well, that's his name, Jenna. Agent Smith. Although, now that you mention it, he's not an original guy. But he's a straight shooter. He'll help if he can." Cole watches me with steady eyes, waiting for my response.

"Thank you. I do appreciate your help, Cole." I hold eye contact. Does he feel the electricity between us? Or is this a figment of my imagination? He reaches over and tucks a strand of my hair behind an ear. Then he cradles my face with his hand and lightly strokes his thumb across my cheek. A jolt runs down my spine. The heat is instantaneous. I guess that answers my question. He releases me, and for a moment, I'm lost in his deep, green eyes.

"You got it. Now scram." He smiles.

I stumble out of the car and toss his borrowed hat and coat on the passenger seat. I've barely shut the door, and he's speeding away.

Nadir is waiting out front, leaning against a wall of band posters. He looks puzzled and slightly terrified. "Is that who I think it is?"

"The infamous dead Canadian? Yes."

"You two looked friendly."

"It's a long story."

Nadir takes in my ripped leggings and bloody knee.

"What happened? Did he—"

"Cole? God, no." I take a step, but my leg has stiffened up, and the knee joint is locking. "I'm fine. Really."

"You don't look fine."

"Nothing the first aid kit can't handle. Guess what I got?" I unzip my bag and show Nadir the burner phone. "A certain dead Canadian's fingerprint."

Nadir grins and claps his hand like a five-year-old who just received a new toy. *"Braedon's print?* Damn, Jenna, you're a badass! I'll schedule time in the print lab—"

I shake my head. "I need to hold onto this phone. We'll have to think of something else."

Inside, Cello's is packed three people deep. Music is blaring from the back room, and burgers are flying out of the kitchen. Sharon is busy showing a new bartender Kyle, the ropes, pouring, mixing, and slinging drinks at a pace to keep up with demand. She's about to embark on her famous "Espresso Martinis" tutorial when she sees me through the crowd. Her face lights up, and she motions me over.

"Hey, Jenna! Come to see the band?" Sharon smiles, laced into a black leather bustier, blonde hair teased within an inch of its life. She looks amazing.

"Actually, no, I ran into a little trouble—" I slip under the pass-through, behind the bar. Sharon takes in my dirty clothes and a bloody knee. Her eyes grow wide with concern. Then she plants her hands on her hips, like Wonder Woman about to fight an army of thugs.

"What the hell happened? Who did this? Were you mugged?"

Sharon is the ultimate mother hen. Telling her the truth about my evening is out of the question.

"Of course not. I was jogging, and I fell." I reach under the bar for the first aid kit and a Ziploc baggie. "It looks way worse than it is. I just need to patch myself up real quick."

"Jogging? I see." She doesn't believe me, but thankfully she lets it slide.

"Hey, I just got an idea," Nadir says. He has a "Eureka" look on his face. "Can I borrow that cocoa powder? And some scotch tape—"

I know where he's going with this.

"You think you can MacGyver the print?"

"I think so." Nadir grins.

"What are you talking about?" Sharon says, confused.

"It's a school thing," I say as I grab a roll of the clear packing tape we use to box stuff from under the cash register. Then I pluck the bag of cocoa powder from the martini station and tuck the first aid kit under one arm.

"Now all we need is a make-up brush," Nadir says. "Any chance you—"

"Are you nuts?" Sharon says, grabbing her handbag. She pulls out a compact makeup brush. "Do I look like a girl without game?"

"You're a lifesaver!" Nadir says.

"Make sure you bring that stuff back! I've got a table of high rollers on their third round of espresso martinis!" Sharon calls after us as we fight our way through the crowd.

A gaggle of metal chicks has lined up outside the women's restroom. They reapply lipstick and fluff their hair in the hallway mirror while waiting their turn to use the bathroom stalls.

"Sorry, ladies, staff!" I barge in front. They startle, teetering on high heels like a flock of flamingos. I drag Nadir past the line and into the largest booth, the one with a baby changing table. Honestly, who thought anyone was going to bring a baby to Cellos? I pull the shelf down and place the tape, cocoa powder, and first aid kit on the clean plastic shelf. Then I ease down on the toilet. My leg is throbbing, and blood has crusted over my knee.

"Me first," I say, biting my lip. "Is there some aspirin in there?"

Nadir hands me the pills, and I swallow them dry. Then he evaluates my wounds and gets to work, dabbing my knee with an alcohol swab, cleaning away the grit and dirt.

"You're right. It looks worse than it is. While I'm doing this, can you put the phone print-side up on the shelf thingy?"

I carefully retrieve a latex glove from the first aid kit and pull the burner phone out of my bag. A zap of pain shoots up my leg as Nadir hits a nerve.

"Ouch! That stings." I nearly drop the phone but manage to slide it onto the shelf, print side up.

"Sorry." He holds an antiseptic towel against the scrape. "Now, can you keep pressure on this until the bleeding stops?"

"No problem," I say through gritted teeth.

"There, now just stay still while I get the print." He shrugs off his backpack and pulls clean sheets of paper out of his notebook, sliding one under the phone. Next, he carefully sprinkles cocoa powder onto the paper, dabs Sharon's makeup brush into it, and lightly dusts the powder over the phone's plastic surface. Dead center on the back of the phone is a perfect thumbprint.

"Jackpot!" he yells and rips a piece of packing tape off the roll. Then, with a surgeon's precision, he lays the tape over the phone, smooth as silk with no air bubbles. I hold my breath as he lifts the print and holds it up, revealing the dark swirls of Cole Braedon's thumb defined by cocoa powder.

"Oh, you are good, Naughty...."

"Thank you!" He transfers the print to the second sheet of clean white paper and eases the tape down. Then he places the paper in his notebook and shoves it in his backpack.

"How long will it take to run the print?"

"Not long. I need to digitally scan the pattern and run it through a database or two. How's your knee doing?"

"It still hurts, but I think the bleeding's stopped."

He examines my knee, then presses a large butterfly bandage over the wound and closes the med kit. There's a loud bang on the door.

"What are you two doing in there?" I recognize Sharon's sweet but firm tone. Nadir opens the stall door and hands Sharon the first aid kit and her retracted makeup brush. She looks at the mess we've made on the changing table in horror.

"I can explain," I say lamely.

"Can you?" Sharon says. "Because this looks like one of your weird capers, Jenna."

"I told you they were up to something," says a metal chick dressed in thigh-high boots and an AC/DC T-shirt.

"Who asked you?" Sharon tucks the first aid kit under one arm. "I suppose you want Kyle to do your shift tomorrow?"

"If he doesn't mind—" I manage to say sheepishly as I gather the used first aid supplies, wipe the changing shelf down, and lock it back into place.

"Good, I already asked him. Listen, I have to get back to the martini table. They're blowing money like it's Saturday night in Vegas. Good luck with your case." Sharon winks, grabs the cocoa powder, and darts out the door, hurrying back to the bar.

"Come on, Nadir. We need to be long gone when she finds out her make-up brush is covered in cocoa powder."

My knee stings as I hobble toward the entrance.

Outside, Wally the bouncer flags down a cab for us to share. As we slide into the back seat, I feel a pang of guilt asking Nadir to run Cole's fingerprints. If Cole wanted me to know his true identity, he'd tell me. Then again, he made it pretty easy for me to get his print. He has to know I'll try.

Cole's burner phone chimes and I flip the cheap plastic lid open. There's a text waiting.

Number One: *Meet Smith at 3 p.m. tomorrow at Battery Labyrinth. Tell him - The weather is so unpredictable.*

So Braedon came through with his FBI contact. Hopefully, Smith can tell me how Rick Muraro was connected to a hitman for a cartel. But before I head to my first meeting with an FBI agent, there's someone I need to see.

Chapter 23
Graduation Day

The throbbing in my knee kept me up most of the night, leaving me groggy, cranky, and running late. I arrive for my meeting at Bar Kiev at ten past noon and find the door locked. After I bang loudly several times, a gray-haired man with deep lines on his face, clutching an enormous push broom, answers. He takes a look at me and frowns.

"Closed!" he snaps in a thick Russian accent.

"Sergei is expecting me."

"Name?" He squints, and the lines on his face slope down.

"Jenna Stack."

A curious look of surprise registers in his flinty eyes.

"You girl Sergei teaches to shoot gun?"

"That's me."

The man steps aside. As I enter the windowless bar, the pungent aroma of strong disinfectant mixed with even stronger booze assaults my nostrils and stings my eyes. Bar Kiev is narrow but deep. A mahogany bar stretches along the right side ending at an open area in the back. All of the tables have been set aside for cleaning. Behind the bar are dozens of glass decanters filled with vodka, each infused with a different flavoring ingredient. Floating in the various bottles are lemon slices, chili peppers, strawberries, and whole vanilla beans. At night, the vodka looks exotic and tempting, but now with the house lights up, the murky concoctions seem more like a series of failed science experiments. I try not to think about how often I've accepted a drink from those silty vats.

"Jenna! Over here!" a gravelly voice booms out across the quiet room. My unlikely friend Sergei Harkov sits at a booth against the far wall in the back. The Russian ex-gangster and colleague of Wolfson's also doubles as my gun instructor. Usually, we meet at the range once a week to practice shooting and discuss self-defense techniques. But I called him last night and asked for a meeting. It occurred to me that with his connections, he might know something about Rick and his father, Manny the Rock.

"Sergei!" I walk to the table, and he stands up and kisses me on both cheeks. Sergei has a narrow, pointed face with a large, ragged scar that runs from his thinning hairline, through his left eyebrow, and into his eyelid, causing it to pucker unnaturally. When he smiles, as he is now, his two gold teeth glitter in the light.

"Now, vat so important, you need Sergei?"

"There's a situation I need your help with—"

"Of course, I help favorite student." Sergei smiles broadly and checks a large gold watch on his wrist. "Sit," he commands in his heavy accent and shouts something in Russian to the old cleaning man. Most of the time, I can make out what Sergei is saying, but when he speaks quickly, I get lost. The mystery is solved when the man arrives with two glasses and a bottle of clear liquid.

"First, ve drink!" Sergei holds up a glass.

I shake my head. I need to stay sharp for my meeting with Agent Smith.

"Not today. I have an appointment. I was hoping we could talk."

"Sergei here for you." He drinks a glass of vodka and pours another. Then he tosses the second one back and slams the glass on the table. He throws his head back and lets out a hearty laugh. "Russian nectar!"

"Really? This early in the day?"

"Good anytime. Okay. Shoot!" He makes a shooting gesture with his fingers and lets out another robust laugh.

I take my phone out and scroll through the pictures I took at the crime scene. I open the one of Rick standing with Manny the Rock in front of the law office.

"Do you know this man?" I hand him the phone and point at Manny.

Sergei cradles the screen in his sinewy hands.

"Sure. Back in day, Manny the Rock big man. Mob lawyer. Very good. Shame about kid." He taps his finger on the screen. "Disgraceful."

"So you heard about Rick Muraro's death?"

"Die like common junkie." Sergei shakes his head with disapproval.

"Where did you hear that?" I'm surprised. Only the medical examiner's office and Denning are supposed to know Rick's actual cause of death.

Sergei shrugs. "Grapevine—friend in coroner's office."

"Listen, Sergei. This can't leave the room. But Rick didn't overdose accidentally. Someone gave him a hot shot and then shot him in the back."

Sergei whistles. "How you call that? Overkill?"

"Definitely. And his estranged wife, Natalie, is being framed for the murder."

"This Natalie, friend of yours?"

"Yes. I'm trying to help her. What do you know about Rick Muraro?"

Sergei looks at the photo and frowns.

"I only met boy ven he vas young. Big disappointment to Manny. Still, no man should outlive his son." He shakes his head sadly.

"I heard Rick and his father didn't get along. But nobody seems to know why."

"Sergei knows." He smiles proudly. "Manny built good, solid business. Set up for kid. But nothing vas ever good enough. Rick vas disrespectful, greedy, impatient. There vere rumors... drug trade, crazy risks. Manny not like that—not at all. He try to counsel him. But kid no listen."

"Do you think the Mafia was involved in Rick's murder?"

"Nyet. No vay," Sergei says, clenching his jaw. "Not unless Manny signs off."

"Could Manny have had him—"

"*Killed?* Nyet. Manny is gangster, not monster. Besides, Mafia hate drugs. Shoot, yes. But OD? Not Mob-style."

"What about the Izar Cartel? Is it their style?" Cole already told me an overdose is in line with cartel tactics. But I want to hear what Sergei thinks.

"Bad people. How you know them?"

"It's a long story, but a hitman named Romero shot at me."

The blood drains from Sergei's cheeks, and he releases a puff of air. "Izar Cartel try kill you?" His voice is heavy with concern.

"Yes. But I got away."

Sergei nods, his expression serious.

"You find trouble again, Jenna?"

"I guess so. So what do think? Was the cartel involved in Rick's death?"

Sergei pours himself another drink and tosses it back.

"I hear nothing. But easy to believe. Cartel much vorse than Mob. You understand difference, Jenna?"

"I think so...."

"Important for safety. I explain." Sergei runs his finger over the scar on his forehead. "Mafia old money. Powerful, but vith *rules*. Cartel new money. Flashy. Something they must prove. Manny is like Mafia. Rick like cartel. You understand?"

"I'm starting to get the picture."

"Cartel ruthless, Jenna. No rules. Promise you vill be careful?"

First Cole, now Sergei. Two of the most dangerous people I know have warned me about the Izar Cartel. My mouth feels dry, but I manage to spit out, "I promise."

Sergei slaps his hands down on the table.

"I just remember. Today is vonderful day. Graduation day for Jenna."

"Graduation?"

"From Uncle Sergei's gun range academy." He thumps a hand down on the table for emphasis. "I have present for you—" He walks over and ducks behind the bar. After rustling around, he returns with a box.

"Oh, Sergei, you shouldn't have."

He waves his hand dismissively. "Gift for best student, meant for later. But I think you need now. Open, please."

I pry off the lid. Inside is a gun; a simple, black Glock 19, small but efficient, with fifteen rounds.

"For me?" I'm so touched by the gift I choke up.

"Not just any gun." Sergei's tone grows serious. "Special gun. You know vy?"

"Not really." I lift the grip and feel the gun's weight.

"This gun does not exist. No history. No numbers. Poof."

He waves his hands like a magician.

"Untraceable?"

"For protection." He nods. "I hope you never use it. But if you do, vipe down, drop on ground, valk avay. Understand?"

I look up and see something I've never seen in Sergei's eyes—*fear.* This tough ex-gangster, who has seen and done things I can't even begin to imagine, isn't just warning me to be careful. He's afraid for me. Suddenly everything sharpens like someone's turned the contrast up on my life.

"Got it. Wipe, drop, and walk away." I put the gun in my right hand, slide in the magazine, check the chamber, snap the magazine back in place and click on the safety.

"Good. Remember vat Sergei taught you?"

"Distance is your friend?"

"Very good. Someone point gun, vat you do?"

"Move fast. Lateral, diagonal. Stay out of the line of sight."

"Keep on you for now. All times. Yes?"

"I will." A chill runs down my spine as I tuck the gun into my bag. I've never seen anything get to Sergei before. The Izar Cartel has him spooked.

He rechecks his flashy gold watch. "Now, one more gift today."

Sergei disappears into his office. After a few minutes, he reappears and sits across from me. "About brother, Tyler Stack—"

Already on edge, the mention of Tyler rips through what's left of my composure. Sergei has access to information from both sides of the law. But even if he's learned something that can help us, I have no way to reach my kid brother. I can't even visit him. Tears sting my eyes, and I push them back.

"I'm so worried, Sergei. He's in solitary confinement—"

"I know," Sergei says gently and hands me a small, black mobile phone. "When I say *now*, you push redial." He checks his watch and holds up a finger.

"What is this about?" Confused, I take the phone and wait.

"Now." He points a bony finger at me.

I hit the redial button. There's a short ring. Then a familiar voice answers.

"Jenna?"

"*Tyler?* Is that you?" A flood of relief overwhelms me, and the tears start to flow.

"It's me. I'm good. I'm okay."

Sergei smiles and refills his glass before walking away, allowing me to talk to my brother in private.

Chapter 24
The Labyrinth

After a bumpy subway ride downtown, I arrive at the edge of the Financial District near Battery Park with fifteen minutes to spare. Street vendors line the sidewalk, hawking food from around the world: Thai BBQ, Indian, Greek, fish and chips, and Korean-Mexican fusion. My stomach grumbles; I'm starving. According to the gospel of Wolfson, *eat when you can*, so I stop and order carnitas tacos topped with onions, tomatoes, and cilantro. I inhale the food and toss the wrapper before heading into the park.

The Battery is twenty-five acres of greenery and memorials located at the southern tip of Manhattan, where the East River meets the Hudson. People stroll along the walkways, enjoying the fall weather before winter drives everyone inside. I pass tourists holding maps, families picnicking, dogs sniffing, joggers working up a sweat, and even a few lovers holding hands.

I'm supposed to meet Smith at a quiet spot not far from where tourists line up for the ferry to Ellis Island. When I see the red brick of the Castle Clinton Monument, I veer off the main walkway to a tiny, crooked gate marked with a sign—*The*

Labyrinth. I let myself inside and follow a smaller path surrounded by wild growth. This part of the park is unfamiliar.

Crows cackle in the trees, and a gust of wind whips my hair. My mind jumps to thoughts of Agatha Christie's novels and murders in the English countryside. The path opens onto a green lawn scattered with dead brown leaves. Carefully placed stone pavers create an eerie circular pattern.

Across the small expanse, a man sits on a wooden bench, wearing a casual light blue windbreaker and reading a newspaper. His skin is weather-beaten and freckled, and his reddish hair is slightly unkempt. This must be Smith. He looks like a tired office worker, not an FBI agent, but he's the only person around.

"The weather is so unpredictable," I say, trying to sound casual.

The man looks up with narrow, faded eyes. "Jenna Stack?"

"Yes. Agent Smith?"

Smith inclines his head, indicating I should take a seat. He folds his newspaper and extends his hand. We shake, and his palm is cool and dry.

"Peaceful, isn't it?" He leans back on the bench and gazes out at the quiet garden. There's a strange longing in his voice.

"Yes. It's very serene."

"It's important that we never forget."

That's right. I remember reading that The Battery Labyrinth was built to commemorate the first anniversary of 9/11. Tucked between the statue of Giovanni da Verrazzano and the Korean War Memorial, the little respite is well hidden by dense plants and spindly, grayish green trees. The lovely setting suddenly strikes me. Before pressing Smith for information, I let a moment pass to pay my respects and honor the memorial's purpose.

"Thanks for meeting me."

"Professional courtesy," is all he says.

"How *do* you know Cole?"

"Braedon does some work for us now and then. Our paths cross." Smith stares out into the park. A few pigeons peck nearby. "Cole told me the basics of what happened. Any idea why the cartel targeted you at the Muraro house?"

I shrug. "I was taking a closer look at the crime scene."

"And why were you doing that?" He continues to face forward, keeping his eyes on the grassy area.

"Someone is trying to frame my friend for the murder—"

"Mrs. Muraro? I saw the pathology report." Smith shakes his head. "I doubt the cartel would go to such trouble. Not Izar's style."

"So I've heard. What is their style?"

"Terrorism, blackmail, making gruesome examples of people who cross them. I know the Izar Cartel well."

I shudder thinking of what constitutes a gruesome example in *this* guy's book. "Why is the Izar Cartel in New York anyway?"

"We aren't sure. But they're an international organization, so that isn't strange, although they usually keep a low profile."

"Was Rick Muraro involved with the cartel?"

"I never saw any sign that he was, but it makes sense." Agent Smith shrugs matter-of-factly. "Why else would a known assassin try to take you out? You came a little too close for comfort, Miss Stack." He looks up at the sky and sighs. A seed floats down on the wind like a tiny helicopter. He reaches his hand out and catches it. "Aren't these the darnedest things?"

The details are adding up. The cartel taking out Rick Muraro explains the pleading message on the dictation program, begging for more time. But what about the gunshot in Muraro's back? And why frame Natalie for the murder? Cole's theory must be right. Someone else is entangled in this mess. But who?

"Agent Smith, if Rick was involved with the cartel, do you know *how*?"

"Call me Marty. Yes, I'm starting to think I do." Smith takes a deep breath. "You see, we've been tracking movement along the Canadian bor—"

A dull hiss fills the air between us, followed by a thud. Warm liquid sprays across my face. A jolt of fear rocks my spine.

Then, Smith topples over in slow motion. Pigeons scatter into the air. A scream chokes in my mouth. Smith lies in a heap on the ground. Blood drips from his body, trickling along the stone pavers. He's been shot. My breath comes in ragged bursts. I shake Smith, but he isn't breathing. A pool of blood widens under his head, and his lifeless eyes stare out at the carefully placed stones of The Labyrinth.

Whoever shot Smith can't be far away. My clothes are spattered with blood—a terrible sense of dread lodges in my gut. I rush to the nearby bramble, double over, and vomit. Stomach acid burns my lips. I wipe my mouth and try to catch my breath. I need to do something, call someone.

My phone rings. It's an unknown number. I pick up the call.

"H-hello?"

"Jenna Stack?" says a deep, male voice with a soft accent.

The sound I make is unformed. I take a breath and try again. "Y-yes?"

"Leave Smith now. Walk in a direct line through the foliage. Then cross the bike path to the road."

"Who is this?"

"Just do as you're told. I'll be waiting."

"I can't. I have to call for help."

"There's nothing you can do for Agent Smith. Do as I say *now,* or you'll be joining him. My man Romero is still close by."

A wave of shock rises. *Romero? The hitman?*

Frozen in place, I'm unsure what to do. The labyrinth is empty except for Smith's dead body. A cluster of leaves explodes behind me. I recognize the unmistakable whooshing sound of a silencer, followed by a rush of footsteps.

"Move!" a disembodied voice hisses from the trees.

Stunned and shaking, I do as I'm told, pushing north into the dense brush. Behind me is the sound of labored breathing, like a great lumbering animal closing in on me. Then the air is pierced by a high-pitched scream. Someone has found Agent Smith. When I reach the bike path, a pair of cyclists is headed my way. Knowing my shirt is splattered with blood, I hesitate and zip up my jacket.

My phone rings again. "I suggest you hurry, Miss Stack. Unless you want to explain yourself to the New York City police."

"I'm trying!" I watch from the bushes as the bikers pass and run across the wide strip of road. On the other side, a long, black limousine is parked with the motor running. The back window slides down silently.

"Please, join me," says the same deep voice from the phone. The person inside is hidden in shadow.

Something cold pokes into my back—a *gun*. It's Romero.

He pats me down, rifles through my bag, and examines all three of my phones. Then he finds my gun, which disappears into his pocket. *So much for my protection.* Romero opens the limo door, shoves me inside, and throws my backpack onto the seat after me.

As the door slams, I catch a glimpse of Romero. He's built like a heavyweight boxer with a square head, bent nose, and jet-black hair. His cheeks are pock-marked, and his mouth turns downward in a menacing frown. He lives up to my expectation of what a hitman looks like.

Romero shuts the door and slides into the driver's seat. Automatic door locks engage with a loud click. I'm trapped.

A stranger sits across from me on the far side of the dimly lit cabin. His face is obscured by darkness. He wears an expensive gray silk suit. As he leans toward the partition separating us from Romero, I get a better look. He has a lean face, sharply angled bone structure, black eyes, a closely trimmed beard, a mustache, and stylish, collar-length hair. He sports jewel-encrusted cufflinks and a large, gold ring on his pinky finger.

This must be Darius Candelas Izar.

"Drive," he commands softly before sliding the partition closed. He pulls a vanity mirror down from the ceiling. Then he hands me an old-fashioned handkerchief. "Clean yourself up."

"Oh God—" My reflection in the mirror is horrific. I wipe the blood spatter from my eyes and mouth with trembling fingers.

"May I offer you a drink?" Izar says as if we're at a dinner party. Who threatens someone, kidnaps them, and then offers them a beverage?

Romero turns the limo onto West Street, heading uptown, away from the sirens rushing toward the park. My mind flashes to something I heard in a movie once. Never let a kidnapper take you to a second location. My stomach clenches.

"Where are we going?" I try to sound confident, but my voice wavers.

He looks me over. "A drink will calm your nerves."

"How do I know you won't poison me?"

"Oh, come now, Miss Stack. I don't consider you an enemy *yet.*"

"Funny, you have a strange habit of threatening to kill me."

Izar laughs, and the sound is cold.

"I see you are a wit. Let's not be too dramatic. I'm simply a businessman, a guest of your country." He pours a dark liquor into two leaded crystal glasses and hands me one. I take a sip. It's brandy, mellow, slightly sweet, and complex.

"What do you want from me?" I swallow the rest of my drink,

and the heat moves through my body, taking the edge off the shock.

"I want something *for* you, Miss Stack." His accent is cultured and elegant, his manner aloof. "For you to live a long, productive life. But I assure you, if you continue investigating Rick Muraro's death, the chances of that happening will grow increasingly slim."

"You're Darius Candelas Izar." If he won't say it, I will.

"In the flesh." He raises his glass in a mock toast.

"Why did you kill Agent Smith?"

"I have my reasons. Let's just say...." He takes a sip of his drink and looks out at the Hudson River. "Smith disappointed me."

"And Rick Muraro? Did you have him killed too?"

"I have to admit, in that case—I'm not entirely sure."

"How can you *not be sure* if you killed someone?"

"Be careful, my dear." He looks at me with a flash of heat in his black eyes. "I am in a somewhat tolerant mood. But that could change quickly."

The cold certainty in his voice makes me claustrophobic. "Am I next?"

"As they say in my country, *métete en tus asuntos*. If you mind your affairs, I see no reason to dispose of you. But if you continue digging into things that don't concern you or go to *la policía*...." Darius Candelas Izar watches me coldly. "Well then, I'm afraid you will leave this earth rather abruptly. I trust you believe me?"

"I believe you." Killing is nothing to this man.

Izar slides open the glass partition and signals. Romero passes my Glock through the opening. His gold pinky ring glints in the sunlight. The ring is stamped with a familiar symbol. I push down my rising panic. Isn't that the cloaked skeleton worn by Elena Solaris and the shopgirl Camila?

"Ah, I see you are admiring my lovely saint?" Izar waves my gun casually as he shows me his ring.

"That corpse is a saint?"

"Santa Muerta. She's popular in cultures with a certain reverence toward death. Even before Santa Muerta, the Aztecs worshipped *Mictlantecuhtli* and *Mictecacihuatl*, the lord and lady of Mictlan, the realm of the dead."

"Why death?" I try to hide my terror.

"It is simply a way to honor a force beyond our comprehension. For the deceased to be accepted into *Mictlan*, offerings to the lord and lady of death are necessary." Izar runs a finger along the gun's barrel, examining the cold, black metal. "This gun of yours is an instrument of death, is it not?"

My mouth is dry from fear.

"I—I guess so. I never thought of it that way before."

Izar unclicks the safety and hands me the loaded gun—pointed at his heart. There's no fear in his eyes, only a calm certainty I won't pull the trigger, and he's right. Shooting Izar would be a death sentence. I click the safety back on and shove the gun into my bag.

"A wise choice, Miss Stack. I trust you will heed my warning and avoid becoming an offering yourself?"

"Believe me, Mr. Izar, the reason I went to that house and met with Agent Smith has nothing to do with you. I'm trying to save an innocent person."

"That's good to hear." Izar taps on the partition, and the limo pulls over. "Just one more thing." He reaches for my backpack and pulls out the phone Cole gave me. He flips it open and scrolls through the history. "A disposable phone and with just one number programmed. Let me guess...."

Fear grips me. Does Izar know Cole helped me escape Rick's house the other night? Is Cole in danger?

Izar smiles and presses the programmed number.

"Mr. Braedon, I presume? This is Izar. I'm going to text you an address. If you want to see the girl alive, come alone... And, oh yes. *You owe me a favor.*"

Izar hangs up, takes a silk handkerchief from his pocket, and wipes his prints off before tossing the phone in my backpack.

"Don't hurt him," I say, terrified.

"Please, Miss Stack. I'm a civilized man. Go live your life and remember our little talk. Mr. Braedon should be here shortly."

Romero unlocks the door. I have more questions, but Izar is letting me walk away. Best not to push my luck. My legs are unsteady as I step onto West Street. The sun is low in the sky. What time is it? I pull on my backpack. There's a loud thud as something blunt strikes the back of my head. My ears ring. I try to stay upright, but my knees buckle. The last thing I see is a patch of grass rising toward me before everything turns black.

Chapter 25
Safe House

Agent Smith and I are standing in the center of The Battery Labyrinth. The air is cool and misty. Through the haze, I see the grassy circle. But the stone pattern isn't laid with small, flat pavers. Instead, large boulders rise out of the mist and block our way.

"Follow the path." Smith gestures for me to enter the maze.

"But I can't see where it leads."

"You will." He smiles serenely.

Suddenly the ground begins to move, and the boulders shake and groan. I open my eyes, startled and disoriented. *It was just a dream.*

For a moment, relief washes over me until I realize I'm in an unfamiliar bed, wrapped in sheets, with a blanket thrown on top. A hand squeezes my shoulder like a vice. My heart races. A male figure is looming over me.

"Get off me!" I squirm to get away, but his grip tightens.

"Jenna! It's me!"

I stop thrashing long enough to recognize familiar green eyes surveying me with concern. Izar and Romero are gone. I'm alone with Cole Braedon in an unfamiliar apartment. What is this place?

"Cole? Don't scare me like that!" I struggle to sit up and get tangled in the sheets. Uh oh. I'm naked. I clutch the thin fabric.

"What the hell? Where are my clothes?"

"Listen, you're okay."

"What happened? I think someone hit me." I feel the back of my head. There's a lump, and it's tender. "Owwww!"

Cole takes my shoulders in his hands and steadies me. *"The past doesn't exist anymore.* Understand?"

Somehow, his strange words make sense and calm me down. I nod.

"Where am I?"

"Easy now." Cole narrows his eyes. "This is a safe house. Your clothes were covered in blood. I had to make sure you weren't hurt—"

"You saw me naked?"

"Only a little bit." He grins.

The previous few hours rush back into my mind; Romero taking my gun, Izar threatening me, Agent Smith falling, the spray of blood.

"Oh, God. Agent Smith is dead! I remember now. We were at The Labyrinth. A shot came out of nowhere."

"I know." Cole clicks on the television to NY1. "The shooting at The Labyrinth is the lead story. Poor Marty."

"It's my fault. We need to go to the police station. I should make a report." An involuntary shudder moves through my body. I hate losing control, especially in front of someone like Cole Braedon, who is always so calm and collected. Hot tears sting my eyes, but I catch them before they fall.

Cole takes me by the shoulders. "No one's blaming you, Jenna. Nothing you did would have kept him alive. Anyway, you can't go to the police. Agent Smith was deep undercover on a big case. The FBI will decide what to share with the locals. Believe me. They don't want you complicating things."

"How do you know that?" I struggle to a seated position.

"I told you, I know a lot of things. Besides, I'm working with them, at least this week."

I look around the room for the first time. We're in a small studio apartment facing an alley with a fire escape. A kitchenette and a living area with some office equipment, a laptop, and a paper shredder are on a folding table next to a bed. On one side of the room is an open closet with men's clothing hanging inside.

"I should get dressed." I wrap the sheet around me.

"Sorry, but your clothes need to be destroyed." He gestures to a paper bag in the corner, folded with odd markings.

"What the hell, Cole!"

"As I said, Jenna, the Feds don't want you complicating things. I bought you some stuff." He points to an Anthropologie bag on the table.

"How do you know my size?" That is the only thing I can think to say This day is so surreal.

"That's top secret." He grins. "Look, why don't you get cleaned up? There's a robe in the bathroom. I'll get some take-out and be right back."

"No!" I reach for his arm, panicked.

"It's okay." He looks at me with enough confidence for both of us. "You're safe here. I promise."

My hand gripping his arm is covered with dirt and blood. I take a deep breath. "You're right. I need a shower."

"I'll be back before you're finished." Cole slips out the front door.

As soon as I hear the lock tumble into place, I slip into the bathroom. It's small but clean, with white subway tile, a tub with a shower, and a medicine cabinet above an old-fashioned pedestal sink. The mirror is slightly cloudy. Agent Smith's blood is spattered across my face and hair. I turn on the shower, and the water heats up fast. Every muscle in my body hurts as I step under the warm spray. The blood-stained water washes down the drain, and I see Agent Smith's face, staring at The Labyrinth. One moment he was alive, the next dead, slumped over, eyes clouded and sightless. It all happened so quickly. Could I have done more? Tears begin to flow, slowly at first, then uncontrollably. I squeeze my eyes shut, trying not to go down the rabbit hole of events. I recognize the effects of PTSD, emotional numbness, intrusive thoughts, paranoia, nightmares, and hyper vigilance.

One thing's for sure. I never want to see a gun again.

In my dream, Agent Smith told me to follow the path, despite the obstacles—to see where it leads. I make a silent promise to him.

I'll find the clues and solve the case no matter where the path takes me.

A knock on the bathroom door makes me jump.

"Jenna? Are you okay?" Cole says.

"Fine." I check my reflection, straighten the robe, and comb through my damp hair. A cloud of steam puffs into the room as I open the door.

There's a take-out bag on the kitchen counter and a familiar, pungent smell: Thai food. *My favorite.* Does Cole know that? Too bad I've lost my appetite.

Cole looks at me intensely, like a specimen he's observing through a microscope. Then he unexpectedly walks over and steers me to the bed. He kneels beside me and looks into my eyes.

"You're going to be okay, Jenna." His voice is deep and commanding. "You're a survivor. You'll get past this."

"What about Smith? He'd still be alive if not for me." I touch my cheek, convinced I can still feel his blood on my face.

"You're wrong, Jenna." Cole takes my hand. "You know that."

"But I had a gun. I should have stopped it somehow."

"That's the shock talking. Believe me."

"How can you be sure?" I'm desperate to be convinced.

"Smith was an experienced agent. He'd been undercover for months. I'm guessing his cover got blown. If that's the case, his days, his hours, were numbered. He was a good man, a good agent. And I'm sorry you had to be there, but there's nothing you could have done." Cole pats my shoulder and heads for the kitchen. He brings me a plate of fragrant noodles, a napkin, and chopsticks.

"But—"

"Let it go, Jenna. First, you need to eat something."

"I can't." I dab the tears from my eyes with the napkin. I've cried more in the past week than in my entire life. Just hours ago, I was happily eating tacos on my way to meet Smith. It all feels so distant now.

"You can and you should. What's that crazy rule of Wolfson's?" Cole says as he deftly twirls noodles onto his chopsticks.

"Eat when you can," I whisper.

"That's it." He tilts his head back, drops a generous pile of food in his mouth, and chews with relish. "Mmmmmm. Now you try."

"Okay," I smile half-heartedly and carefully whirl the sticky noodles onto my chopsticks. My stomach grumbles in antic-ipation.

"Go on—eat," Cole insists.

I give in and take a bite. The food is warm and satisfying, with a hint of smoky char. But the chopsticks are meticulous and distracting. I wish I had a fork when it dawns on me. There's a method to Cole's madness. He brought me chopsticks on purpose; to force me to focus my mind on the task. I'm hungrier than I realized as I struggle to master the chopsticks. Within a few minutes, I finish the entire plate.

"Good?" He smiles.

"Delicious. *Pad see ew*, right?"

"Impressive. You know your noodles, don't you?"

Cole takes the dishes to the kitchen and washes the plates with military efficiency, which strikes me as odd. Who cares if dirty dishes sit in the sink? Pulling two bottles of water from the fridge, he hands me one.

"Now, tell me everything that happened." He sits close to me.

After a few deep breaths and a sip of water, I arrange the events in my mind.

"I met Agent Smith at The Labyrinth. He seemed tired, kind of world-weary. We were talking. Then there was a gunshot, not loud, more like a hiss—"

"The shooter probably used a silencer. Did you see him?" Cole watches me with unblinking intensity.

The scene replays in my mind. The memory is fresh and raw.

"No, I just saw Smith fall. There was blood. Izar called my phone, and Romero pushed a gun into my back. Izar was waiting."

"And you're sure it was him?" Cole holds up his phone. There's a picture of a well-dressed man with sharply angled features and a mustache.

"Yes, that's him."

Cole shakes his head in amazement. "Darius Candelas Izar is one of the most dangerous men in the world. You're lucky to be alive, Jenna."

"I heard him call you just before I blacked out."

"That was a display of power. He was playing God, not by the same rules as everyone else. He's a monster."

"He looked younger than I expected. How did he become so powerful?"

"Izar is a prince of thieves. His father was a Colombian cartel leader who moved cocaine, and his mother's family ran a Mexican cartel that distributed the finished product to the US. Their marriage united two criminal organizations into the single most powerful, well connected, ruthless cartel south of the equator." Cole looks at me hard with an unwavering gaze. "Their untimely deaths put Izar in charge of an empire worth billions."

"Billions? You're serious?"

"Dead serious. Now, what did he say to you?"

"He told me to stay out of his business."

"Good advice. What else?"

"I asked if he killed Rick Muraro."

"You asked him that?" Cole's eyes flare with alarm.

"He said *I'm not sure.* Weird, right?" In retrospect, maybe it was stupid to ask, but I can't help but be a little proud of myself. "Why would he lie?"

"Why do sociopaths do anything?" Cole seems lost in thought. "What else do you remember?"

"He wore a gold ring with a La Muerta symbol, just like the medallion worn by Elena Solaris. I saw the same necklace on the shopgirl at Facèré Boutique. That can't be a coincidence—"

"It's not," Cole says with a stunned look. "Elena is Izar's half-sister."

"His *sister*? What the hell? When were you planning on telling me that?"

"Look, Jenna. Any intel is on a need-to-know basis."

"That Elena is cartel royalty? Don't you think I needed to know that?

"We aren't sure what her relationship is with the cartel. For all we know, Izar sent Romero to kill *her.* Besides, I had no idea Izar would kidnap *you*. Investigations take time—jumping to conclusions can get you killed."

"You're right, sorry." I believe him. How could he have known?

"I need a drink." Cole walks to a cabinet. He takes out two heavy crystal glasses and an oddly shaped bottle with a long neck.

"Is that *Tres Cuatro Cinco Extra Añejo Tequila?*" I'm stunned. That stuff is 87 proof and half a grand a bottle, a legend in bartending circles.

"I thought you might appreciate it." Cole grins. He pours a shot and hands it to me. Then he takes a seat and cradles the glass of amber-colored Tequila in his palm. "Now, let's solve this together."

"All right. What do you know about Elena?" I sip my drink, which is hot and mellow at the same time. Wait until Sharon hears about this.

"Elena Solaris is the illegitimate daughter of the cartel's patriarch, Matias Candelas Izar. The product of a long-term relationship with a favorite mistress. She grew up among the cartel until Matias sent her away to boarding school in Switzerland. She changed her identity. Re-invented herself."

"What about now? Does Elena work with her brother?"

"We aren't sure. We're still figuring out the players. She and Darius were never close. But she's a silent partner in Facèrè Boutique, which appears to be a money mule."

"We covered that at school—a network of businesses that move cash, diamonds, and gold for a criminal enterprise."

"That's right." He nods approvingly. "But we aren't sure how much Elena knows about Izar's business or Rick's death. She could be a victim too."

"True, Elena seemed upset about Rick's death, and she had a solid alibi the night of the murder. Maybe you should see this." I open the camera on my phone. "I took photos of the crime scene before Denning arrived."

"Of course you did." Cole smiles and shakes his head. He takes the phone and swipes through the pictures intently, stopping at the photo of Rick's schedule. "Rick was planning a trip to Massena? Near the Canadian border?"

"He has a cabin up there. He was going to meet a woman."

"How do you know?"

I reach over and scroll through the pictures until I find the message. "See? He was dictating when he was murdered."

Cole reads the words, mesmerized.

I'm picking up Milania the day after tomorrow—
Goddammit! You? No! You can't do this to me!
It's not what you think! No, no, no—

"You're kidding me." Cole sits bolt upright with a startled expression.

"What?"

"Milania!" He grins.

"Who is that? Is she important?"

"She's not a person. The program misheard. Rick wasn't picking up *Milania*. He was picking up *Milonga*."

"Milonga? Who's that?"

"Not a *who*—a *what*. Milonga is cartel slang for cocaine."

Now I sit up, startled too. "Rick was trafficking coke? Agent Smith said they were tracking movement along the Canadian border. But why Canada?"

"Sometimes the cartel hires bikers to drive drugs from Mexico up to Canada, then back into the States."

"That doesn't make any sense."

"Actually, it does. The smugglers cross from Mexico into the US at less fortified border outposts in the west, drive up to, and then across, Canada, and re-enter the US on the east coast by boat. It's a highly sophisticated and profitable system."

"Does that mean Rick worked for the cartel?"

"Maybe. But why trust a coked-up amateur?"

"What if Elena and Rick started something on their own?"

"Doing an end run around the cartel would explain the hitman. Family or not, you don't cross Izar."

"I suppose if he killed Agent Smith in broad daylight, he'd have no problem murdering a backstabbing future brother-in-law."

"Jenna? This is a long shot...." Cole's voice is hopeful.

"What?" The tequila has taken the edge off, and I'm feeling fine.

"Somebody, Rick's partner or an accomplice, might still pick up that shipment tomorrow. Can you think of who he'd send to do dirty work? Someone tough and a little sleazy?"

One person comes to mind.

"There's a private investigator who worked for Rick's law firm. I spent a few hours with him. They were friends."

"What's your impression of him?"

"Definitely tough. Kinda shady. The type that isn't above rooting through people's trash to get what he needs. But I liked him. He was smart and funny and obviously cared a lot about Rick."

"What's his name?"

"Jack Russell."

"Like Jack Russell Terrier? You're kidding?"

"I swear, that's his name. But if he's involved, I doubt it's knowingly. His bark is worse than his bite."

Cole smiles at my lame joke.

"Okay, tomorrow we tail Jack Russell."

I can't help but laugh at Cole's even lamer joke. Finally, there's a sliver of light at the end of the tunnel. There's no way Natalie was involved in some crazy drug ring. With Cole's help, we might crack this case. He leans over and clinks his glass against mine. We both finish our expensive Tequila.

"It feels fantastic to have a lead." The words burst out of me.

"We'll need to get up early." Cole walks to the closet, pulls out a men's button-down shirt, and tosses it to me. "You can sleep in this."

"Sleep?" My eyes dart around the room. One bed. No couch. "Here?"

"What's wrong? Have you got to work or study or something?"

"No. It's just… there's only one bed."

"A gentleman would offer to sleep on the floor," he says. "Luckily, I'm no gentleman." Cole takes a blanket out of the closet, rolls it up in a long tube, and places it in the center of the bed as a divider. "Better?"

"Um, sure." I grab the shirt and duck into the bathroom. Luckily, the tails fall to the middle of my thighs.

When I step back into the room, Cole is stripping down to his underwear without a thought. He's lean and fit, with ropey muscles and not an ounce of fat. But across his torso and back are a crisscross of scars, and he's covered in ink. Some look like Russian prison tattoos, faded and crudely done. The ones on his hands are in the process of being removed. Others are newer, more colorful, and artistic. I climb onto my side of the bed before asking.

"Where did you get those old tattoos—White Swan?"

He narrows his eyes. "How do you know about that?"

I shrug. "The first time we met in that alley, I researched the tattoos on your hand. I ended up at White Swan. Were you there?"

"I was. And I'll tell you about it sometime, but it's not exactly a bedtime story." Cole flicks the light out and gets into bed. He smells like musk and tobacco, and I can feel his warmth nearby. I close my eyes and listen to his steady breathing, hoping it will lull me to sleep.

"Cole?" I'm unsure if he's still awake. "Do you ever get sick of this life? Of the safe houses, the secrets, the death?"

He lets out a long sigh. "It's all I know."

"There must have been a time before, when you were a boy?"

"Honestly, Jenna, I don't remember."

"I wish I was more like you," I say sleepily.

"Me? Why?"

"You're so focused, not afraid of anything."

"You'd be surprised."

"Name one thing that scares you," I challenge him in a whisper. I want to put my arms around him. But I don't.

"Maybe someday. Right now we both need a good night's sleep."

Chapter 26
Road Trip

The sound of a truck rumbling by wakes me from a deep sleep. There's no sign of Cole, but the aroma of fresh coffee leads me to the kitchen. A steaming carafe sits on the counter. I pour myself a cup of much-needed caffeine and forage for milk in the fridge—my stomach grumbles. I hope Cole went for breakfast. Dave's goofy ringtone sounds off. Where's my backpack? Oh yes, Super Spy bagged my clothing. My backpack too. Then I spot the box behind the coffee pot. Inside is my stuff. A quick note has been thrown on top.

J -
Back soon.
Fill the new bag with essentials only.
I think you'll find a crossbody more practical in the field.
- C

Crossbody? What the hell? I rummage through the box. The

contents of my backpack are there, except for two items: my lock-picking kit and the Glock 19 Sergei gave me. I guess Cole Braedon doesn't trust me after all.

I check my collection of phones. Every one of Dave's pet sitters seems to have left a text. There's also a new voicemail from high-maintenance Mrs. Brochelle.

"Gary tracked grass onto my kitchen floor after Mr. Biggle's walk! You know I love Gary, but I'm allergic to grass. Please remind him to remove his shoes and wipe Mr. Biggles's paws next time."

I text Mrs. Brochelle an apology and Gary a gentle reprimand. Seriously? Is this what it's like to be Dave? Next, I fire off a series of rapid replies to today's questions.

Sandy: *Am I walking Jellybean Sat?*
Me: *Blumes r out of town. No walk for JB.*

Gina: *What temp is koi water supposed to be?*
Me: *59 to 77 degrees.*

Jerry: *Where is kitty litter?*
Me: *Laundry room.*

Grass stains and kitty litter? Really? Do other detectives have to deal with this kind of crap? In a matter of minutes, I'm all caught up. Thank goodness for technology. As far as my personal phone goes, there is no news about my internship. Tyler and Nadir are quiet. Give them time, I suppose.

I can't spend all day in Cole's borrowed shirt, so I peek inside the Anthropologie bag. There's a pair of jeans, a black button-down shirt, a stylish utility jacket, a pair of ankle boots, and dark socks. Wrapped in tissue is a lacy pair of underwear and a bra that doesn't leave much to the imagination.

At the bottom is a large, sturdy-looking leather bag with a thick strap. I guess this must be the crossbody. There's also a small plastic travel bag from Duane Reade with deodorant, a toothbrush, toothpaste, and a comb. The necessities and nothing more.

Moments later, I'm dressed and the whole ensemble, even the undergarments, fits me perfectly. How is that possible? Does Cole have a dossier on me down to my measurements? Or is he just really good at sizing up women?

By the time I've packed my new bag and brushed my hair, Cole slips through the front door.

"Your breakfast, madame." Cole deposits a white paper bag on the counter. "You look great."

My stomach does a little flip-flop at the compliment. I take a seat on one of the tall kitchen stools. Maybe a meal will settle the butterflies down.

"I'm missing a couple of things—"

"You mean like this?" Cole opens a drawer and slides my lock-picking set across the counter. "A Southard twenty-two-piece set? Nice. Are you any good?"

"Pretty good. I've been practicing."

Then he holds up my gun. My mind flashes to Izar telling me about Santa Muerta while waving the deadly weapon so casually.

"And where'd you get this little gem?" Expertly, Cole drops the magazine out and checks the chamber. "Glock nineteen, never been fired."

"Sergei gave it to me."

"Wolfson's Russian pal? Really?"

"He's given me shooting lessons. He said it's untraceable."

Cole examines the gun, puts the magazine back, and flips the safety lock. "Okay, keep it." He hands me the weapon.

The memory of blood spreading under Agent Smith's head

makes me shudder. The thought of ever touching a gun again is terrifying. "I'd rather not."

Cole considers his words carefully before speaking. "Listen, Jenna. Guns are terrible creations. I get that, and *I agree*. But if you're going to be a detective, they will come into play. If you pretend guns don't exist, you'll end up dead. Understand?"

I consider what he's saying. I can hate guns and still use one to protect myself if necessary.

"You're right." I pack the Glock, lock-pick kit, and phones in my new bag, where there seems to be a compartment for everything.

"Three phones? A bit of overkill, don't you think?"

"You should know; you gave me the burner. Speaking of which, won't there be cell records showing I was in the park when Agent Smith was killed?"

Cole shakes his head. "The best a cell tower can do is put you in the vicinity of The Battery, along with thousands of other New Yorkers. Besides, why would anyone pull your records? Nobody knew about the meeting except you, me, and Smith. Right?" He looks at me expectantly.

"I didn't tell anyone, if that's what you mean."

"Good. Now let's eat." He hands me a breakfast burrito. Inside are scrambled eggs, potatoes, bacon, salsa, and cheese. It's steaming hot and delicious.

"So, has Wolfson tapped you for one of his coveted internships yet?"

"Mmm hmm, I'm waiting to hear—"

"About Bell River?"

"How did you know?"

Cole shrugs and smiles. "I know you, that's all. If you think you can save Tyler, you'll try. And who knows? Maybe you can."

"Listen, Cole, how *did* you get that forensic evidence you sent me?"

"I know a lab tech upstate. He searched the records and turned up that file. Something's not right in Bell River, Jenna. Have you ever heard the saying where there's smoke, there's fire?" Cole finishes his burrito and crumples the wrapper.

"Sure," I say warily. "Wolfson did a whole lecture. Idioms, not just for Idiots."

"Well, I can smell the smoke from here. If someone set your brother up to take the fall for the Vitner murder, then Bell River is a dangerous place. Remember, the closer you get to the truth, the more risk you take. So keep that phone handy. I'm number one, remember?" He grins and grabs a laptop from the far side of the counter. The computer screen lights up, and he types in the longest password I've ever seen. An unfamiliar program opens. He types into the search box: Jack Russell.

"Is that even legal?" I ask.

Cole ignores my question. After he eliminates a few contenders with the same name, a picture of Jack appears on the screen.

"Found him. Your friend was an orphan, grew up in foster homes, got a job as a runner for Manny the Rock's law firm, worked his way through detective school, and lives in East Williamsburg."

"Really? Kind of a young scene for him, right?"

"He's been there since the nineties, bought cheap, long before the hipsters gentrified the neighborhood."

"I told you he's smart."

Cole dials a number using his computer. A weird pop-up appears.

"Yes?" says a robotic voice.

"This is Peregrine. Confirmation code Omega two three one seven. I have a clean-up."

"Confirmed."

He shuts the laptop and starts packing his stuff into an over-the-shoulder bag.

"What was that about?"

"You're the detective in training, Jenna. Guess."

Cole grabs a black trash bag from the corner and tosses it into the bathroom. No doubt filled with my blood-spattered clothing and my backpack.

"You're eliminating the evidence?"

"You got it. Fingerprints don't wipe themselves down, and blood evidence doesn't destroy itself, either." Cole grabs a thick wad of cash and a gun out of the kitchen drawer. "FBI, standard issue Glock twenty-two," he says and slides the weapon into a holster under his arm. "Now we need to get moving."

Cole's car is in a nearby parking garage. It's early, so the streets are quiet, with just a few people walking their dogs. The trendy neighborhood does not scream FBI safe house. Instead, there are chic boutiques, and cafes with security gates pulled shut. We cross the Williamsburg bridge, closing in on Jack's apartment and obeying the speed limit to avoid drawing attention. Finally, we reach a street lined with converted warehouses and older apartment buildings.

Cole pulls over by a loading zone across from a three-story brick building that probably hasn't changed much in the last hundred years.

"Any sign of Jack's car?"

I scan the street. "He drives an old blue sedan. I don't see it."

We watch the door in tense silence for several minutes until

Jack emerges from the building wearing a leather jacket and heads for an enormous, shiny black SUV.

"Looks like he's upgraded," Cole says.

Jack pulls out abruptly, and we follow. Cole hangs back, keeping his distance but matching the SUV's speed. I've never followed anyone before, and it's exhilarating.

"So now what? Do we tail him? For how long?"

"As long as it takes."

"What if he drives to Atlantic City?"

"Then we drive to Atlantic City."

My phone buzzes, and I glance at the text. A chill runs down my spine.

Nadir: *Braedon's fingerprint is a dead end. Nothing in any database. FBI, Interpol. The dude's a ghost.*

How is that possible? Cole's prints have to be on file someplace. I type back my answer.

Me: *Keep looking.*
Nadir: *Tried everything. No place left to look.*

Panic rises in my chest. I glance at Cole. He's all business, staring straight ahead, following Jack. Who *is* this guy? Agent Smith did say he worked for the FBI. But I can't confirm anything else about him. He's like a phantom. Am I just a pawn in some weird game? What am I doing alone in a car, headed God knows where, with this man? Cole would never hurt me—would he?

Jack drives down Vandervoort Avenue, past squat industrial buildings covered in graffiti, toward the BQE. The SUV traverses the steel and glass of upper Manhattan before crossing the vast expanse of the George Washington Bridge. Cole hangs back, weaving like a shark through traffic, staying in Jack's blind spot.

"Looks like he's headed out of town," Cole says. "Who're you texting?"

"Oh, just a client," I say, struggling to sound casual.

I think about Natalie, in jail, desperate for someone to help her. Right now, I may be her only hope. I push down my fear. I'm along for this ride, wherever the road takes me.

Chapter 27
X Marks Massena

As we follow Jack across the George Washington Bridge, Cole stares at the black SUV with unwavering concentration. The traffic congestion lightens as we enter New Jersey and before long, we're headed north on Route 17. The road opens up, bordered by thick green trees. Cole lets Jack widen the distance as we merge onto the Major Deegan Expressway and pass under a series of bridges, heading toward Albany. Sometimes I'm convinced we've lost the trail, but Cole always manages to catch up.

"Looks like Jack is picking up where Rick left off," Cole says. "He's headed toward Massena."

"Maybe," I say. "But for all we know, he's taking a vacation. You're the one who said jumping to conclusions was dangerous."

"True. I'm surprised you were listening." Cole smirks. "But who goes on vacation with no luggage?"

The highway becomes a blur of gray tarmac and yellow dividing lines as we follow Jack northward, keeping our distance. Whenever his black SUV stops for gas or coffee, we follow. I'm amazed by the casual way Cole zeros in on the guy. There's little room for cover, but Cole seems to know when Jack will stop and how long each task will take. We have plenty of time to go to the bathroom and get drinks or food before pulling discreetly back on the road and catching up to our prey. The monotony of the pursuit is somehow calming. My anxiety about Cole lessens. No matter who he is, I'm stuck with him for the foreseeable future. I guess he'll tell me his story when he's ready.

"You're good at this," I observe while sipping a bottled iced tea.

"In our business, it's a critical skill. The key is to avoid a prolonged appearance in the rearview mirror of your target. That means hanging way back and making random movements."

I'm distracted by the fact that he said *our* business—like we're a team. I'm also surprised by the weird sensation his words evoke. I'm attracted to Cole, drawn to his intensity. Even if this epic road trip doesn't answer any questions, being on this case together is thrilling. I imagine giving into my feelings, but it's a fantasy. I need to be careful, at least until I know a lot more about the guy.

Outside, the towns are getting smaller and smaller. I recognize the little diners, gas stations, hardware stores, and churches, similar to my hometown. I couldn't wait to move to New York. How ironic that I'm trying so hard to get back to Bell River. "Do you mind if I ask you a question?"

"Shoot," Cole says.

"How did you get into this business exactly?"

He hesitates a moment, keeping a steady hand on the wheel.

"Same way you did. Somebody hurt someone I loved."

That answer throws me off for a moment. So Cole had someone in his past who got hurt the way Tyler did?

"Who was that?"

"My sister. It's a long story. I'll tell you about it someday."

"I've got plenty of time now." I gesture to the long stretch of road ahead.

"Not today, Jenna. Okay?"

Cole's made himself clear. I've pushed enough. I'll add that to the list of stories he's promised to tell me *someday*.

Our surroundings grow increasingly rural, peppered by lonely motels, farms, quaint bridges, and bubbling streams. The landscape is familiar, almost comforting. Finally, the highway ends, turning into Massena's Main Street. We pass a high school, Walmart, and Home Depot as we follow Jack through the sleepy town. The SUV turns onto a winding country road. Clusters of tall, leafless maples form a gray wall stretching into the distance.

"You're going to lose him," I say nervously.

"No, I won't," Cole says. "Watch. He's slowing down, probably coming up to his destination. We have to be cautious." We round a corner just in time to see Jack's car turn left at a red metal mailbox. Cole slowly cruises up to the mouth of the driveway. Down a treelined driveway is a chalet-style hunting cabin.

Cole backs up, turns onto a service road, and drives up a slight hill until the cabin appears below us. There's a fence and a wooded area with a view of the front door. We watch Jack park his SUV, walk up the steps, unlock the door, and disappear inside. Why am I feeling deja vu?

"Cole, I know this place." I pull out my phone and show him the picture of Jack and Rick dressed in fishing gear. In the background is the cabin.

He squints skeptically. "Where did that come from?"

"Rick Muraro's home office. Maybe Jack's just going fishing?"

"That's a pretty elaborate security system." Cole points to cameras along the fence. He reaches into the backseat and unzips a black duffel bag. I spot some telescopic rifles as well as a variety of handguns. Holy crap! That's a lot of guns. I'll bet Cole knows how to handle every single one.

"Rick was a security nut," I say, trying not to think about the arsenal in the back seat. "He had cameras at his office and his house."

"Good to know." Cole reaches into a side pocket of the bag, pulls out a plastic baggy, and fishes out a small disc-shaped metal object.

"What's that?"

"Magnetic tracker." He opens his palm and shows me the disc. "This is going to make tailing Jack much easier for us. The trick is getting it on his car." He smiles and holds up a small tube.

"I'm afraid to ask...."

"This little wonder is a laser to disable the cameras. You just aim directly into the lens. Stay here." He opens his door and slips out of the car.

"Wait!" I call, but he's already at the fence, crouching low. There's a laser flash as he shines the beam into the first camera. He swings onto the wall with a swift, athletic movement and drops down to the other side.

Staying low, he crosses the yard and slides under Jack's SUV to attach the magnetic tracker to the car's undercarriage.

At that moment, the front door opens, and Jack steps out carrying two gym bags. My heart beats like a jackhammer as Cole quickly flattens to the ground. Then he slowly rolls underneath the SUV.

Jack lumbers down the steps and drops the heavy bags on the driveway. He opens up the back hatch of the SUV and loads the bags one at a time, grunting as he hoists each one. Cole pulls himself out near the engine and stays low as he darts toward the fence. As he slips behind some bushes, a twig snaps.

Jack stops fiddling with his cargo and peers into the woods. He takes a gun out of his belt and points it in Cole's direction. I hold my breath as Jack scans the perimeter.

"Oh God, please stay safe," I whisper, praying Jack doesn't spot

Cole in the undergrowth. There's only the sound of crickets rising and falling in the dusk.

After a long moment, Jack closes the hatch, climbs into the driver's seat, and maneuvers back down the dirt road.

Once the coast is clear, Cole races back, vaults the fence with the same athletic prowess, and slides behind the wheel.

"Close call," he says, grinning.

"Jesus, Cole! That was terrifying."

"You scare too easy." He smiles and plugs his phone into the dash. Then he opens a tracking app and tilts the screen so I can see the map. A tiny light blinks along a route. "Bingo. That's Jack's SUV."

"That was *so* risky." I'm still rattled by the close call.

"It was either the tracker or call in a drone."

"You can call in a drone?"

"Not on a hunch." Cole winks and pulls back on the road, following the blip on his phone southwest toward Lake Ontario.

"That reminds me," I say, watching the blinking light. "You never said what scares you."

Cole cocks his head and glances at me.

"You really want to know?"

"I do."

Cole hesitates, mulling over whether to confide in me. Then he looks at me with haunted eyes.

"Rats. I hate rats."

Chapter 28
Musophobia

For the past twenty minutes, Jack's SUV has traveled through the outskirts of Massena, disappearing around corners and appearing ahead. Cole expertly hangs back out of sight, quiet and focused, tracking his prey. As the sun sets, Jack turns onto a rugged dirt road in a desolate forested area. I lower the window. I can smell water. Cole waits until the SUV's headlights disappear before following. We're deep in the darkest woods, with no streetlights, just empty back roads and the mystery of the forest. An owl hoots a long, lonely cry.

"Where are we exactly?" I look out at the dark tree line.

"Near the St. Lawrence River on the border of Canada," Cole says in a low voice. "Fishing trip, my ass. There are bodies buried in these woods or at the bottom of the lake."

"Bodies? What makes you think that?"

"Look at this place," he hisses. "There's no one for miles, no one to hear you scream. It's the perfect place for a drug deal, or worse."

"I guess you're right..." Panic rises in my chest. If Cole wanted to kill me, my body would never be found. I didn't even tell anyone I was leaving town with him. What was I thinking?

"We need higher ground to get a visual." Cole points to the tracker. Jack's red dot has come to a stop. He evaluates the map for a moment, then takes a bumpy fire lane to a small clearing, parks, and turns off the headlights.

Below us, the river reflects the moonlight. There's an old hunting lodge along the water near a dilapidated pier. Jack's SUV is parked beside the building with the interior light on. After a moment, he steps out of the car and leans on the hood.

"What's he doing?" I strain to see in the darkness.

"Waiting." Cole reaches across me. I'm startled by his quick movement, and my muscles tense. He places one hand gently, reassuringly, on my leg. With the other hand, he pulls a pair of binoculars out of the glove box.

"Just grabbing these." Cole presses against me, and I feel the heat of his breath. Electricity shoots through me. A second ago, I was worried he'd bury me in the woods, and now I'm attracted to him again. What the hell is wrong with me? They say fear and arousal are similar sensations. But that's no excuse. I'm a professional investigator, or at least training to become one. Concentrate on the task at hand, Jenna—find out what Jack is up to, solve the case, keep alert, and stay alive.

Cole focuses the binoculars on the SUV, watching in silence for a moment before handing them to me. Then he pulls what looks like an antenna from his bag and slaps it on the roof. He grabs a scanner from the back seat and flips it on. There's a blast of static as he dials through the channels.

"What is that?"

"Sort of like night vision radar; it picks up sound waves," Cole says. "Keep an eye on Jack. Tell me what you see."

I look through the binoculars. "There's a broken-down pier,

but it doesn't look like the wood could hold a person's weight, much less secure a boat."

"Ever hear of a crib dock?"

"No." I scan Jack's face and try to gauge his expression, but he's just checking his phone.

"They're heavy-duty docks built for loading and unloading cargo. Smugglers are experts at making them look run down. I'm betting that ratty old landing is a fine example." The scanner crackles. The faint sound of a motor fills the interior of the car. Cole cocks his head, straining to listen.

"Hear that?" He grins.

"Yes." I stare through the binoculars looking for any sign of movement. The water starts rippling. "There! I see it. There's a boat coming."

The sound gets louder as a boat slowly chugs along the shoreline and pulls up to the sinking pier. I hand Cole the binoculars.

"That's a trawler. They've got sophisticated navigation systems and can move through shallow water." He hands the binoculars back to me.

Jack signals with a flashlight, and the trawler echoes the pattern.

"Something's happening. They're signaling each other."

"I see that," Cole says and starts filming with his camera.

The boat pulls into the dock, and a heavyset man wearing a shearling-lined jacket jumps down from the deck. They shake hands, and Jack leads him to the SUV. The hatch goes up, and Jack unzips one of the duffel bags. The boat captain holds up a rectangle wrapped in plastic. I zoom in on the exchange.

"Money! Jack's bags are filled with blocks of cash," I whisper. "That's why Jack stopped by the house."

"Figures," Cole says. "What are you up to, Jack Russell?"

The captain signals the boat with a sharp whistle. His crew, a group of hard-looking biker types, haul a duplicate set of duffels to the SUV.

"What's in those bags?"

"By their size, I'd guess around fifty kilos of cocaine. Worth a little over a million on the street. But I need to get a closer look."

"I'm coming with you."

Cole shrugs. "Suit yourself."

We slip out of the car and make our way down the gentle incline, creeping toward the empty hunting lodge. Cole edges along the back wall and tries a door. He fiddles with the lock for a second, and the door pops open. He gestures for me to follow, and we step inside.

The room is black. Vague shapes become clear as my eyes adjust to the darkness. There's broken furniture scattered around the room, a wide fireplace, and some dead animal heads hanging on the walls. There are also hooks at regular intervals for hanging game or fish, and fishing nets. Through the filmy windows, Jack and the trawler's captain are talking by the car, lit up by the SUV's interior.

A sleek, dark shape scurries across the floor. Angling my flashlight down, my breath catches in my throat. The floor is moving. The strange sight confuses me for a moment. Then I realize what is creating the effect. *Rats.*

"Holy shit!" I blurt out. Disturbed by our intrusion, the rodents scramble in all directions, moving like quicksilver over the furniture. The place is infested.

"Goddammit," Cole says, staring at the slithering rats. He stumbles back, breathing hard.

"Are you all right?" I whisper.

"Fine," he hisses, eyes wide.

Usually cool as a cucumber Cole Braedon is sweating and barely holding himself together. He takes a deep breath and sweeps the rats away with his boot, creating a path. Slowly, we make our way across the room and to the cloudy window. A small group of men gather outside near the SUV.

Jack faces the boat captain, arms crossed, chest puffed out. Cole films the exchange with his phone as I strain to make out the words.

"I'm in charge now, Bob," Jack growls confidently. "It's that simple. Take it or leave it."

So helpful, lovable Jack Russell is not only involved, he's taking over. Too bad. I kind of liked the schmuck.

"Relax, man. I've got a lot to lose here." Captain Bob lights a cigarette and inhales.

"And a lot to gain." Jack opens his phone and shows him the screen. "Tell your people this is just a taste. We're ready to double our arrangement. When can you bring the next shipment?"

Captain Bob squints at the screen. "Depends on the weather. I gotta check with my supplier. Maybe March?"

"Good. Consider this a token of my appreciation, something extra just for you." Jack pulls an envelope from his pocket. Bob looks inside. I don't know anything about piles of cash. But judging from Bob's expression, it's a lot.

"We'll be in touch." Bob extends his hand, and the two men shake. Then Bob and his crew head back to the trawler and Jack returns to his SUV wearing a satisfied smile. The boat's lights flash as the trawler pulls away. Jack climbs behind the wheel and disappears down the road.

Suddenly, I feel angry at Jack for fooling me and mad at myself for being fooled. How could I be so stupid?

"Okay, let's go," Cole says and starts back across the cabin. Out of nowhere, there's a loud snapping sound, and he stumbles in front of me. The wood floor groans and splinters as he plunges into the basement. As I rush to the hole's edge, the rotten floor bends, making an awful sound.

"Are you all right?" I peer down.

There's movement below as Cole scrambles to his feet.

"No," Cole chokes out. "I'm not fucking all right." His hands are upraised, his breath labored. There's a look of shock and horror on his face.

As my eyes adjust to the darkness, I gasp.

Cole is standing knee-deep in filthy water. And swimming around him, their wet bodies churning the dank pool, are so many rats I can't believe my eyes. His breathing heaves until he's hyperventilating as the rodents scurry around him in the darkness.

"Okay, I'll look for a way to get you out."

A rat starts running up his back.

"NO! Oh, God!" he shouts.

"Cole!" I call his name again, but it's as if he's hypnotized.

"Jenna, get me out of here." His voice is sharp and thin as glass. The man who always knows what to do is frozen, unable to move or react. He looks up at me with sheer terror in his eyes. "*Please*, Jenna!"

"Hold on—" I look around for a way to help him and grab a floor plank, but the wood won't budge. I search the room desperately. I rip down a fishing net and test the rope with all my strength to ensure it's not rotted. Looping the end around one of the game hooks on the wall, I crawl back on my stomach to the edge of the hole and throw the net down into the rat-infested basement.

"Cole?" I reach my hand out. "Climb up. The rope will hold you."

He grasps the net, fingers rigid, eyes wide with fear. The net is strong but twists and creaks under his weight. Rats scurry onto his boots, and he kicks them away. Slowly, hand over hand, he pulls himself out of the filthy basement. Twice he loses his grip and starts to fall, but he manages to hang on.

Finally, I grab his waistband and pull hard. He hoists himself onto the floor, face drained of color, trying to catch his breath. I try to touch him, but he flinches and pulls away. I don't know what to do.

"I'm okay," he says, rocking himself. He's trembling, forcing his breath to slow down. I take his hand and pull him to his feet.

"Come on. You're safe now. Let's get out of here."

He avoids eye contact and stumbles to the door.

Outside, the moon has risen, and clean air fills our lungs. I'll never forget the haunted look on Cole's face as he climbed out of the pit—a man escaping from Hell. All my fears about Cole Braedon dissolved at that moment. I may not know who he is, but he bleeds like the rest of us.

Chapter 29
The Trouble With Cash

Back in the car, Cole checks the tracker. Jack and his SUV are already heading to New York. He texts his contact at the FBI with trembling hands. He's still shaken from his fall and the rats.

"Want me to drive?" I say lightly, testing the waters.

"No," he answers gruffly and pulls onto the road. He unwinds the window and freezing air rushes into the car.

"There's nothing to be—"

"I said no!" IIe grips the wheel, muscles coiled.

"Fine." I try to hide my hurt feelings by crossing my arms, but my jacket is uncomfortably wet and caked with dirt.

Cole stares at the road intently. It's pitch black, and his knuckles are nearly white from gripping the wheel in concentration. Slowly, his breath calms as his blood pressure drops. He glances at me.

"Sorry, I didn't mean to snap," he says in an even tone. But his eyes don't lie. He looks as if he's seen the devil.

"Is the FBI going to arrest Jack?" I try to distract him from thinking about the rats.

"No. It makes more sense to follow him; see what develops, where he unloads the cargo, and who he contacts."

"So Jack had a motive to kill Rick and frame Natalie."

"Looks like it." Cole loosens his grip on the wheel, but there's still a hint of a tremor in his hands. "Muraro must have encroached on the cartel's territory, maybe poaching their supply chain. It explains their interest in Rick."

"I should call Denning and tell him we have another suspect —"

"No." Cole glares at me. "The FBI will bring the local cops in when it's appropriate. Right now, this information is on a need-to-know basis. What is it with you and that Denning guy anyway?"

"Nothing. He's just a cop I know. I called him when I found Rick's body."

Cole rolls his eyes. "Well, he's a real pain in my ass. Last time I was in town, he complained about me to the Feds." He laughs, but the sound is abrupt and tense. "What a boy scout."

"Sorry, I had no idea." I sink into my seat a little bit, embarrassed.

"Listen, Jenna. I told you I'd help, and I will. I'm on your side, but we need to play our cards close to our chest, understand?"

"Sure, but don't forget I'm here for Natalie."

"Is that the only reason?" He smiles.

I ignore Cole's question as he turns the car northeast.

"Are we heading back to Massena?"

"Yes," he says. "We need to check out that house."

We ride in silence until he turns onto the service road by Rick's cabin and parks.

"Wait here." He opens the door quietly. "I'm just going to make sure the place is empty."

"Be careful," I whisper as he disappears into the darkness.

The sky is black, and strange sounds come from the woods. A

couple of times, a laser flash cuts the night. Then Cole climbs back into the driver's seat.

"Nobody's home and I've disabled the security system."

With the headlights off, Cole backs up and maneuvers down the treelined driveway, parking in front of the cabin. As we climb out of the car, I notice he's holding his arm.

"Are you hurt?"

"I'm fine."

But he's not fine. I can tell. He's still shaken. He notices my concern and shoves his hands deep into his pockets, hiding his tremor.

We walk up the steps, and Cole examines the lock.

"Think you can pick this?" He seems almost reluctant to ask. But holding the small tools requires a steady touch.

"Sure, looks simple enough." I hand Cole a penlight, and he steadies his hand against one arm. Crouching down, I dig the lock pick set out of my bag. Time to focus.

First, insert the tension tool along the plug and apply light pressure. Next, choose a pick. Judging by the lock, a city rake will work. Carefully, I slide the wavy shaft into the cylinder. The driver pins are stubborn, forcing me to work the rake back and forth delicately several times. There's a tell tale click.

I look up at Cole in time to catch the hint of a wistful smile.

"Very impressive." He unholsters his gun and pushes the door open.

I blush and put my tools away clumsily. Thank God the porch is dark.

Cole flicks on the cabin lights, and the whole place illuminates like a Christmas tree. The inside of the house is just as grand as the exterior. The main room is large, with a vaulted ceiling. I count eight chairs at the glass dining table. The living room is furnished with modern leather couches, a white shag area rug, and an enormous television. A floor-to-ceiling stone fireplace occupies one entire wall, and a grand floating staircase disappears on the second floor. This place must be worth millions.

Cole looks around for a moment before zeroing in on a storage room. He pushes the door open and flicks on the light. The room is stacked with sealed plastic boxes piled high in neat rows.

"Drugs?" I say, guessing.

"Nope." Cole holsters his gun, pulls one of the boxes out, and pries off the lid. The container is filled with blocks of cash bundled in plastic wrap.

"Money? There's so much of it."

"Drug money waiting to be laundered. It looks like Rick had a logistical issue on his hands." Cole takes his phone out, snaps a photo, and types a message to his colleague or whoever he's been updating. "It's a pretty common problem in the drug trade. Money takes up a lot of space, and the cash has to be laundered through a legitimate business. You can't just deposit all that cash at the bank." Cole closes the box and pauses momentarily, rubbing the stubble on his chin. He looks exhausted, he's covered in bruises, and his clothing is wet and filthy. "We might as well sleep here tonight," he says. "No chance Jack is coming back."

"Good idea." I'm no prize, either. Lying on my stomach in that hunting lodge left me covered in filth. A shower and some sleep sound like heaven.

The door to the bathroom is wide open. There are clean robes and towels and a glass-enclosed rain shower. Cole stands in the doorway, staring.

"Why don't you clean up first? I'll throw your clothes in the wash." I walk past him, turn on the shower, and a cloud of steam fills the air.

"All right." Cole's shoulders relax, but he doesn't move.

"Come on. You'll feel better." I motion him inside the inviting bathroom.

Without a word, Cole peels off his clothes and steps into the shower. I've never seen anyone strip down at the slightest prompting the way Cole does. Even bruised and traumatized, his body has an air of fierceness in the way he moves. But admiring his physique at a time like this seems incredibly wrong, so I force myself to stop looking and scoop up his pile of dirty clothes instead. Then I close the door and search for the laundry room. On the far side of the kitchen is a stacked washer and dryer. After emptying Cole's pockets on the counter, I throw his clothes in the wash with a ton of soap and set the dial to "deep clean."

The fridge is empty, but the freezer is jammed with food, including bread, meat, and ice cream. The cabinets are stocked with nonperishables like peanut butter and jelly, ramen noodles, tuna fish, and soup cans. There's a rack of expensive wine, so I pull out a red and unscrew the cork to let the vintage breathe.

I make a couple of peanut butter and jelly sandwiches and set everything up in the living room.

The shower water is still running. What is Cole doing in there?

"You okay?" I knock lightly. "I made some food."

No answer. I crack open the door. Cole is standing at the sink with a towel wrapped around his waist, hands gripping the basin, body shaking. Beads of water drip to the floor. He's fighting off a panic attack.

"Those filthy r-rats, I can't get them out of my head—" Cole whispers.

I turn off the shower, grab another towel and tousle his hair. Then I gently pat down his arms, torso, and back. There are bruises and scrapes on top of old scars and tattoos. The guy is a mess. He stands in a daze. I pull a fluffy white robe off the hook and help him into it.

"Come on, Cole." I lead him to the living room. He sits down, still in a fog, squeezes my hand tight, and won't let go.

"I- I just—"

"Talk to me."

Cole looks down, damp hair falling across his haunted eyes.

"I just can't stop the thoughts."

My mind flashes to the shower at the apartment safe house, when I couldn't stop thinking about Agent Smith.

"What kind of thoughts?"

"The rats. There was a place in White Swan—"

"The Russian prison?"

"A room in the bowels of the place, windowless, with a low ceiling and chipped yellow paint. We called it *The Pit*." His body shudders, and he crosses his arms tightly. "The floor was a foot deep in water. I was beaten, burned, and interrogated. The guards left me there in the dead of winter. At night, rats came… dozens of them. They crawled on me—" He gasps for breath.

My gut twists. Cole was tortured? I gently pull him against me, and he buries his head against my shoulder, shaking. How the hell did he survive, let alone escape from that place? Now I understand his reaction. Stroking his back, my fingertips touch his scars through the soft robe. I try to find the right words to comfort him, the same way he reassured me just twenty-four hours ago.

"It's okay. You're safe. The past doesn't exist anymore."

Cole lifts his head and looks at me with sadness, then his expression shifts. His deep green eyes hold mine with an intensity I've never experienced before. My heart nearly stops, and I feel a heat rising between us. Fear, excitement, and attraction all swirl through my mind and body like a storm.

Then Cole Braedon kisses me, his lips hungry as he presses his mouth against mine. This is a terrible idea. I should pull away. Instead, I feel myself being swept under by a deep wave of desire.

He slips his hand under my shirt, and my body responds. There's a sense of desperation as he kisses my neck, working his way along my shoulder. I want to let go, but a part of me is terrified.

It doesn't take a genius to figure out that getting involved with Cole Braedon is a bad idea. I don't even know his real name. But my body thinks otherwise. It's been so long since I've been with a man. Should I?

Suddenly the washing machine chimes, and I struggle back to reality. What I need is to buy some time.

"Listen, why don't you eat your sandwich while I take a shower?"

"Hurry back." He smiles with a longing look.

I strip off my clothes in the bathroom and step into the shower. The warm water washes off the grit of the last few hours. Should I sleep with Cole Braedon tonight? The butterflies in my stomach don't lie. Our chemistry is undeniable. The thought of his body against mine and the intensity of his gaze makes me feel weak. I'm nervous as hell, but I'm also an adult. I can handle it.

Yes, I decide. I'm going to do it.

I towel off and pull on a robe, tingling with anticipation. My hair is damp, and my skin is flushed from the heat. I toss my dirty clothes in the washer and start the cycle. Then I adjust my robe to drape off my shoulder provocatively, just like in the movies. *Hey Cole, guess what? I'm naked under here.*

So, here we go. I'm alone with an incredibly sexy man in a secluded place, my hair and skin are clean and fragrant, and my mind is made up. Tonight's the night. I take a deep breath and step into the living room.

There's a faint snoring sound. Cole is lying on his side, sandwich devoured, fast asleep.

～

A bright shaft of light comes through the glass windows, streaming into my eyes. I blink, trying to orient myself. Above me is a wholly unfamiliar, vaulted ceiling. Where the heck am I? I jolt upright in a panic. Too fast. My head is swimming, and my muscles are sore. Why is my brain so fuzzy? Pushing up on one elbow, I'm aware I've spent the night on a leather couch in a fluffy bathrobe. Then it hits me. I'm in *Massena, New York*, at a cabin in the woods with Cole Braedon. A bag of Cool Ranch Doritos lies on the coffee table beside an empty bottle of wine. No sign of Cole.

Slowly the evening comes back to me. Cole told me about his torture at White Swan Prison. Then he kissed me hungrily, and I kissed him back. My already queasy stomach flutters at the memory.

My God! Then what? Oh, that's right... I took a shower, and *he fell asleep*. After that point, the whole evening is a bit of a blur. The last thing I remember is polishing off a bottle of Cabernet while watching a Hallmark Channel movie about a matchmaking dog. It seemed like a good idea at the time. Now, not so much. My head is killing me.

Maybe Sharon is right. Why do I do these crazy things?

Clanging noises explode in the kitchen. My hangover amplifies every sound. I hope that's Cole making coffee. Oh no. *Cole!* I wrap the robe around myself tighter. Should I say something about last night? Spotting my clothing neatly folded on a chair next to my bag, I beeline for the bathroom, grabbing my stuff on the way. In the mirror, my hair looks like a bird built a nest in the night, and my eyes are circled with smeared mascara like a raccoon. I clean myself up and dress as quickly as possible.

"There's a cup of coffee on the table," Cole calls out. "And some water."

"Thanks." I'm thirsty like I've been in the Sahara desert, so I drink the water first. My head feels a bit better after hydrating.

Next, I taste the coffee. It's surprisingly good. Cole's still rattling around in the kitchen.

Now, where are my boots? Checking under chairs and in the corners, I'm on my hands and knees when Cole walks back into the room, dressed and carrying two bowls.

"Apples and Cinnamon or Maple and Brown Sugar?"

"What?" I tilt my head, confused.

"Oatmeal." He holds up the bowls.

"Um, apples. I guess?"

"Eat when you can, right?" He places a bowl on the table and takes a seat. He scans his phone as he eats, like nothing happened between us. But something did happen. He kissed me, and I kissed him back. The wounded, passionate man from last night is gone. He's in his own world, ignoring me.

Maybe I'm being immature, but our kiss seemed important. I sink into a chair, feeling confused and frustrated. I eat my breakfast, waiting for a sign, but he taps away on his phone while spooning oatmeal into his mouth. What is the deal with this guy? Well, if he's not going to say anything, I'm not either. I finish breakfast and start gathering the trash and dishes from last night.

"Don't bother," Cole says.

"Let me guess. You're going to call the magical clean-up squad again?" My voice sounds tense and irritated.

"Actually, yes." He furrows his brow. "Now get ready. There's a long drive ahead, and I've got things to do on my own." He dials a number to order the clean-up. "On the road in five, Stack."

My mouth opens, but no words come out. This is the guy I almost slept with last night? He's right back to business. I pull on my jacket and double-check that I have all my stuff.

"Ready when you are," I call out, avoiding eye contact by checking my messages. Two can play this game, Braedon.

Scrolling down my list, I see a text from Paul Hill.

Paul: *Still waiting on appeal for Natalie's bail. Saw her yesterday. She's in rough shape. If you have any leads, call me.*

I want to tell Paul everything, but Cole's warning to keep quiet echoes in my mind. I bite my lip and text back.

Me: *Got a lead. I'm working on it. Tell Natalie to hang in there!*

I'm not lying. We're onto something. But what, exactly? How do the pieces all fit together? My phone vibrates.

It's a text from Sergei. That's surprising. He says E is for evidence, and Ta Ta is for texting, as in goodbye to your freedom. He never puts anything in writing.

Sergei: *Manny wants to meet you.*

Those five words send a chill down my spine. Manny the Rock wants to meet *me*? I've encountered some unusual characters in the past few months. A few have even tried to kill me. But there is something different, even ominous, about being summoned to prison by a known member of the New York Mafia.

"Guess who wants to meet me?"

Cole looks up from his phone. "Who?"

"Manny the Rock." I hold up my screen so he can see.

Cole looks stunned. "That's… interesting."

"Right? What does a Mob lawyer want with me?" Finally, I spot my boots under the couch and dig them out.

"Okay, you got me. Where's the meet?"

"He's in Eastmoor Correctional." I pull on my boots and check my bag. Going to that prison is always rough, knowing Tyler is trapped there. But if Manny can help Natalie, it'll be worth the pain.

"That's on our way back to the city." Cole looks at me with a calculating expression. "Do you mind if I tag along and see what he wants?"

I shrug, acting aloof. The hangover helps.

"Why not? Just don't say I never gave you anything."

Chapter 30
Manny the Rock

Cole and I breeze through visitor check-in at Eastmoor Correctional Facility like a couple of old pros. We both know the rules; no hoodies, jewelry, ripped clothing, open-toed shoes, hats, or spandex. The list goes on. After screening and ID checks, we enter a waiting room with dirty beige walls. There are women with antsy kids, a few attorneys, and some random adults clutching paperwork. Once our names are called, an unfriendly corrections officer pats us down. Finally, we're shown into a sad visiting area, furnished with plastic tables and chairs bolted to the ground, to wait for our prisoner to arrive.

Manuel Muraro, aka Manny the Rock, is going through a similar routine on the convict side of things. I've done the procedure at least a dozen times as a visitor. I wonder how many times Cole has been on both sides of this scenario.

We sit at our assigned table. As always, Cole positions himself with a view of the door. Prisoners trickle in, accompanied by guards who walk them to waiting family members and friends.

"Look, maybe you better let *me* do the talking," Cole says, leaning toward me. "We need to find out if Rick was working with the Mob and what his connection was to the Izar Cartel. I know how to talk to guys like Manny."

"Sure, right after we find out who set up Natalie," I respond in a firm voice. Manny the Rock asked to see me, not Cole, and I have my own agenda.

"Come on, Jenna. The murder, the drugs, the cartel—it's looking more and more like they're all connected."

"Maybe, but Natalie is sitting in jail for a crime she didn't commit. As far as I'm concerned, finding out who killed Rick, and framed her, is the priority."

I fold my arms and stare defiantly at Cole.

"Fine." He looks at me as if he's created a monster. "We'll do it your way."

"And Cole? Don't piss off the wiseguy. We need him."

"Wow, when did you get so bossy?" Cole's gaze shifts beyond me, and he sits up abruptly. I follow his eye line. An enormous guard is escorting a heavyset man in his sixties to our table. So this is Manny the Rock? He has a broad face, wire-rim glasses, a full head of silver hair, and a hardened expression. The guard waits as Manny sits down in the tiny plastic chair. Manny nods at the guard, who walks over and stands by the door as if he's been dismissed. Interesting. Who's really in charge here?

Manny sits across from me, shoulders wide, wearing drab green prison clothes.

"Mr. Muraro? I'm Jenna Stack. My condolences on the death of your son." I extend my hand, and we shake. He and Cole exchange an almost imperceptible nod before he turns his attention to me.

"Your guy?" He inclines his head toward Cole.

I pause for a moment, confused, then catch my stride.

"Yes, my guy." I glance at Cole, who shows remarkable restraint.

"Trust him?" Manny purses his lips slightly, measuring us up.

"Completely."

"Okay then. As Sergei says, *doverlay no proveryay.*"

"Trust but verify," Cole translates.

Manny smiles and leans back in his chair. His eyes crinkle up with surprising good humor. He folds his hands on the table.

"I understand you're a friend of Talie's?"

"Talie?"

"Natalie. My son Rick's wife. You're trying to help her?"

"Oh, yes. I'm doing my best. She's safe at the moment, in custody at MCC."

Manny and Cole exchange a solemn look.

"Nobody is safe in lock up." Manny flinches as his big hands contract into fists. The idea of Natalie in prison clearly bothers him. "Sergei says you're good people. I'm not sure who else I can trust in this situation. So it's gonna be you." He leans closer. "I've got some information. God willing, it'll help Talie."

A wave of relief washes over me.

"Good, we want the same thing." I lean in, matching his body language.

"Let me just be clear," he begins. "Because I know there are rumors. Rick was a real pain in my ass, didn't listen, and turned my practice from a respectable resource for a certain type of businessman into a front for the worst type of criminal."

His Mob law firm was respectable? That's an interesting way of seeing things. I glance at Cole. He half smiles.

"What kind of criminals?" I ask lightly. Better to just roll with it.

"My clients weren't angels. But they had a set of rules. There were certain types of businesses they didn't touch. The men Rick got tangled with – drug pushers, smugglers, and worse – they have no code, nothing. They're like animals. It broke my heart to see him representing people like that. It caused a rift between us. But he was my kid, and I loved him. You got that?"

"Of course, you had standards, I understand." There's something in his frank manner that makes me believe him.

"Now Talie, she was always too good for Rick. But I didn't know that at first. He was my kid. I'm a lawyer. He asked for my help."

What is he talking about? I glance at Cole to gauge his expression, but his face is stone still, except for his eyes. They scan the room continuously as if he expects someone – a guard or another prisoner – to attack us at any moment. Until now, I hadn't considered how triggering being inside a prison might be for him.

"What did Rick need help with?" I make my tone sound casual.

"Protecting his assets. You see, we lawyer types are pretty good with money. We hide accounts and move amounts. It's one of my personal specialties." He grins. "Do you know what a shell corporation is?"

"Like an offshore account, but for a business?"

"Close. They serve a similar purpose. A shell corp is used to protect assets, hide dealings, and clean dirty money. Think of the shareholders as the people with the secret bank account number. Whoever controls the shell controls the assets. You follow?"

"Sure, I follow. But what does that have to do with Natalie?"

Manny sighs. Whatever he's been carrying weighs on him.

"I helped Rick set up a shell in his and Natalie's names. Pretty standard stuff, and if anything happened to Rick, Talie would have the corporate assets in her name."

"That doesn't sound so bad."

"It's not. But I did something else, for Rick's protection, in case the marriage went south."

"What did you do?"

"I had Talie sign a resignation letter for Rick to hold onto. That way, he could remove her from the company at any time just by filing the document."

"Are Rick and Natalie the only shareholders?"

"They were at the time. But that's what got me worried." There's pain in Manny's eyes. "When I heard about Natalie's arrest, I had a friend look into things. Rick never filed that resignation letter. It's out there somewhere. And who knows who Rick could have added to the account—"

The magnitude of what Manny is saying hits me. Natalie could be the only thing standing between the money in that account and some criminal who wants it. What did she say the first time I met her? *When I left I took some papers that will protect me, help me negotiate with him.* Does Natalie have the letter?

"How much is in the account?" Cole says, concerned.

"Three million when I set it up. By now, it could be a lot more."

"*Three million?*" My voice rises a notch in surprise.

"The only way for a shareholder to get that money is the resignation letter or Talie's death certificate," Manny continues. "I hope I'm wrong—"

"But if Rick added someone else to the account, someone dangerous..." I glance at Cole. He's thinking the same thing I am.

"Then Natalie is in deep trouble," Cole says.

"I had no idea I was putting a target on Talie's back." Manny shakes his head, clearly torn up over the situation.

"Mr. Muraro?" I try to put my next question delicately. "You said Rick was involved with criminals. What about the Izar Cartel?"

"You mean his girlfriend, Elena? I had my boys look into her. As far as I could tell, she was estranged from her family. And who was I to judge? We all come from somewhere."

"What about the Mob? Are they involved with the cartel?"

Manny laughs from deep down in his belly.

"Are you kidding me? No way the Mob's working with the Izar Cartel. Why would you ask me such a thing?"

"Because the Izar Cartel sent a hitman after Rick," Cole says abruptly, leaving silence in his wake.

Manny squints his eyes in confusion. "Why would they do that?"

"He was running drugs into New York. Cocaine, to be exact."

"*Non c'è modo.*" Manny's expression turns to shock. "I knew he was hiding money for the worst kind of people. I knew he was a user, but running drugs?"

He turns to me with a questioning glare.

"I'm sorry, Mr. Muraro, it's true. I saw the drugs and the money. Rick was definitely involved in drug smuggling."

"We're not sure if Rick was stepping on the Izar Cartel's turf or working with them, but one of their hitmen gave him a hotshot." Cole's voice is low, confidential. "That's what killed your son. Not the gunshot you read about in the paper."

"That son-of-a-bitch." Manny's face crumbles into conflicted emotions, and he slams his fist down. The guard looks over, but Manny makes a calming gesture with his hands and collects himself. "Listen, my son was no criminal mastermind. God rest his soul. It took him three times to pass the bar. Even then, I had to grease some palms. If he was into something big, someone else, someone smarter, was pulling the strings." He removes his glasses and cleans them with the tail of his green prison shirt. For a moment, he's quiet, brown eyes damp, skin gray. "I never meant to put Talie in danger. I wanted to reach out to her when she and Rick broke up. But I didn't want her to see me like this. Better she makes a new life, right?"

It's strange, but I feel sorry for this man. Now I understand why Natalie had such a hard time believing Manny the Rock is a killer.

"I think you might be underestimating her," I say. "Natalie's tougher than you think."

The guard gestures to Manny, tapping his watch. We're running out of time.

"Listen, Miss Stack. I asked you here because I need you to look out for Talie." Manny puts his hand close to mine without touching and looks me in the eye. "If something happens to that sweet lady, I'll never forgive myself. Find that letter. Destroy it. Make sure she's out of harm's way. You'll do this for me? Whatever it takes to keep Talie safe?"

"Of course, I promise."

Manny nods his head solemnly. "Then I'm going to help you."

"*Help me?*" I look at Cole, but he's watching Manny with a reserved look, waiting to see where this goes. "I'm fine. I don't need any help."

"But your brother does. Tyler's a good kid."

The hackles on the back of my neck rise. Of course, Manny knows my brother is at Eastmoor. Judging by the guard's demeanor, Manny is practically running the place.

"Tyler *was* a good kid. Now I don't even recognize him half the time."

"That's not his fault," Manny says. "You have to be tough in here. You can't let these animals push you around."

"I understand, but it's getting worse. Now he's in solitary. What's next?"

"Listen, you make it right for Talie. I'll look after your brother. Tyler's with *us* now. You understand me?"

"No!" I try to hide my fear. "I appreciate what you're trying to do, Mr. Muraro, but the last thing I want is for Tyler to be indebted to… *anyone.*"

Manny opens his hands in a gesture of surrender.

"No strings attached. Even trade. You help Talie. I help Tyler."

I don't know what to say. Manny turns to Cole.

"You think she can trust me on this?"

"I believe she can," Cole says.

"All right, Mr. Muraro. We have a deal." I shake Manny's hand.

"It's been an honor to meet you, sir," Cole says with reverence.

"Too bad we never met outside," Manny replies.

"A real shame." Cole smiles.

The two men exchange one last knowing glance. They're from a world I doubt I'll ever fully grasp, but they understand each other completely.

As we stand up to leave, Manny signals the guard. He holds up a couple of fingers, indicating he needs another minute.

"One more thing, Jenna. Most of the inmates in this place claim to be innocent, but nobody ever is. In Tyler's case, there's a rumor. Word is, your brother was framed."

"*Framed?*" My heart speeds up, and blood rushes in my ears. "By who?"

"Small-town cops looking for a scapegoat." He looks at me with sadness.

"Thanks, Manny. We'll look into it." Cole grabs my elbow and steers me to the door. My heart is racing. Small-town cops set up my brother? He means *Bell River*. So Cole was right. There's not just smoke. There's fire. And if what Manny says is true, I'm right. I'll need to work Tyler's case from inside the Bell River PD and I won't know who I can trust. As Wolfson said, go back to the beginning—Ouroborus.

A storm rolls up behind us as we drive back toward the city. The sky deepens into a mass of thick, ominous clouds. It's late morning, but it looks more like dusk. Rain spatters against the window in long, oil-colored streaks. The temperature drops, and I turn the heater on full blast to try and stay warm.

"You've been stewing for the last ten miles," Cole says. "What Manny said back there about your brother? That the Bell River cops set him up? It's a rumor; take it with a grain of salt."

"You found lab evidence that wasn't admitted at Tyler's trial. How else could that happen?"

"I agree Tyler may have been set up," Cole says, brooding. "But we don't know who's behind it."

"How am I supposed to get Tyler out of prison if there was some sort of conspiracy to put him inside?"

Cole frowns for a moment. "You're a detective, Jenna. You'll figure it out. Besides, the truth will out."

"Are you quoting Shakespeare?"

"Maybe."

"I imagined you as more of a le Carré guy."

"That's because you don't know me very well *yet*."

Cole exits the FDR highway in the 60s. We glide through the streets of Manhattan, wet with shiny fresh puddles. Oil and water mix to create greasy rainbows on each shallow surface. It's a huge relief to be back in the city, away from the cabin in the woods, the drugs, and the rats. Cole falling into that hole still has me shaken. The look on his face was so terrified and hopeless.

"Can you get yourself home from Midtown?" He interrupts my thoughts. "I have something I need to look into for another case."

"Sure." I don't bother to ask what case. I know he won't tell me. "But once you drop me off, I'm calling Denning. Natalie's a target, and he's the only one who can keep her safe at this point."

"Go ahead. Just don't mention Jack and the drugs. Got it? I don't need some boy scout messing up my investigation."

Wow, I guess Denning really does get on Cole's nerves.

"I need to tell him about the missing resignation letter. I didn't want to say anything in front of Manny. But I think Natalie may have it."

"Fine, throw the boy scout a bone. Too bad Manny didn't know more. We still don't know if Rick was working with the cartel or behind their back."

"Well, we know Jack is involved," I offer.

"True, but that guy seems more like a wanna-be player than a bloodthirsty mastermind." Cole strums his fingers on the steering wheel.

I stifle a laugh. "I guess you're right. And don't forget about the two-killers theory. If Rick used the business for illegal activities, Paul Hill had a motive. Jack had a motive—"

"And Natalie had a motive. She had a lot to gain and no alibi. All she has to do is destroy that letter and she's a very rich widow."

Cole's words remind me of how bad things look for Natalie. Unless I find something solid, a jury might find the whole thing too compelling. I lapse into silence, my mind swimming with possibilities.

Cole turns down 5th Avenue and stops at a light. People are out in their boots and raincoats, splashing puddles as they cross the street. A lady with one of those plastic rain scarves tied over her hair crosses in front of the car and scowls in our direction.

Across the street is a high-end department store with an elaborate window display. Silver mannequins dressed in black pose among lush tropical plants. Each figure wears an animal-themed mask accessorized with a handbag, scarf, and shoes in a matching animal print. There's a zebra, a giraffe, and a leopard. I stare at the window, mesmerized—the leopard scarf draws my attention, deep velvety black spots on a tan background. What is it about that material?

Then all of a sudden, the answer hits me.

"Pull over!" The words burst out of my mouth in a rush. Cole responds like lightning and darts out of traffic. He screeches to a stop. Too bad Denning never takes me as seriously as this guy does.

"What?" He turns to me, concerned.

"I know who killed Rick. I'm so stupid. Why didn't I see it before?" I'm breathing hard, and my mind feels like a game of Tetris with all of the pieces tumbling into place. I close my eyes and struggle to see it all.

"Take a deep breath, Jenna. Don't think, tell me—"

"The opening party at Facèrè Boutique. It was the same night Rick was killed. Look—" I scramble to find my phone and open Instagram.

"Just tell me, Jenna." Cole pushes the phone away.

"In the pictures from the party, Elena was wearing a leopard print scarf—like that." I point at the mannequin wearing a similar scarf. It's almost identical.

"Okay," Cole says. "So how does that connect to the murder?"

"Because the night I walked into Rick's house, Romero shot at me, and I dove to the ground."

"I remember. I was on the phone with you at the time."

"That's when I saw it."

"Saw what?"

"*The leopard scarf!* I saw it on the floor. The same scarf Elena was wearing that night at the boutique opening—"

"I'm still not tracking." Cole's eyes are steady. He's following my words, but there's no sign of comprehension.

"Don't you see? Elena lied. She was wearing that leopard scarf at the opening party. So how did it end up pushed way under the desk in Rick's office? I saw her when she arrived at the house. She wasn't wearing a scarf. That means she must have been in Rick's office the night of the murder *after* the picture was taken at the party and *before* I arrived at the scene. She was the one who found Rick's body."

"My God, Jenna." Cole pulls his phone out and begins to text as he talks excitedly. "It's like Manny suspected. Rick added someone to the shell corporation—Elena. But they weren't married yet. So when she found Rick, she needed to get Natalie out of the way—"

"So Elena decided to frame her. She grabbed Natalie's gun, shot Rick in the back, and stashed the gun in the pet carrier. Then she returned when the cops arrived and acted like the grieving girlfriend."

It all makes sense. And for the first time, I'm relieved Natalie is being held without bail. As long as Elena is out on the street, Natalie isn't safe.

"I'm calling Denning now—"

"If you're going to see the boy scout, I'm coming with you," Cole says.

"Fine." I dial Denning, but he doesn't pick up, so I text him.

Me: *Urgent! I need to talk to you now, John.*
Denning: *What about?*
Me: *Meet me at Bar Kiev.*

Chapter 31
Anatomy of a Triangle

This time, Sergei answers the heavy door at Bar Kiev himself. He kisses both my cheeks in greeting before looking Cole up and down.

"Is this guy you hit on head in park?" Sergei crosses his arms and scowls.

"The same. We're friends now. Cole, meet Sergei. I showed him your photo during the Ab el Malik case when I thought you were a Russian hitman." I step aside, and the two men face each other.

Cole extends his hand, and Sergei grasps his palm and squeezes. They stare each other down for an absurd length of time.

"*Rad vstretit' tebya*," Cole says in Russian.

"*Eto moya chest*," Sergei says gruffly.

Finally, their hands release. The weird macho staring contest is over.

Sergei motions us both past the dark bar. It's too early for patrons, but a burly bartender is setting up for the evening, polishing glasses and preparing mysterious garnishes. He eyes us as we walk past.

"Your detective friend not here yet, Jenna," Sergei says, leading us to the back lounge. A few of the tables are occupied by shadowy figures.

"Okay, we'll wait."

"You have a nice talk vith Manny?"

"I don't know how to thank you, Sergei. I owe you."

Sergei bows his head graciously.

"Vodka?" he offers and indicates a table.

"Always," Cole says.

That puts a big smile on Sergei's pointy face, and he disappears behind the bar. Cole takes a seat next to, rather than across from, me. I catch a whiff of the fancy laundry soap from the cabin on his clothes, and my mind flashes to our passionate kiss. Nothing seems to bother Cole, but a flurry of contradicting emotions rises in my mind. Intent on keeping my composure, I nervously blurt out the first thing that comes to mind to start a conversation.

"So you're a vodka man, huh?" I cringe at how lame that sounds.

Cole leans back, wearing the atmosphere like a second skin.

"I'm whatever man I need to be, Jenna. You know that."

"I'll keep that in mind." My heart sinks at the reminder. Cole is a chameleon. He does whatever is necessary to get what he wants. Was he acting last night, pretending to be vulnerable to keep me close and quiet about what we uncovered in Massena? I know his fear was real, but what about his passion?

"By the way, good choice," he continues, referring to the location. "It's private, the proprietor is an ally, and I'll bet you know the layout by heart."

That perks up my mood, and I flash him a smile.

"I suppose I do have a home-court advantage."

"Not to mention your boy scout cop will hate it."

As if on cue, Denning arrives, escorted by Sergei. He's wearing a rain-spattered leather jacket. Sergei sets down three glasses and a large bottle of vodka steeped in chili peppers before leaving us to our business.

Denning sinks into a seat across the table and glances at Cole with cold eyes. "What's *he* doing here?"

"Nice to see you again, detective." Cole grins and pours out three glasses of infused vodka.

"I'm working." Denning shakes his head.

"Yeah? Me too." Cole downs a shot. "Ooh, spicy. Just the way I like it."

Denning ignores him and glares at me. "What's so urgent, Jenna? I was across town."

"I think I know who framed Natalie."

"Who?" Denning's expression is skeptical.

"Elena Solaris." I pick up a glass of vodka and toss it back.

He looks at me, then Cole, who keeps grinning.

"What makes you say that?" He isn't convinced. "Have you got proof?"

"Not yet. But it all adds up. Manny the Rock asked to see me."

"So I gave her a ride. Right, J?" Cole throws his arm around the back of my chair. I don't mind the attention, but he's acting weird. And he never calls me J…is he trying to goad Denning?

"Okay, I'll bite," Denning snaps. "What did the old timer have to say?"

"Manny was worried about Natalie; he told me he set up a shell corporation, to protect Rick's assets, with Natalie as a shareholder."

"I'm listening." Denning glances at Cole, still irritated.

"He also had Natalie sign a letter removing her from ownership."

"Manny Muraro told you all that?" Denning glares at me hard.

"As riveting as this is…I've got to get going." Cole leans toward me, cups my face with his hand, and kisses me. Not a passionate kiss but a romantic one, soft and lingering. "You're good, Jenna? I *loved* our little getaway."

"Ah—" My cheeks blaze red as I recover from the kiss.

"I'll be in touch. Quite a detective, isn't she, boy scout?" He grins and walks away, nodding to Sergei before slipping out the front door.

Denning has a strange look in his eyes. I can't tell if he's hurt or just confused. Cole isn't exactly his favorite person, but what does he care who I kiss, or more precisely, who kisses me?

"Please don't tell me you're involved with that guy," Denning growls.

"I'm not. We're just friends, kind of. He's probably just trying to annoy you, although I don't know why you'd care."

Denning's expression is twisted. "I'd care if something bad happened to you, Jenna. And that guy is *bad news*. He's shady, and he's dangerous."

"I'm not a fool. I can take care of myself." I'm not entirely sure what I'm saying is true. Is trusting Cole foolish? Maybe, but I'm sick of being underestimated by Denning. It's annoying.

Denning looks down as if trying to collect himself. A lock of dark blond hair falls across his forehead, and his brow knits for a moment.

"Okay, where's this letter?" he says.

I'm not ready to tell Denning I think Natalie might have the letter. So I avoid the question. "Manny doesn't know, but it hasn't been filed. And there's an account for the shell corporation with a lot of money."

"How much?"

"At least three million. Probably a lot more."

"That doesn't exactly help Natalie's case." Denning's jaw tightens. "That's a motive for murder."

"Not if Rick added someone else to the account and they're after the money."

"Where did all of this money come from?" Denning says.

"I don't know. Maybe drugs?" I say, being purposely vague. Cole asked me to keep quiet, but I need Denning to connect the dots. So I press my point home. "Listen, what if the cartel gave Rick the fatal overdose and someone else shot him with Natalie's gun to frame her?"

"You think Elena Solaris shot her own boyfriend? Do you have proof?"

"The leopard scarf under Rick's desk. When you went back to the crime scene, you must have found it."

"Along with bullet holes..." Denning's eyes narrow. "How do you know about that?"

There's no way to avoid confessing, so I take a deep breath and blurt it out. "Because I went back to the house to look around."

He stares at me with a deadly calm. Then he picks up a glass of vodka and tosses it back.

"I thought you didn't drink on the job."

"You're driving me to it," he says in a low voice. "So you went back to the crime scene—what happened?"

"I saw that scarf just before someone shot at me."

"What?" Denning's hands squeeze into fists. "*Who* shot at you?"

"A hitman named Romero. He kidnapped me and took me to his cartel boss, Izar, who hit me on the back of the head. But it didn't kill me, luckily. Then Cole drove me to see Manny. On the way back, I remembered the leopard scarf."

Denning shakes his head slowly like he's losing his mind one brain cell at a time. The vein on the side of his temple is pulsing. "Jenna..."

This is not going the way I planned. Honestly, I wasn't going to tell him all of the details. He's just so good at questions.

"I know you probably want to kill me, but I have proof." I open Instagram on my phone. "This is the Facèré Boutique opening. See the clock on the wall? It proves that Elena is wearing that scarf an hour before she showed up at the murder scene. How did it get under the desk?"

"Give me that." Denning takes the phone and his blue eyes harden.

"Don't you see? Elena grew up in the cartel. She'd know the ins and outs of the business. Manny said Rick was too dense to mastermind things himself. Think about it. He hooked up with Elena. He was planning to marry her. I'd bet you a dozen Cellos' burgers she was his partner."

"Which means—" Denning squeezes his eyes shut as the truth hits him.

"She's on an account holding drug money. She needs that resignation letter. It's the only way to access the cash."

"Not the only way. If Natalie's dead—"

"You need to check on Natalie in jail."

"Damn it. Natalie isn't in lock up anymore. It turns out Paul Hill is a pretty good lawyer. She got out about an hour ago—"

"What? We have to find her!" I pull out my phone and call Natalie. No answer. I grab my stuff and stand up. "I need to warn her."

"Come on. I'll drop you off at her apartment on the way to the precinct. In the meantime, I'll track down Elena."

Denning and I make our way to the street. As I climb into the passenger seat of his car, there's a text from Nadir:

Nadir: *Doc Forbin just got a hit.*
Me: *What?*

Nadir: *Elena Solaris bought a ticket to the Maldives. 11 p.m. departure.*
Me: *Any other activity?*
Nadir: *She's been quiet since. Unusually quiet.*

"What is it?" Denning asks.

"Elena is running to the Maldives."

"No extradition," he finishes my thought, then quickly calls in a BOLO for Elena Solaris. He pulls into traffic, weaving through the busy Manhattan streets, hands tight on the wheel. I know the feeling when something's been under your nose the whole time, and you missed it. It's torture. And now Natalie's in the city alone. I've got to find her before Elena does.

Chapter 32
Unexpected Arrival

Pushing past a neighbor exiting Natalie's building, I race up the stairs and nearly collide with her on the fourth-floor landing.

"Jenna?" Natalie looks startled, balancing a box of belongings while struggling with her keys. She's thinner and more drawn than I remember. She sets the box down and throws her arms around me.

"I'm glad to see you too. Are you okay?" I squeeze her tightly.

"Prison was awful," she whispers and looks past me down the stairs. "Where are Olive and Pepper?"

"They're with Gary. Don't worry, they're fine." I look down the stairwell, scanning the building nervously. All the doors are closed, no unusual sounds. Still, being at Natalie's apartment is not a good idea, given the circumstances.

"I knew you'd get me out of that terrible place," Natalie says, fighting back the tears.

"To be fair, it was Paul who got you released."

Natalie blushes at the mention of Paul's name.

"He's been wonderful. He even picked me up and drove me home."

"Listen, Natalie. I think you should come with me."

"Now? But I just got home—"

"I know, but something's come up. I don't think you're safe here."

Natalie seems to register that I'm dead serious.

"Okay, can I just put my stuff down inside?"

I glance down the stairs. Everything is quiet. "Sure."

Natalie turns her key in the lock and pushes the door open a few inches before picking up the box of belongings.

"They gave me my stuff back, everything but the gun. I'm glad. I hope I never see—Oh my God!" Natalie gasps.

I step through the door behind Natalie. Her apartment wasn't exactly tidy the last time I was here, but now the place is trashed. Boxes are tipped over, furniture upturned, papers scattered over the floor, and drawers emptied. The place has been ransacked. Elena, or her people, must be looking for that letter.

Then the door slams shut behind us.

Jack Russell stands in the entryway holding a coal-black Beretta M9. Beads of sweat shine on his forehead. His eyes are wild as he waves the gun in Natalie's face.

"Okay, princess, go sit on the couch," he says gruffly.

Natalie obeys, placing the box on the floor, the color draining from her face.

"Jack. I should have known," I say.

"No lip, baby detective." He gestures with the gun. "Turn around."

Slowly, I face the wall. "So, you're working for Elena?"

"Shut up." Jack pats the side of my hip and checks my jacket pockets and boots. "Always check the boots, right? Mistake number one, you ain't carrying no backup weapon."

When he's finished patting me down, Jack rifles through my bag and tosses my phones on the counter. "What have we got here?" he says and pulls out my gun. That's twice someone's taken the damned thing off me. No wonder people get killed with their own weapons.

Isn't the FBI supposed to be following Jack? Where are they?

"The cops are on the way, Jack."

"I seriously doubt that," he growls. "Now, go sit next to the mouse."

I join Natalie on the couch. She's gripping her hands together so tightly her knuckles are white. There's a terrible resolve on her face as if she knows what will happen next.

Jack brings a chair over and sits across from us.

"Now, we're all going to have a little talk." He runs a hand through his thinning hair and waves the gun.

"What's happening, Jenna?" Natalie's body trembles with fear.

"It's going to be okay," I promise her, knowing it might not.

Natalie nods almost imperceptibly.

"You know why I'm here, baby investigator?" Jack looks at me with cold eyes, gun pointed at the center of my body.

"I think so. At least I have a theory."

"Why don't you explain it to the mouse here?"

Even now, Jack's ego is working overtime. He's going to school me, which gives me a weapon to use against him.

"You were right, Natalie. Rick was involved in some bad things, but not alone. Jack was helping him."

Jack waves the gun at me. "Go on."

"Remember Rick had you sign some papers?"

"He had me sign a lot of things." Natalie blinks, confused.

"There was one paper, in particular, a resignation letter?"

"I remember. He and Manny said it wasn't a big deal. I played along but could tell the letter was important to them."

"I'm pretty sure Jack's looking for that letter."

"Smart girl." Jack leans in with the gun, menacing but just out of reach. He's unshaven and more disheveled than usual. He seems stressed, and that makes him even more dangerous.

"Natalie?" I ask gently. "Did you take the letter?"

"Yes." She bites her lip nervously. "I know it was wrong, but I just wanted to keep Olive and Pepper. Before Rick could change the combination on the safe, I grabbed some papers, anything I thought might give me some leverage."

A satisfied smile creeps across Jack's face. "Where's the letter now?"

"In a safety deposit box."

"Yeah? Where?"

"My bank. On Third Avenue."

"And where's the key?"

"In my purse." Natalie gestures to the box of her belongings.

Jack glances at his beat-up wristwatch.

"Okay. Here's what's going to happen." He points the gun at Natalie. "You get all of the papers you took from Rick's safe while Jenna stays here to keep me company. If you call the cops, if anyone comes near this place, if you take longer than thirty minutes—" He points the gun directly at my head and slips a finger along the side of the trigger. "I'll kill her. You got that?"

Natalie swallows hard and nods.

"Now go!" he barks.

Natalie grabs her purse and scampers to the door. I feel an enormous sense of relief that she's gone. Now I only have myself to worry about—time to figure out a way to get the upper hand.

Jack sits across from me, a sheen of sweat on his brow, shirt damp.

"It's not too late, Jack," I say. "The cops—"

"Don't think I won't pull this trigger, kid," he threatens menacingly. "I like you, but this is business."

I scan the room, desperate. My gun and phones are too far away. Jack would shoot me halfway there. A large metal lamp is much closer, almost within reach. Maybe I can get Jack agitated enough to let his guard down?

"You're over your head, Jack. Elena is playing you."

He should ignore me and stay focused on the task at hand. But he can't resist.

"Oh yeah? Tell me all about it. Show off your baby investigator skills."

"I know Elena killed Rick."

"Ha! Wrong. The Izar Cartel killed Rick for setting up his own supply chain. Elena grew up down there. She helped him figure it all out. They outsmarted those cartel bastards. Too bad they found out."

"But Elena shot Rick with Natalie's gun, right?"

"Wrong again!" His eyes are wild. "I did that."

A shock runs through me. *Jack shot Rick?* "But you were friends!"

"Yeah." Jack shrugs. "And I did feel bad about that. I'm no cold-blooded killer. But he was dead already. We had to make the facts fit our needs. You know?"

"We? I thought she was the mastermind, and you were the dumb henchman?" There, that should piss him off.

"Well, you guessed wrong, smart aleck." Jack's mouth jerks involuntarily, and the gun slips a little in his clammy hands. "Elena was there, all right. She came home early, found him dead, and figured out the cartel got wise. She called me in a panic—classy broad like that finding her man murdered by a drug cartel. The gunshot was my idea." Jack smiles proudly. "Give the cops an easy solve so the business could keep running. Smart, right?" As he recounts the events, Jack's body language relaxes.

Pulling the truth out of Jack is a double-edged sword. He'll kill us both as soon as Natalie returns. But I'm buying time. If I can keep him talking longer, I might have a chance.

"I must admit, Jack, it was a good plan. What did Elena promise you?"

"Rick's part of the action. I'd been helping out already, knew the players, and all the details, to keep the business going."

"And the Izar Cartel? What's to stop them from killing you?"

"Rick played fast and loose. I'll fly below their radar. Once I rebuild the network, Elena can negotiate. Rick never listened to Elena; she's smart."

I hear the faint sound of footsteps from outside the door. Natalie must be back. We don't have long now. Jack will never let us walk away. I glance at the lamp, steeling myself to lunge before Jack can shoot. My chances of success are almost nil, but I'd rather go down with a fight. Then the door flies open.

"*You?*" I manage to spit out.

Chapter 33
This Walk-Up Is Killing Me

Elena Solaris steps into Natalie's apartment. She's decked out in a camel-colored pantsuit and tan kidskin gloves, hair pulled back in a low chignon. Gone are the mascara-stained eyes and mournful demeanor. This is not the flashy, heartbroken mistress I met at the hotel. Today she looks like a high-powered international business-woman. Of course, she does. That's exactly who she is.

She walks to the counter and looks at the three phones with a lifted eyebrow. Then she picks up the gun Sergei gave me and runs a gloved finger over the barrel. "A Glock 19? Not very lady-like." She smiles. "They say at the range you're a good shot."

"You checked on me?"

She shrugs and places the Glock back on the counter.

From his expression, Jack's surprised to see her too, which could work in my favor. Any hope I harbored that Denning would apprehend her at the airport just died. It's two against one, and that one is me.

"I told you I had this handled." Jack scowls. "I've got Natalie out gettin' you those papers right now."

"Yes, I know," Elena says coolly. She faces Jack, one hand lightly draped on her hip. "I *told* you not to go to Massena, didn't I?"

"Come on, Elena. Don't be like that," Jack says.

"I thought we *agreed* to lay low for a while?" Elena runs a sharp nail along her expensive lapel.

I eye my phones, so tantalizingly close. If only I could press record. She's practically confessing. On the downside, my chances of surviving this encounter plummeted with her arrival.

"That woulda been a waste," Jack says. "Besides, I had to show those bikers who's boss now. Ya know?"

Elena rights the only remaining seat in the room, the maroon wing chair. The same one I sipped coffee from on Monday.

"Actually, I do. My Uncle Pablo used to say, let the rats run free, and the streets will be filled with them." She sinks down, crosses her long legs, and draws an exquisite pearl-handled gun from her purse. She points the business end directly at me. My mind flashes to Natalie's limited-edition Beretta. I wonder if this, too, was a gift from Rick?

"Come on, Elena. You're not mad, are you?" Jack shrugs. "The show must go on, right?"

"Shush," she scolds. "The ladies need to talk."

Jack's face burns crimson, but he quiets down. Elena is clearly in charge.

She slides a perfectly manicured nail along the Beretta's trigger, almost like a caress. I wonder how crazy growing up in a cartel makes you?

"What do you want from me?" I say, trying not to show fear.

"Now, Jenna," she begins. "You nosed around my house, my friend's boutique, my hotel room, and now you're at Natalie's apartment with my... business partner. Why are you so interested in my affairs?"

"I don't know, Elena. I guess you had me at dead fiancé. Or maybe it was the part where you framed an innocent woman?"

"Did you come to that conclusion all by yourself?" She flicks a cold glare at Jack. "Or has someone been chatty?"

Jack avoids making eye contact.

"You left quite a breadcrumb trail, Elena," I say carefully, wondering how long before Denning figures out she didn't get on that plane.

"Tell me, dear." She smooths her hair with a free hand. The ghoulish La Muerta medallion glitters against her bronze skin. "What exactly do you think you know?"

"That Rick was shot to cover up the cartel hit. And you framed Natalie. You need that resignation letter to access the cash in that account."

"My, that's quite a shocking story." Elena flutters her eyelashes, transforming herself into a beautiful victim with a gesture. Then she smiles glibly. "However, there's absolutely no proof I was involved."

"You left something at the crime scene."

Her black eyes widen. Finally, a reaction. "You're lying."

"A leopard scarf." I watch her reaction closely.

Elena's eyes flash with fear as the penny drops.

"I don't know what you're talking about."

"Come on, Elena. There's a picture on Instagram. Did you freak out when you found Rick dying? Were you so busy calling Jack that you didn't notice the scarf had fallen?"

"That's hardly proof." Elena raises her gun to sit level with my heart.

"No, but it's pretty damning. What other mistakes have you made?" I look across at Jack intentionally.

"Yes, he can be a problem at times. But he's loyal."

"That's right, Elena," Jack says.

The front door creaks, and Jack points his gun in that direction while Elena remains focused on me, unblinking. Natalie stands on the threshold, clutching a large manila envelope against her chest, eyes wide.

My mind flashes to the envelope that got me into this predicament in the first place. Delivering the custody papers for Olive and Pepper turned out to be a dangerous favor. I'll be lucky to get out of this mess with my life.

"Elena?" Natalie whispers.

"Wonderful timing." Elena's eyes light up with glee. She points the gun at Natalie. "Don't be shy. Step inside. Show me that delicious resignation letter."

Surprised and frozen in fear, Natalie doesn't move.

"Natalie," I say calmly. "Elena needs that letter. Do you understand? Go ahead and give it to her."

Natalie crosses the room in halting steps and hands Elena the envelope.

Elena pulls out the resignation letter and holds it up to the light.

"Excellent," she smiles. "Signed and notarized. Now, go sit down with your bothersome friend."

"It's okay," I say as Natalie sits beside me, trembling.

Elena tucks the letter into her pocket and tosses the envelope to Jack.

"The bank will have a record of Natalie's visit. When you're done, leave that on the floor. Understand?"

"Done with what?" Jack says, confused.

I suddenly feel sick. I know what. I'm expendable, and Natalie's a liability. The one thing we have going in our favor is the noise factor. Gunshots in this neighborhood will draw the cops. I doubt Elena wants that kind of attention.

Then Elena smiles slyly and opens her bag. She withdraws a

familiar object, a suppressor, also known as a silencer. She walks to the counter, picks up my gun, and carefully screws the metal tube onto the barrel. Then she hands the weapon to Jack.

"Because, my friend, you're going to kill them. Use this."

Jack looks pale as he takes my gun from Elena. Natalie clings to my arm, terrified.

"*Kill* 'em? Do we have to?" Jack carefully tucks his own weapon into his waistband.

"Of course," Elena says, exasperated. "If you want to be a big drug kingpin, you will have to do some unpleasant things."

Natalie shrinks behind me, on the verge of panic.

"Yeah, but the mouse ain't gonna say anything. Maybe we can make some kinda deal with the baby detective here." He motions his head toward me.

"With *her*? She's working with the FBI, you idiot."

There's no denying it; maybe I can use that fact to turn things around. I need to try something quick or crazy before Elena murders us all.

"That's right." I keep my gaze steady. "The FBI is following you, Jack. They're outside the building right now."

A smug look of recognition crosses Jack's face.

"That's who that was! I lost a coupla jarheads at my corner bodega this morning. I didn't know they were feds, but they didn't exactly blend in."

Unbelievable! How can Jack be so dumb and competent at the same time? I'm running out of options here. This is not where I thought I'd end up today, seated in a room with a wanna-be king-pin, a crazed cartel princess, and my own gun pointed at my client and me. I have to outwit the oddest crime couple ever.

Think, Jenna, think!

"We need to protect our business, Jack," Elena says. "They've got to go."

Protect *our* business? Jack doesn't know Elena is planning to flee the country. What else doesn't he know? Maybe I can pit them against each other.

"You think your brother will let you stay in business, Elena?" The words have an effect. Rage flares up in her eyes.

"Brother?" Jack is lost, trying to track the conversation.

"Darius Candelas Izar. I had the displeasure of making his acquaintance recently."

Jack's jaw drops. "Wait. Izar is your *brother*?"

"Technically, he's my half-brother."

"But... I don't understand." Jack sits with a stupefied expression on his face.

Elena begins to pace. "How do you think I knew how to set up the operation, Jack? By some sort of osmosis growing up in Colombia? I learned the business from the inside, watching and waiting for my turn. But Darius didn't want his illegitimate little sister to have any power. They sent me away. So I waited, and I *plotted*. Rick was the perfect cover. Only too happy to help. We could have been a bridge, uniting the great crime families of Colombia and New York."

"But Rick got greedy," I encourage her.

"He moved too much product, spent too much money, and he developed a coke habit. My half-brother noticed. There's no reasoning with Darius."

The final pieces of the puzzle are falling into place.

"So Izar found out Rick started his own operation and had him killed. But your brother couldn't be sure you were involved, right Elena? That must have been dangerous for you." I keep my eyes on the gun as Natalie cowers beside me.

"Dangerous? You can't even imagine. I told Darius that Rick tricked me into telling him childhood stories and used the information to build a business. I pretended to be stupid and hapless. It made me sick, but you learn to survive when you grow up as I did. My brother never saw my potential. He had no trouble believing me a fool." She glares at Jack. "And now, thanks to your stupidity, *partner*, the FBI is closing in on us."

"No way," Jack protests. "I lost those bozos. And I've got the stuff stashed someplace safe."

Jack is falling farther behind the narrative.

"If the FBI catches up to you," I continue to fill in the facts, "your brother will know you crossed him. You'll be as good as dead."

"That isn't going to happen," Elena says.

"Because you're going to disappear?" I need to keep them talking.

"With this helpful paper." She pats her jacket. "And a little luck."

"What about the business, Elena?" Jack protests.

"There won't be any business unless you clean up these loose ends," Elena says coldly and walks toward the door, leaving the dirty work of murder in Jack's hands.

Jack points the gun directly at me. There's tension in his eyes. He's torn.

"Can't you see, Jack?" I say in a low voice. "Elena's setting you up. Your fingerprints are on that envelope, and she's leaving the country. Once she drains that account, she'll kill you too."

Beads of sweat appear on Jack's brow. He looks sick.

"Okay, you two face each other." Jack motions with the gun, thick fingers curled around the trigger. With that damn suppressor, the gunshot will be muffled. Nobody will come running.

I slowly stand up and pull Natalie to her feet. Jack steps behind me and points the gun at Natalie to get the right angle.

Instead of cowering, Natalie faces him.

"The blame for all of this will be on *you*," I say as he steadies his aim.

"Nobody will believe that," Jack says.

"Yes." Natalie speaks up for the first time, a look of terror on her face. "They will."

At that moment, Jack hesitates. Time to drive the fear home.

"The FBI followed you to Massena," I say. "That's motive. You'll be the prime suspect in Rick's murder. Elena will be long gone. You'll go to prison."

"We're out of time," Elena says impatiently, standing by the door. "Do it, and let's get out of here."

I can read the moment Jack realizes I'm telling the truth. "Are you saying Rick was still alive? That I killed—" His voice catches in his throat.

"No, Jack. You didn't kill your friend. The hot shot killed him, not the bullet. But the cops will put the pieces together and think you did both. And if you shoot *us,* that will be murder. Elena will be long gone, and so will your business."

The doubt in Jack's expression transforms, and he swings his gun toward Elena. "You!" he shouts, waving the barrel in her direction.

Elena, cool as ice, squeezes the trigger of her pearl handled gun.

Jack clutches his side, blood streaming through his fingers. The gun slips from his grip as he slumps over. I dive for the weapon and roll. Elena shoots again. This time the bullet tears through a couch cushion, and stuffing explodes into the air. Natalie shrieks and drops to the ground.

"Stay down!" I call to her. She ducks behind the couch.

I spring out of Elena's line of sight, moving low and lateral, as Sergei taught me. Then I aim and fire off two shots. Elena shrieks. There's the sound of wood splintering and a puff of plaster dust as bullets lodge in the wall behind her.

A look of shock spreads over her face as she clutches her arm. A trickle of blood runs down from her shoulder, staining her crisp blazer. I clipped her!

Elena runs out the door. High heels clack loudly down the stairs.

Jack groans, holding his side. The bullet grazed his ribcage.

We need to stop the bleeding.

"Natalie!" I shake her, but she doesn't react. She's in shock.

"S-she was going to kill us," she says, dazed.

I race to the kitchen and grab a clean towel. Then I pull a stunned Natalie over to Jack. "Listen, keep pressure on the wound. Then call 911 and Detective Denning. Can you do that? I need to go after Elena."

"Elena?" The name of the woman who caused all this horror and destruction snaps Natalie out of her daze. She presses the towel to Jack's side with her elbow and starts dialing. "Go on, Jenna. Get her!"

I unscrew the silencer and shove the gun into my pocket. Then I charge out the door, following the clacking sound of stilettos echoing up the stairwell.

Chapter 34
Late Season Tomatoes

Blood is smeared on the banister and there are drops on the steps as I race down the stairs after Elena. The trail disappears on the ground floor. She must have stopped the bleeding somehow. I burst onto 46th Street, searching frantically for any sign of her. At the end of the block, a camel-colored pantsuit rounds the corner onto 2nd Avenue. I bolt after her. At the busy intersection, my luck holds. Elena is in heels, and I'm wearing the sensible boots Cole bought me. Even with her long legs, I can close the distance as she weaves through the crowd.

Then she crosses the avenue and heads uptown. I sprint after her to an open plaza. There's an active farmer's market, and the courtyard is packed with stalls and people. Vendors sell fruits, vegetables, fresh bread, and honey. Just the kind of place I'd stop and explore if I wasn't busy chasing a criminal. And the place is filled with shoppers. Mothers wheel baby carriages through the busy tents. Couples purchase gourmet coffee and fresh berries. Kids run around laughing and chasing each other.

Elena disappears into the maze of aisles and colorful booths.

Her dark hair and lanky frame are visible for a moment. Then she's gone. Damn it!

Weaving my way through the activity, I search for any sign of my prey. If Elena plays her cards right, she can lose herself casually in this crowd. I hear a commotion, people yelling, and the sound of crashing. Elena's leaving a path of chaos for me to follow.

"Excuse me, oops, sorry!" I muscle past the startled shoppers. Up ahead, Elena squeezes through a narrow channel in the crowd, slipping further into the maze of stalls, clutching her injured shoulder. A woman with a plastic shopping bag blocks her path, slowing her down for a fraction of a second. I leap forward until my fingers brush the tail of Elena's jacket. She feels my touch and panics, shoving the woman aside. But that gives me enough time to grab her coat and yank hard. There's a loud rip.

Elena topples on her heels, arms flailing, handbag flying. The pearl-handled gun arcs up in the air and clatters onto the sidewalk. We smash into a vegetable stand and land on a display of late-season tomatoes. Red skin, juice, and seeds splatter everywhere as we crash.

I clamber on top of Elena and pin her down.

"Noooo," she howls, slippery with tomato juice, eyes wild. "You have no idea what they'll do to me. Let me go! Please!"

Tears stream down Elena's face as she thrashes in the red sticky pulp. I loosen my grip. Big mistake! She wriggles an arm free and yanks my hair so hard I smack my head on the pavement. Then she scrambles to her feet and dives for the gun. But I sweep my leg out and kick it away. I scramble to grab her, but she knees me in the ribs. The air huffs out of my lungs. Her shoe flies off and clips my cheek. I remember my Krav Maga training. Inflict maximum damage in the minimum amount of time. I pick up her stiletto and slam the sharp heel down hard into her thigh.

"Owwww!" Elena howls like a wounded animal and collapses

to the ground. Diving on top of her, I pin her again. She fights, bucking with her body. I draw back my elbow, ready to strike her jaw, when someone grabs me from behind. I resist with all of my might, trying to break free. There's no way I'm letting Elena escape.

"Jenna, it's me, John!"

Denning? Strong hands lock around my shoulders and squeeze.

Slowly, I roll onto my back and catch my breath. A sea of faces stare down. Handcuffs click, and through bleary eyes, I watch Denning pull Elena up and hand her off to a uniformed cop. He picks up Elena's gun.

Then he offers me a hand, but I can't move. I'm lying in a pile of broken crates, squished tomatoes, and vegetation. Everything hurts.

"Oh no!" Denning's expression turns to panic, and he drops to the floor next to me. "Are you hurt? Bleeding? Show me where."

Laying on the sidewalk covered in tomato guts, I take mental stock of my body. I'm sore, and my head hurts, but nothing's broken. The spot where my forehead hit the cement throbs. But it's just pulp, no blood.

"I'm okay. No cuts or broken bones."

"You scared me for a second there." Denning's face relaxes as he gently helps me to a sitting position.

"How did you find us so quickly?"

"The airport was a dead end. I was on my way back when Natalie called. She told me what happened. So when I saw a commotion in the street, I figured it might be you and I stopped."

"So my public disturbance plan worked?" I brush tomato pulp off my shoulder.

"It sure did." Denning tucks a strand of damp hair behind my ears.

There's a burst of activity on the street. Additional officers are arriving, securing the scene, and talking to witnesses, but they're all local. Denning pulls me to my feet and examines the tender spot on my head.

"Ow!" I wince at the pain.

"Let's get you checked out, just in case." He slips an arm around my waist, pulling me close.

"If you insist." The crowd parts to let us through.

"I'm impressed, Jenna. The way you fought for Natalie was top-notch."

Top-notch? No wonder Cole calls him a boy scout. Still, he's being awfully sweet, and the softness in his tone is new.

"Thanks Denning. That means a lot."

"So I'm not going to book you for possession of an illegal firearm. Okay?"

Oh, God. I forgot the damn gun in my pocket. He can't be serious.

"Um, thanks?" My cheeks blaze red right on cue.

Denning lifts me over a toppled market stall as if I weigh nothing.

"You know, I'm starting to think you can take care of yourself." He smiles. For a second, it's like a summer breeze just blew through the marketplace, warm and inviting.

"I always could. You just didn't notice." I smile back.

There's a rapid camera flash as we step out of the wreckage. Someone's taking pictures. I guess I should be worried about how awful I look, but I'm not. Instead, I feel elated. Even though my muscles ache and I'll be sore tomorrow, I saved Natalie and solved the case. Not too shabby for an afternoon's work.

Chapter 35
Bienvenue à la Maison

Dave's apartment is spotless. Every pet-sitting crisis has been resolved, and the completed jobs are marked off on the Tails of the City assignment board. I've stocked up on his favorite essentials like oat milk and fresh zucchini for making carb-free zoodles. I even bought fresh flowers to brighten up the living room. I've had a good night's sleep, showered, and camouflaged my cuts and bruises with makeup. Now with the addition of a bit of mascara and lip gloss, I look refreshed. Dave has been texting nonstop from the cab since he left the airport. He's caught French fever, so I keep having to check every message in Google Translate.

Dave: *Presque à la maison!*
Me: *You're almost home. Yay!*
Dave: *C'était tellement amusant!*
Me: *I'm glad you had fun. Speak English!*
Dave: *A venir maintenant!*
Me: *OMG, stop with the French!!! You're in America now.*

I frantically type his last text into Google Translate.

Dave: *Coming up now!*

The distinct sound of luggage wheels echoes in the hallway just before the door opens. Dave and Matty walk inside, looking chic in matching new shirts and stylish jackets. Someone's been shopping in Paris. Dave rolls in an extra suitcase, probably filled to the brim with French clothing. That must have cost a fortune to lug over the ocean.

"Salut, mon petit chou," Dave proclaims. "Comment ça va?"

"Er, fine?" I say, scrambling to re-open Google Translate.

"Don't mind him." Matty smiles. "He lost his mind in Paris. Be ready to have a morning croissant with coffee drowned in sugar and cream for the next month, at least. He's also gone mad for crêpes."

"Just because I like to absorb the culture." Dave tosses a scarf over one shoulder, pretending to take offense. "This is for *you*."

He hands me a shiny white box with a gold ribbon. Inside is a stunning silk scarf with a colorful abstract watercolor pattern.

"Thank you! I love it." I hug Dave, relieved to have him back.

"So, how did everything go while I was in *Europe*?" Dave smiles.

"Great! Dogs and cats living together. It's all good."

"What's that?" Dave points at my forehead. Damn, I thought I covered the bruise. Of the two of us, I'm not sure who's the better detective.

"This? Nothing! I just knocked my head, um… reaching for something I dropped. You know, clumsy me." I'm not lying technically, just fibbing slightly.

"Really?" Dave crosses his arms and gazes at me with an I'm-not-buying-it look. "You must have hit your head pretty hard."

"Yeah, I banged it good." I laugh, but the sound is hollow.

"Funny. I thought maybe that bruise was connected to this." Dave throws a copy of the *New York Post* on the table.

"What do you mean?" I ask as innocently as possible.

"I picked it up in the taxi," he says, arms crossed. "Imagine my surprise when I opened the Metro section."

I fan through the newspaper to a full-page spread with photos. The second I see the headline, I cringe. Busted.

The copy reads *Lawyer's Mistress Charged in Drug-Related Murder Cover Up.* "I'm innocent," says the pull quote over a picture of Elena's face looking surprisingly angelic. She's standing next to her new lawyer, a sharky, thousand-dollar suit guy who looks like a male model. Below are pictures of Elena, Rick Muraro, Natalie, Olive and Pepper, Paul Hill, the brownstone, and Natalie's gun.

"Um, weird," I manage to say.

"Turn the page," Dave says, tapping his foot impatiently.

Reluctantly, I flip to the next page and hold my breath. There's a picture of Elena being arrested amidst the wreckage of the vegetable stand. In the foreground is me, covered in pureed tomatoes, holding Denning's hand. The caption reads *Manhattan Detective John Denning with student criminologist Jenna Stack, who helped apprehend the accused.*

"I can explain...." But despite my words, I can't, not really.

Dave snaps his fingers and points at the picture. "Time to come clean. I want all the details. Most importantly, what are you doing holding hands with that sexy cop, Denning?"

"It's a long story."

"That's my cue to leave," Matty says. "I have to check on Buster, and I'm sure I'll get a full report. Good luck, Jenna." He kisses Dave goodbye, winks at me, and darts out the door.

Dave sighs and stands with one hand on his hip. The look on

his face says that I'm a lost cause. "Okay, girl. Spill it. And don't hide anything. I'll know."

One bottle of Pinot Noir later, Dave and I are nestled in the living room, watching old episodes of Glee and eating dark chocolate truffles from *La Maison du Chocolat,* Paris. I've been power talking for the last fifteen minutes, telling him the whole sordid tale from the moment I delivered that envelope to Natalie to my current head lump. "So that's how I ended up chasing Elena into the market." I finish my narration and my glass of wine simultaneously.

"And you never doubted Natalie's innocence?"

"Ya know, I didn't. The same way I'm certain Tyler is innocent, I just knew Natalie was being set up. But I never could have predicted how much danger she was in."

"You know you're a hero?" Dave's expression has changed to something akin to wonder.

"I don't know about that. I was just glad to help."

"And you swear you didn't sleep with Cole Braedon?"

"I swear. But it was a close call."

"And Denning held your hand even though you were covered in vegetables?"

"Yes, and he didn't arrest me for possession of a firearm. And he insisted the paramedics check me out too."

"Hmm," Dave says, deep in thought. "Well, it's official. You've got a triangle going on, and you're in the middle."

"A triangle?" My phone dings announcing a text. I glance at the message, then I sit up in shock.

Unknown Number: *Hey, sis. It's me. Manny got me a phone! And he's teaching me chess.*

This isn't the usual inmate texting app announcing an inmate is trying to reach me. This is a proper text from a proper phone. Manny kept his word. He's looking after Tyler.

Me: *Awesome!*
Unknown Number: *Gotta run, love you.*
Me: *Love you too, Ty.*

I hand Dave my phone and try not to cry. It's been so long since Tyler acted like a normal kid, excited about life and ready to learn. Even though Manny the Rock is a gangster, he's done something I can't do for my brother. He's made him feel safe. Dave reads the text before reaching out to take my hand. He really does look like an angel sometimes with his kind eyes and golden complexion.

"Listen, sweetie. Are you still planning to go to Bell River after what that gangster, Man-boulder, said? About the cops being in on framing Ty?"

"You mean Manny the Rock? Of course. If I'm accepted, I'm going."

"I know you, Jenna. Nothing I say will stop you from trying to save your brother. But if your new Mob pal is right, things could get dangerous. Promise you'll tell me what you're up to. You know I'll help any way I can."

"Promise." I don't know what I did to deserve a friend like Dave.

"Good." Dave slides a cream-colored envelope across the center of the table. "Then you might want to have a look at this."

"What is it?"

"An invitation. I found it in the mailbox on my way up."

I open the envelope and slide out the invitation printed on thick paper in cursive text:

You are invited to the opening of a new law firm

Hill & Stone & Associates
Please help us honor the past and celebrate the future
Cocktail attire

"Now, let's talk about something important." Dave smiles and pops a truffle into his mouth. "What are you going to wear?"

Chapter 36
Aftermath

The first thing I notice when I arrive at the party is that the old Muraro and Hill sign above the door has been replaced. A new, more contemporary typeface reads:

Hill & Stone & Associates
Attorneys at Law

Somehow, seeing the words makes it real. Rebecca passed the bar. She and Paul are officially taking over the firm. I have a feeling they'll help a lot of people.

I smooth out my black lace dress, adjust my bolero jacket, and walk inside. The reception area looks different, bigger somehow. The walls have been repainted a tasteful egg-shell white. The furniture is new; modern couches and sleek chairs in amber leather complimented by minimalist coffee tables and recessed lighting. The look is tasteful and serious, but welcoming.

The cocktail party is in full swing. There's a bar beside a table of colorful appetizers on silver platters; coconut shrimp, bacon-stuffed mushrooms, and chickpea bruschetta with sun-dried tomatoes. A DJ dressed in classic 1980s Madonna-style attire plays retro music. People are laughing and drinking. A bit of impromptu dancing has broken out in one corner.

"Jenna!" a voice calls out. Natalie waves, looking adorable in a fluttery pink A-line dress. After the shock of almost getting killed, Natalie had another surprise. She's now independently wealthy. The FBI arranged for her to testify against Elena. As soon as the dust settles, she'll get to keep a good chunk of Rick's estate.

She rushes across the room, dragging Olive and Pepper behind her, and hugs me. "I was hoping you'd come!" The dogs look up, wagging their tails. I pat their heads, and they disappear under the appetizer table, nosing for treats.

"Natalie, you look amazing," I remark, and I mean it. She's practically glowing.

"What do you think about the digs?" Paul Hill says and steps next to Natalie. He smiles at her, looking relaxed and confident. I almost don't recognize him. A glance passes between them, and he lightly touches her waist. I guess something else is changing around here.

"It's wonderful." I take in the room. "Very elegant."

"Thanks, Jenna." Rebecca Stone joins our little group. She's dressed in a stylish, dove-gray business suit. "You know, now that Jack is gone, we could use an investigator around here. We've got our first big case coming up."

"I might take you up on that, but not until I graduate." I smile. "What's the big case?"

"We're representing Jack Russell, pro bono," Paul says. "Rebecca's been talking to the FBI and doing a great job. We're trying to get Jack immunity, and she might pull it off."

"It's pretty high profile," Rebecca says. "We already have new clients streaming in the door. Call us when you're ready, Jenna.

You're a problem solver with integrity. We could use someone like you." Rebecca heads off to play hostess, and I beeline to the bar, leaving Natalie and Paul talking quietly as if no one else in the world exists.

There's a little shrine set up against the wall, memorializing the law office's history with pictures of Rick and Manny back in the day. I wasn't sure what to expect, but the party is less weird and more uplifting than I anticipated. Neighbors and clients file in and out, offering their condolences and well wishes.

I step in line for cocktails at the bar, shrugging off my jacket.

A tall man dressed in a casual tan suit accepts a beer and turns around. It's John Denning, looking dashing with his strong jaw, five o'clock shadow, and sharp, intelligent blue eyes.

"Jenna Stack." He smiles. "You look lovely. How's your head?"

"Fine. I seem to have retained my finer motor skills," I say and order a dirty martini. "What should we drink to?"

"Well, let's see," Denning says. "How about staying out of trouble?"

"Seems like a long shot." I smile.

He actually laughs, and we touch glasses. I sip my martini. It's ice cold and tart.

"Oh, I almost forgot," Denning says. "I just came from a consultation with Wolfson. He told me to give you this." He hands me an envelope imprinted with the official seal of the University of Manhattan. I tear it open and pull out the letter.

"Oh my God, I got it!" I squeal with delight.

"Let me see." Denning takes the letter from my fingers.

"They approved my application. My internship came through!"

"Congratulations." Denning grins. Then his face changes in a flash. The familiar glowering brow returns, and I can see he's doing the math in his head. "BRPD? You're interning at the Bell River Police Department?"

"That's right." I throw back the martini and signal for another.

"The town where your brother was arrested?"

"That's the one. My hometown."

"I guess you were right. You can't stay out of trouble." He runs a hand through his sandy hair. Then he pulls me over to a quiet corner. "Listen, Jenna, I know I've been tough on you. And I can't help but think Wolfson gave me that letter to deliver for a reason. I don't want you to go. It could be dangerous."

I look into Denning's eyes. He's telling the truth. He's worried about me. But there's something more, something intense and smoldering. Suddenly I feel naked and exposed as if he knows me down to the bone.

"I *have* to go, John. Can't you see that? He's my brother."

Denning seems conflicted. I feel the chemistry between us pulling me like a magnet. He feels it too. There's passion in his eyes. He steps so close, I can smell his aftershave. Is that Old Spice? How weirdly old-fashioned. But even as I fight the attraction, the heat rises in my body.

"Jenna, the thing is, I—"

"Am I interrupting?" a deep masculine voice shatters the moment. "I certainly hope so."

I break eye contact with Denning and find Cole Braedon standing next to me, dressed in a charcoal gray slim-fit suit with a dark shirt and tie, a cocky grin on his face.

"You!" Denning says. "What the hell are *you* doing here?"

"I helped crack the case, remember?" Cole says, amused at his effect on Denning, who looks like he is about to lose it. Cole catches Rebecca's eye and waves. She smiles and waves back. "We're negotiating with Rebecca Stone for Jack Russell to turn state's evidence. She's a helluva lawyer."

"And you're a snake," Denning says, frustrated. "I ought to warn them."

"You're overreacting, boy scout," Cole says. "What's that you're holding?" He plucks the letter out of Denning's hand and scans the text. "You got that internship after all. You know, I've never been to Bell River, but I hear it's charming. Maybe I'll pop by for a visit."

As the two men glare at each other, I snatch back my letter and finish my drink. I'll need a little buzz for what comes next.

"John? You seem to think I'm a damsel in distress."

"Come on." He looks at me sheepishly. "I never said that—"

"Shhhh." I hold up my hand. "I'm not finished."

"Yeah, boy scout," Cole says with a wide grin. "Quit mansplaining."

"And Cole? You waltz in and out of my life acting like you're the hero. But you couldn't have solved this case without me."

"Jenna, I—"

"You're both wrong. I have good instincts, and I don't need saving. I've got this. Just wait and see." Satisfied, I pull on my jacket and walk out the door. I don't bother turning around to see their reaction. Dave's words ring through my mind. *Love triangle? With these two?* I don't think so. If this is a triangle, it feels like the crazy one off Bermuda where ships go missing.

Outside, a cool, crisp breeze welcomes me. Clusters of people pass by, laughing and chatting as they head for restaurants or out for the night. I call for a ride and settle down on the stairs to wait. I touch the letter tucked in my bag and text Nadir.

Me: *Guess what?*

Nadir: *Let's see, new case?*

Me: *Better. An old one.*

Nadir: *No way! Did you get it?*

Me: *Yep. I'm going to solve the Bell River Murder.*

More From Hanna Wren

Don't miss *The Bell River Murder*, the next thrilling installment in the Jenna Stack Mystery series!

About Hanna Wren

Hanna Wren is the pen name authors Amy Eyrie and Alix Sloan use when writing together.

Visit HannaWren.com to learn more about them and find Hanna Wren on social media. While you're there, join the Hanna Wren mailing list for updates and freebies.

And if you enjoyed this book, please help other readers discover the Jenna Stack Mysteries by leaving a review on Amazon, Goodreads, or any place you review or talk about books.

www.ingramcontent.com/pod-product-compliance
Lightning Source LLC
Chambersburg PA
CBHW020127310726
48970CB00006B/1760